MURDER AND THE
GOLDEN GOBLET

*Amy Myers titles available from
Severn House Large Print*

Murder in Hell's Corner
Murder in Friday Street
The Wickenham Murders

MURDER AND THE GOLDEN GOBLET

Amy Myers

Severn House Large Print
London & New York

This first large print edition published 2008
in Great Britain and the USA by
SEVERN HOUSE PUBLISHERS of
9-15 High Street, Sutton, Surrey, SM1 1DF.
First world regular print edition published 2007 by
Severn House Publishers, London and New York.

British Library Cataloguing in Publication Data

Myers, Amy, 1938-
  Murder and the golden goblet. - Large print ed.
  1. Marsh, Peter (Fictitious character) - Fiction 2. Marsh,
  Georgia (Fictitious character) - Fiction 3. Private
  investigators - England - Kent - Fiction 4. Fathers and
  daughters - Fiction 5. Detective and mystery stories
  6. Large type books
  I. Title
  823.9'14[F]

  ISBN-13: 978-0-7278-7698-0

Printed and bound in Great Britain by
MPG Books Ltd, Bodmin, Cornwall.

Author's Note

Much of this story of Sir Gawain and King Arthur, as regards their connections with Dover Castle in Kent, is to be found either in legend or in historical records. The bones and skull of Sir Gawain are indeed mentioned by Caxton and John Leland, antiquarian to Henry VIII, as being on show at the St Mary-in-the-Castle. A nineteenth-century edition of Malory's *Morte D'Arthur* states that the bones have disappeared since Leland's time. My theory of what might have happened to those bones after Leland had recorded their presence is, however, fictitious, as is (so far as I know!) the goblet, although since Malory claims that Gawain was given the last rites it isn't at all unlikely that a goblet survived...

I have also added a fictitious dimension to Dante Gabriel Rossetti's work. Although he was indeed in Paris with Lizzie Siddal, and did indeed use Arthurian subjects for his work, I have added four such paintings for the purposes of this novel. The contribution made to its plot by John Ruskin is also fictitious, although he was Rossetti's patron. Wymdown, too, will not be found on any map, although its neighbouring villages will.

I am indebted to the following for their help while I was writing this novel, although the use I have made of their information is my own: Phil Wyborn-Brown at Dover Castle, Lorraine Sencicle of the Friends of Dover Museum for her charming story in the *Dover Mercury* about the Lady of Farthingloe, and Mike McFarnell of the Friends of Dover Castle. I could find very few references to the Dover story in other sources, but among the many I have consulted about the King Arthur period and stories, I found Mike Ashley's magnificent *Mammoth Book of King Arthur* of enormous help.

I am also grateful to Bob and Pauline Rowson, and, as always, to my agent Dot Lumley of the Dorian Literary Agency and Amanda Stewart of Severn House for their constant support. The marvellous Severn House team has once again provided its expert help throughout.

One

'Lost at sea, 1961.'

Georgia fought to concentrate her thoughts on the plaque on the church wall and not on the man sitting beside her. Did it mean literally lost: did he silently disappear or was he killed in an accident? A Navy man? Fisherman?

'Survived the ordeal?' Luke asked after the service, as they at last made their way down the aisle in the wake of the bridal couple.

'So far, thanks,' she replied amicably. After all, her aunt's marriage to Terry Andrews was a happy occasion. It was a second marriage for Gwen and everyone liked Terry. It was merely that marriage was a delicate subject between herself and Luke, and one Georgia was trying her best to avoid. She'd taken one big step by moving in to live with him, so surely it would be sensible to have a breathing space before the next?

'Who was Lance Venyon?' her father asked, as he shot his wheelchair past them out of the church, to the annoyance of the photographer who had just positioned Gwen and Terry neatly

7

against the porch.

'Lance who?' she asked him, once this was sorted out.

'The fellow whose name you were staring at in the church.'

Georgia was forced to laugh. Trust Peter to have noticed. His ex-cop's eye never missed a trick. She'd already forgotten the plaque. She had been caught out, so now Luke would guess exactly why she'd turned her face to the wall. 'I've no idea, except that someone obviously holds him or held him in loving memory. Nothing odd about it.'

Peter pounced on that. 'Then why should you feel the need to point that out?'

For want of anything else to do while the fifty or so guests were shunted to and fro in various groupings, Georgia considered this question. 'I was wondering *how* he was lost, a naval rating, a fisherman—'

'Or a yachtsman or day tripper to France,' Luke put in.

Peter wouldn't give up. 'Is that all?'

'I think so.'

'Weak, Georgia,' he replied with some satisfaction – justifiably, she acknowledged.

Marsh & Daughter, her partnership with her father, needed more than 'thinks' or mere curiosity to work on. The past had to speak to them clearly before it decided there might be a case for them to look into. But why on earth should she even be considering that plaque in

8

such terms? The past could throw up ghosts from injustice or unsolved tragedies, but she felt no such vibes in this case, and therefore there was no reason for Marsh & Daughter to be involved. The plaque was a memorial to someone in the past, of great importance to his loved ones, but not to others, save in the general sense that 'no man is an island'. If anything, it was the church itself that reeked of the past.

Wymdown was an interesting village. On a spring day such as this it presented a peaceful face to the world. A duck pond, a village green, a pub, a main street lined with old cottages, some twentieth-century development on the outskirts, and a farm shop. (Georgia envied Gwen for the latter.) Nevertheless the village lay close to the busy A2 dual-carriageway road between Canterbury and Dover, which roughly followed the route of the old Roman road. It was on the higher side of the road, where villages sheltered in the lee of the North Downs, but despite this in winter Wymdown would present a far bleaker picture than it did today. A few miles further towards Canterbury, on the open Barham Downs, the winds could howl to their hearts' content. Over the centuries warrior tribes and armies had gathered there to fight out their grievances – or rather their leaders' grievances. She had walked the North Downs Way once with Luke, and on the Barham stretch when the sun no longer shone it was easy to believe that the past was still stamping its mark on the present, and that given their head the elements would win over all that man could build or try to cultivate on this land.

So who was Lance Venyon? Nobody to worry about today, she told herself, as she and Luke obediently took their places to be photographed beside Gwen and Terry's best man, her cousin Charlie Bone. He winked at her as she equally obediently 'cuddled closer' at the photographer's demand.

'Going to catch the bride's bouquet, Georgia?' he asked.

'Good grief no, I never tamper with fate. I might catch you instead of Luke.'

'Fair enough,' Charlie conceded.

He was in his mid-thirties, as was she, and showed no signs of settling down, as Gwen would sigh from time to time. There was no reason he should, given Gwen's example. She had married at twenty-nine, and had spent most of the preceding ten years or so tramping round the world with a rucksack. She had kept her energetic figure but nevertheless, looking at her now, one could easily take her as a cuddly grey-haired old lady for whom a visit to Canterbury would be the highlight of adventure. One, Georgia thought solemnly, can never tell.

St Alban's Church lay at the end of a long lane leading up from the village centre towards the higher downland. The tarmac ended at the church, and beyond that the lane degenerated into farm track, which must once have been wild heathland. The church was small, with a squat tower, and built of Kentish ragstone. No high towers here, for the winds could blow strongly, and the church was sheltered by ancient yew trees, protecting its secrets. Now that was a ridiculous thought, Georgia acknowledged. All churches held secrets; that's what they were there for. There were two types of secret, however: those of knowledge lost through time, and those that deliberately avoided discovery. Which, she wondered, did St Alban's guard?

'There was a Mary Venyon buried in the churchyard,' Luke remarked idly, as, with the photo session over, they struck out across a footpath to Gwen and Terry's home. Peter and some of the guests were driving round to Badon House, but for the more able at a village wedding it seemed right to walk the footpath. It wasn't a long one, although the drive by road entailed a half-mile back to the village, then up the main street and along another lane, which in effect completed three sides of an oblong. The footpath provided the fourth, and provided a splendid view of the Jacobean chimneys of Badon House as they approached – albeit Georgia's high heels suffered from mud, not to mention the frequent cowpat.

'She's buried right next to your Lance,' Luke added.

'He's not *my* Lance,' Georgia replied. The momentary thought flashed through her mind:

why did he need a grave *and* a plaque? 'He was lost—' she said to herself, unfortunately out loud.

'And must have been found again,' Luke supplied helpfully. 'If the body turned up later, they wouldn't have taken the plaque down, would they?'

Putting love to one side (and there was plenty of that), was it a good idea to be living with one's publisher, Georgia wondered. Luke and she had been together in Medlars for nearly six months, and she had been taken aback – scared? – at how easy it had proved. True, they both had their own bolt-hole: Luke ran his publishing business from the oast-house workroom only thirty yards from their front door. This was *his* working space, just as she had hers in her old home next to Peter's in the village of Haden Shaw a mile or two away.

Anyway, that was enough about Lance Venyon. 'Let's think weddings,' she suggested, 'not graves.'

'Glad you're so keen,' he murmured.

Damn. There was no answer to that, and she had to ignore it. If you step in a cowpat, deal with it yourself.

Badon House was a seventeenth-century building, architecturally altered over the years, and now looking just a little down at heel. Terry had lived here since the 1980s, and it had suited him and his first wife, Anna, admirably, since

12

they, like Gwen, were both great walkers and country-lovers. Terry was at his happiest when his tall, grey-haired figure was either marching pole in hand along a remote pathway on the downs, or delving deep into Kentish history in search of the past. Badon House had suited him in that respect too, since there had been a dwelling on the site for centuries before the present one.

Gwen was now moving into Badon House 'properly', as she explained gravely, for the first time. It was a welcoming home. It was the first time Georgia and Luke had come here, since they had previously met Gwen and Terry either at her former home or at a pub, and Georgia was pleasantly surprised. Wellington boots stood side by side with Victorian jardinières, and on the dresser a chipped Staffordshire eighteenth-century highwayman rode cheek by jowl with a fluffy pink pig. The kitchen range well pre-dated the nineties' vogue for them; one of the lavatories, she later discovered, still possessed an overhead flush, not to mention a tasteful blue rose painted inside the bowl, and the layout of the house had remained all but unchanged since before the Second World War.

'Ah.' Terry's eyes were somewhat glazed by the time they arrived, as the champagne was already flowing. It was a warm day for April, and the party was beginning to spill out on to the brick terrace. 'News for you, Peter. Remember I told you about the medieval foundations we found in the cellars? I've done some more homework. The place is said to have been some sort of dosshouse for monks.'

'Rather far off the road, isn't it?' Georgia commented. 'What would they do up here?'

'Maybe they liked peace and quiet,' Terry laughed. 'Too many wagons thundering by and jolly minstrels disturbing the peace on the A2. Anyway, the church goes way back, and I suppose there were tithes and so forth to collect.'

'Is St Alban's Anglo-Saxon?' Peter asked. There were quite a few such churches in Kent, and several cemeteries too.

'Earlier,' Terry said with some pride. 'There was a Romano-British church or chapel here before the Saxons took it over.'

'A Christian church?' Georgia asked surprised.

'Certainly. Christianity had been around since at least the fourth century, though I guess when the Anglo-Saxons arrived they gave it a bit of a bashing until St Augustine came steaming over to convert them all again. Early Christianity is big in Wymdown. Ever wondered why this place was called Badon House, Peter? King Arthur himself. There's a village tradition that he's still snoozing in them thar hills. Plenty of tumuli and barrows around on the downs, so why shouldn't his royal majesty be tucked inside one, waiting to come back in the hour of England's need?'

'Oh no,' she groaned.

14

Peter was chortling, of course. 'I'm surprised you didn't guess, Georgia. Badon was Arthur's big battle.'

'I don't want to know,' she said firmly. Books on King Arthur had littered Peter's desk for weeks when they'd been investigating and writing up their last case stemming from the Battle of Britain period. She had banned all mention of the gentleman, and for some month or two now all had been mercifully quiet.

Terry chuckled. 'Sorry, Georgia. It's only a tradition. There's not a Round Table in sight in Wymdown.'

'No T-shirts and mugs of Camelot in Kent?' Georgia asked sweetly.

'You may laugh, young woman, but I can tell you,' Terry said firmly, 'there's folk around here reckon they're related to Julius Caesar.'

'You don't have the Ring of the Nibelung in the village pond, do you, or Hobbits running around?'

'Wymdown,' Terry said cheerfully, 'is an odd place. Wouldn't surprise me if I dig up Excalibur round here one day.'

'Keep hoping, your majesty.' Gwen came to join them, linking her arm through her new husband's. 'Meanwhile, Guinevere's here to tell you the Battle of Badon-Lunch is about to begin.'

Hats off to Gwen, Georgia thought, some time later after the magnificent buffet she had produced. Even if she hadn't coped with it all herself, she'd clearly had a hand in it. Peter was equally enthusiastic, when Charlie came to join them on the terrace. 'It's a magnificent old pile, isn't it?'

'Lunch or the house?' Charlie enquired.

'The house,' Peter replied.

'Yes. Terry and Anna couldn't afford to do much to it, and then as soon as he had the money, she died and he didn't have the heart. He's getting interested again now, though. He bought it from a young couple who had ideas about running it as a B-and-B but got divorced instead, and before that it was rented out. So one way and another, poor old Badon House needs some TLC, and tender loving care is what it's going to get under Gwen, if I know my mother.'

'I envy her this garden,' Georgia said, looking at the lawns, trees and flowerbeds stretching, it seemed, into infinity. 'How will Gwen cope with that?' She was no gardener as Georgia knew well.

'Terry's keen enough for two. Also there's an ancient garden retainer.' Charlie pointed to an elderly man, who looked so smart he couldn't have been near a slug in sixty years, Georgia thought.

'Anyway,' Charlie continued, 'the garden isn't quite as big as it looks. There's a ha-ha out there ... and the meadow beyond doesn't belong to Terry. It's grazed, so Ma will have the

16

pleasure of seeing the cows wandering around from time to time. By the way, I asked Terry about your Lance Venyon.'

'He is *not* my Lance,' Georgia repeated patiently.

Charlie grinned. 'Luke says he is. Got the story for you anyway. Lance and Mary Venyon were well known in the village in the late 1950s. Mary seems to have been the domestic type, Lance more of a rip-roaring adventurer. Liked sailing, kept a boat at Hythe. Drowned in 1961. Body later found, duly buried. Wife and daughter moved away shortly afterwards, but wife wanted to be buried next to husband.'

'How on earth did you find all this out?' Georgia felt unexpectedly deflated. A sad story but one that had an ending. Marsh and Daughter's noses twitched at those that lacked closure.

Charlie looked mysterious. 'I have my methods.'

'If entirely lacking in little grey cells,' she threw back at him. 'What methods?'

'His daughter's here.'

Georgia laughed, her interest reviving. 'Really? Where?'

He pointed. 'The lady in mauve and inclining to the non-slender. Elaine Holt is her name.'

Georgia could see the woman he meant. She looked fairly formidable, and the mauve was a mistake – which suggested a lady of firm opinions. She moved towards her, then wondered why on earth she was bothering, and stopped to

17

talk to Peter instead.

'Good do,' he announced with satisfaction.

'Did Gwen do all this food herself?'

'No, some friend of hers helped. Elaine something.'

'Holt,' Georgia supplied. 'Lance Venyon's daughter.'

Peter's eyes gleamed. 'Have you talked to her?'

'No point,' Georgia said. 'A sad story, but nothing for us.'

'Every story should have something for everyone,' Peter said sanctimoniously.

She made a face. 'Then you chat her up. She looks your cup of tea.'

'I will,' he declared, letting this slur go by. She watched as Peter wheeled himself up to Elaine, then her attention wandered, and she was addressed by the elderly man Peter had been talking to. He must be in his eighties, and his mane of white hair was impressive, beautifully soft and smooth. His white eyebrows matched exactly. Mane or not, he looked more lamb than lion.

'I heard you mention Lance Venyon,' he said.

'Did you know him?' she asked curiously.

'Retired vicars tend to have had the privilege of knowing everybody, in a village this size. I took another parish, an urban one a year or two after Lance died, but there's something about Wymdown brought me back here in retirement.'

'Familiar faces?' she asked tritely.

'Perhaps. Though not the Venyons, of course.'

'Were you here when the body was found?'

'I was. Most distressing for his wife, Mary, especially since it was well over a year after the accident.'

'Accident? So it's known what happened?'

'The boat was found drifting, and Lance was most certainly not the suicidal type. I don't think I ever heard the suggestion mooted.'

'What type was he? His daughter describes him as adventurous.'

He considered this. 'Then let's leave it at that.'

If anything was calculated to encourage her *not* to leave it at that, this was. Nevertheless she could hardly say, 'Tell me all.' Discretion was necessary. 'Did you like him?'

His answer was prompt. 'Oh, yes, everyone liked Lance. That was the problem.'

'Problem?' She tried to make it sound casual. What sort? she wondered. A line of lady friends? Work-shy? A series of illegitimate children? Cheated at cards? Ran off with the church funds? She realized with some surprise that her nose was beginning to twitch again.

'Do you have a particular reason for asking?' he asked courteously.

'I have to admit, no. Just general curiosity.'

'Quite understandable.' He didn't volunteer anything further. Feeling rebuffed, though aware she deserved it, she went to claim another glass of champagne. Luke was nowhere to be seen – yes, he was in the garden talking to Gwen. He had nobly offered to drive Peter and herself here, so he was stuck on orange juice. On the way to join them, however, she was accosted by a good-looking man in his twenties; how flattering, her champagne-befuddled head told her.

'Colin Holt,' he introduced himself.

'Elaine's son?' she asked, glancing over to where Peter was deep in conversation with the Mauve Lady.

'Yeah.' He studied her. 'You're Marsh and Daughter, aren't you?'

'Only half of it.' How stupid small talk could get.

'I've read a couple of your books. Is that your dad there chatting up my mother? I heard him ask about my granddad,' he added when she nodded.

'Lance Venyon?' Her interest quickened. Maybe she could get to the heart of the vicar's mysterious 'problem'. 'It sounds as if he was a nice guy,' she began cautiously.

'I wouldn't know. Nor would Mum, really. She was only a babe in arms when he died. But his photos look great.'

'An attractive man?'

'Yeah.'

'Too attractive for his own good?' The champagne was pushing her on, probably unwisely.

'Yeah. Mum always reckoned he was done in.'

'*Murdered?*' She was jolted out of her stupor, as scenarios rushed through her mind.

'Yeah. Did he fall, did he jump or was he pushed?' He grinned at her. 'Take your pick.'

'He was alone on the boat?'

'Who knows? Mum, being aged two at the time, didn't exactly get every detail first hand, but from what I've read, no one's suggested otherwise, except obviously my grandmother. Anyway it's just like Mum to blow it up. Can't be a straightforward accident, has to be more to it.'

Georgia began to dislike this man. 'Perhaps there was.' At the very least there was some mystery here.

He shrugged. 'My grandmother kept all the cuttings. No mention of a police investigation into suspicious death.'

'Not even when the body was found?' At least it was found, she thought, which would have provided some kind of ending for poor Mary. She wouldn't have continued to suffer the worst of all unanswered questions, which Peter and she still endured, after her younger brother Rick had gone missing over twelve years ago. His body had never been found. Georgia pulled herself up quickly. Get away from this subject.

'Did your mother have any reason for thinking he was murdered? Did he have enemies?'

'Anyone like my granddad has enemies.'

'But you didn't know him, so how can you be sure what he was like?'

Another shrug. 'Family, friends, you know how it is. Easy to think of a granddad with whiskers and runny eyes, but when you look at his photos, well, you see him as he was. A go-anywhere, do-anything party-animal sort of chap. One of life's jokers.'

'What did this sort of chap do in life?' Georgia enquired. A joker? Had one of his jokes taken him a step too far?

'Not sure,' he admitted. 'Something in the art world, I think. Not my line. I'm a car salesman.'

He would be. 'A painter?'

'Don't know. Ask Mum.'

'My husband's in art.' A blonde bombshell in her late twenties, too much make-up, too frilly a dress, and four-inch heels too spindly to withstand the onslaught of too much champagne, infiltrated herself with aplomb between Georgia and Colin.

'Is he an artist?' Georgia asked the new arrival's back, since the front was very firmly facing Colin.

'He's got a gallery down in Dover. Sells stuff.' This was tossed over her shoulder in her shrill voice, while Colin got the full force of the follow-up in lower key: 'I'm Kelly. Kelly Cook.'

Georgia decided it was time to fade away gracefully – not that they would notice. And why should they? Colin was at least ten years younger than she was, and Kelly was hunting prey. Georgia faded towards Luke, who was ambling towards the table where Terry and Gwen were awaiting the cake. When it arrived, borne by Charlie, it proved to be a massive replica of Terry's classic old Porsche 356, linked bumper to icing bumper with one of Gwen's Ford Fiesta.

'Different, anyway,' Peter said admiringly. He had owned such a classic before his accident, but he seemed genuinely not to be thinking of that.

'What have you got against poor old King Arthur?' Luke asked, while they waited for the cake to come round. 'Terry says you're a cynic on the subject, yet I gather Arthur's as much of a local as Lance Venyon.'

'Nothing personal,' Georgia explained. 'Don't you remember how obsessed Peter became with him as a diversion from our case about the Spitfire pilots?'

'Yes, but why did he? It's a vast subject to dabble in.'

'He became interested in the Ringlemere Cup, the gold one dug up in Kent a few years ago. Now in the British Museum.'

'That was nothing to do with King Arthur,' Luke pointed out. 'It was Bronze Age, wasn't it? Well before the Romans anyway, let alone King Arthur's time in the fifth century.'

'I suppose in Peter's mind, it got linked

because it was so like the cup found in Corn-wall in the nineteenth century. Near Bodmin Moor I think, which isn't a million miles from Tintagel.'

'All that proves is that there was an ancient trade route going from Cornwall to the Kent coast. We know that anyway. The Pilgrims' Way covers some of it.'

'I sometimes suspect Peter of being a roman-tic at heart. Cornwall to him equals Lyonesse, Tristram and Isolde, Camelot – and King Arthur.'

'What about Wales and King Arthur? Not to mention the rest of Britain, Ireland and half of mainland Europe. Not forgetting Dover.'

'Dover?' she asked. This was a new one.

'Peter must have told you. Malory's *Morte D'Arthur* sets Arthur at Dover Castle, not to mention a battle at Dover against the dreadful Moriarty – sorry, Mordred. Got my villains mixed. You could say Arthur's link with Dover is because the medieval kings of England own-ed the castle, and their spin doctors advised it would be good to represent themselves as the new King Arthur – but then one might ask how did the pre-Malory kings know about Arthur, if there wasn't considerable evidence for his exis-tence?'

'This is very erudite of you, Luke. It must be the orange juice speaking.'

'Nonsense. King Arthur—' he began, as Peter wheeled himself up to them. 'We're talking about your favourite subject,' he said.

'And that is? I can think of quite a few thous-and.'

'How about King Arthur to begin with?'

'I'm more interested in Lance Venyon at present,' Peter replied with dignity. He always had a keen sense of when he was being sent up.

'Because his daughter thinks he might have been murdered?' Georgia asked innocently.

Peter looked disappointed. 'How did you know?'

'Her son, Colin. Why does Elaine think he was murdered?'

'She muttered darkly about various people wanting revenge.'

'Scorned ladies?'

'Possibly, if they were up to sailing boats, pushing people overboard and then swimming off into the blue leaving the dinghy on board.'

'Where did the boat go down?' Luke asked.

'It didn't. According to the vicar,' Georgia said, 'it was found drifting. Colin said there was no indication of a police investigation. I think it's more likely that Lance was too vital a person for Mary to believe that fate has been so cruel as to take him away and so she came up with her own conspiracy theory.'

'Possibly. Jago Priest might tell us,' Peter suggested innocently. 'We'll try him.'

She might have known. Her father was already stampeding ahead, although, so far as she could see, with little cause. It was true her own instinct was prodding her onwards, but it was her job to take the cautious line. 'Who is he?'

'He was Lance's chum during and just after the war years, and even owned this house for a while, though I gather he never lived here.'

Georgia was wary. She was being rushed and would be blowed if she'd pick up on this. 'Try Jago for what, then?'

'I've no idea, Georgia,' he replied blandly. 'Let's find out.'

Two

Why on earth had she come, Georgia wondered. Marsh & Daughter were at that delicate stage of authors' lives when one book is completed, and the next still a jumble of ideas. Usually she and Peter had a number of projects advancing together, until one stood out and demanded attention. This time the projects file had failed to oblige, and each document within it, or each page of notes (Peter insisted on paper backup), had a sheepish look about it, even defiant, as if challenging them to find anything at all interesting within it.

She had to admit that wasn't the only reason she had decided to accompany Peter today. The early May weather was unexpectedly obliging after what seemed non-stop rain, but unfortunately she had no valid excuse for tackling the garden at Medlars while so close by Luke was immersed in his office panicking over his spring list.

'Interesting,' Peter commented, glancing at the house, as he manoeuvred himself into his wheelchair. 'What do we expect from this?'

Georgia considered the neat but somewhat nondescript detached building set some way back from the lane behind high hedges and, from the glimpse through the gateway, shrouded with bushes too. Lewson Street was a hamlet near Faversham, at whose centre was a fine pub. Its houses and cottages were strung out along a long lane leading from a nearby church and back to the busy A2 road.

'The jury's out on this one,' Georgia replied to Peter's question cheerfully, as she rang the doorbell. An academic, perhaps in this green ivory tower?

The man who answered the door was too young to be Jago Priest; he could only be in his late forties. Tall, sturdily built, casually dressed, but smartly. No businessman this, yet no academic either, and any personal memories of Lance Venyon could only be those of a tiny child.

'Mark Priest,' he announced as he greeted them. He was weighing them up carefully, although not unwelcomingly, Georgia thought.

'My father's waiting for you. Come in.' A makeshift ramp for Peter's wheelchair had been laid to the doorstep, which won Mark some brownie points, and he took immediate charge of clearing the path for it to a room at the rear of the house.

'Come in, come in. Make yourselves at home,' boomed its occupant.

It was Jago Priest's size that first struck Georgia. She had expected a frail man in his eighties. This man was certainly that age, but frail he was not. He was tall, still well built, with white hair, which was profuse though hardly rivalling the vicar's mane, and a white beard to complement it. Where the vicar had been restrained, however, this man was jovial in the extreme. When she had telephoned, he had obviously been taken by surprise – not unnaturally considering that Lance Venyon had died well over forty years earlier. Now he exuded welcome, and his personality dominated the room.

Nevertheless the room, or rather its contents, were fighting back with a vengeance, and came a close second. Peter obviously thought the same for he announced approvingly: 'This is somewhere I could feel at home.'

Jago laughed. 'The precious life-blood of a master-spirit, as Milton said, eh? Books.'

That was an understatement. Apart from one framed photo of a striking-looking elderly lady, the books *were* the room. Hardly any wall space

28

was to be seen: two of the walls were entirely hidden, the third grudgingly permitted a window, and the fourth hosted ancient maps. More books were heaped on the floor and were doing their best to encroach on the comfortable-looking chairs and desk, although there a brand-new computer seemed to be eyeing them so sternly that the flood was held at bay. A working room, and an active one, Georgia realized, despite Jago Priest's age.

'My little hobby,' he explained chuckling.

For once lost for the right words, she could only nod weakly, because she had just realized what this collection was all about. Once again, she had run straight into Camelot. This wasn't a higgledy-piggledy random selection of books; they *all*, so far as she could see, had to do with King Arthur, with deviations into early British history, Bronze Age, Roman, Celtic, and Anglo-Saxon. King Arthur reigned serenely over them all.

'It takes some getting used to,' Mark said gloomily, seeing her amazement. 'Imagine growing up with this lot.'

'You're not an enthusiast?'

'No,' he grimaced. 'I deal in facts, not myth.'

Jago didn't seem put out at such betrayal by his son. 'And what is myth and legend but history hiding behind a cloud?'

'Would I be right in thinking,' Peter asked tactfully, 'that these books are divided more or less between the two?'

29

Jago turned to him. 'I can see you have a discerning eye, Peter. This wall has mainly what one might call the Camelot story, the Arthurian story of the Middle Ages, best known through Malory's fifteenth-century *Le Morte D'Arthur*, who drew of course from earlier sources, both French and British, many lost to us now. It is by courtesy of Chrétien de Troyes, writing three centuries earlier, that the Holy Grail stories became part of the Arthurian tradition.'

'Hollywood fodder,' muttered Mark.

'And this,' Jago lovingly touched another wall of books, 'is where Mark and I agree. The historical side of the story. The old faithfuls, *Anglo-Saxon Chronicle*, Gildas, Nennius, Geoffrey of Monmouth—'

'Still largely myth,' Mark defended his corner.

'My son takes the view,' Jago joked, 'that our ancestors got together one day and decided to invent a whole new king to fool posterity.'

This was clearly a battle that had raged for years, Georgia saw with amusement, but there seemed no animosity in it, merely a wariness of what the opponent might say next. The problem was: were they ever going to get Jago to talk about Lance Venyon?

'Dad, your visitors are here to talk about that old friend of yours, not Arthur.'

'Indeed yes, I must remember my manners. You must forgive me.' Jago sat down in his chair, looking his full age. 'Since my wife died two years ago – ' he glanced at the photograph – 'I have little chance to indulge my enthusiasm, and Mark and Cindy, my daughter, are usually my only outlets to sharpen what's left of my wits.'

'Was your wife a King Arthur enthusiast too?' Georgia asked gently.

'Indeed she was. She would say it was because her parents named her Jennifer, which, as you know, is a variant of Guinevere.'

Georgia began to sense even more the kind of upbringing Mark must have had in this overpoweringly Arthurian family. He caught her eye, and obviously read her thoughts.

'I don't live here,' he explained straight-faced, 'so I can take it in small doses.'

Nevertheless, he was clearly on guard and announced he would leave them to make some tea – couldn't stand the strain, no doubt, and who could blame him, Georgia thought?

'Don't pity him.' Jago returned to full vigour, when Mark had left them. 'He pretends to be a doubter, but the mere fact that he tries to disprove my every word by rushing to the history books or the Internet suggests to me that secretly he's as drawn to it as I am. I'll lay a bet with you that when I'm gone this collection goes straight to Tunbridge Wells. That's where Mark lives,' he explained. 'Jennifer and I lived there too when we first returned to England ten years ago. A good town for history, even if Arthur never drank its spa waters. My daughter,

Cindy, is wise enough to keep aloof from our controversy, though I suspect she is more sympathetic to Arthurian history than she likes to let on, whereas the next generation, my dear Sam, is even more of an enthusiast than I am – if that's possible.'

'Perhaps Mark will get his evidence in due course. Our perspective on history can change,' Peter pointed out. 'With a period such as King Arthur's in particular accepted facts can be turned on their head.'

'Just what Lance would have said,' Jago commented quietly.

At last. A chance to get the conversation on track. 'You knew him from his childhood?' Georgia asked.

'No. We met during the war, the Second World War, I should say. We met in 1944. I was twenty-three and he, I think, slightly younger.'

'Were you both in the army?'

'Yes and no. We were in the SAS, the Special Air Service, which was formed in the desert campaign in 1942, but began to spread its wings later in the war. In early 1944 we were with the Partisans behind enemy lines in Italy, and later in Yugoslavia, as it was then called. We were living rough in the mountains a lot of the time which meant there was a lot of time for talking in between ops.'

'About King Arthur?' Peter asked to Georgia's irritation. They needed to keep Jago on the subject of Lance Venyon.

Jago laughed. 'The subject came up, I admit. I had my theories about Arthur even then, and no doubt spouted them enthusiastically. Lance was a good listener; he made fun of me as does Mark, contesting every statement. I don't object to that, it's a good testing ground for my own beliefs. Anyway, Lance must have been more interested than he pretended, because he became a King Arthur fan himself.'

Georgia inwardly groaned. This wasn't looking good. The last thing she had expected was that curiosity about Lance Venyon would lead her straight back into Arthur territory.

'I had been planning to go back to university to do my master's and doctorate on European history,' Jago continued, 'but the war changed everything. I fell in love with Europe, stayed there, took my degrees at the Sorbonne instead, and ended up lecturing in European history in France for many years.'

'What was Lance like as a person?' Peter asked.

'Chalk to my cheese,' Jago replied promptly. 'I would think, but he would *do*. Not that he hadn't a brain. He had, every bit as good as mine, but I was the academic, he was the practical applicator. He was, as one would now say, a people person.'

'His daughter described him as an adventurer,' Georgia put in, 'and his grandson as a party animal.'

'Did they? I'm afraid I lost touch with Elaine

and her mother after Lance's death. They moved away from Wymdown to the West Country, and I remained in France with Jennifer. We were married in 1956, and Mark came along two years later. It's only recently that I've met Elaine again. Now tell me, you write true-crime books, don't you? So why the interest in Lance?'

Georgia seized the opportunity. 'Elaine was told by her mother that he might have been murdered. We wondered if you shared that belief or whether in your opinion it was even possible?'

Jago was clearly startled. 'I find that very hard to believe. Of course I was working in France, but I saw Lance frequently. He came to Paris quite often. I suppose murder might in theory be a possibility, but it is highly unlikely. He often sailed alone, and I never heard any suggestion that anyone was with him that day. In any case, pushing someone off a boat is surely a most inexact way to murder anyone. Suppose they climbed back on board?'

'Murder first, then push over,' Peter said practically. 'I was told Lance's body wasn't found for some while.'

'About eighteen months, I recall. And before you ask, I think it was identified through what remained of the clothes and a ring. Most distressing for Mary, even though she asked Jennifer to come with her as support. I remember talking to Mary at the funeral. Jennifer and I came over from France for it. She told me that despite its condition she knew the body was Lance's. Or was it later she said that? I'm really not sure. Old men's minds wander, Mr Marsh. You will discover that.'

'I'm doing so already,' Peter said feelingly. 'Would anyone have had cause to murder him? I gather Lance wasn't the most faithful of husbands.'

'His lady friends might have lined up to do it,' Jago replied. 'That sounds callous, but then Lance could be too, especially where women were concerned.'

'Any in particular?'

Jago considered this. 'There was a woman in the village he used to go sailing with. Pretty little thing. Broke her heart and she moved away. She was one of those long-distance sailors, around the world in eighty days and all done with one hand. Venetia something, her name was.'

'Venetia Wain?' Georgia asked with interest. She'd not only heard of her but read her books.

'That's it. And of course there was Madeleine who lived in France. Now she was a temperamental lady, although I don't see that extending to pushing someone off a boat. There were other ladies passing through his life too. Poor Mary. Jennifer was most disapproving whenever Lance went too far and boasted about his amours in her presence.'

'What was his line of work after the war?'

35

Georgia persevered. 'Could that have provided a motive for killing him?'

Jago reflected. 'I would think that more probable. You could be bang on the nail with that angle, *if* he was murdered, which I still can't get my mind round. As for his line of work...' He paused, to Georgia's slight irritation. A slight sense of theatre here?

'His grandson thought he was in the art world,' she said firmly, 'but not a painter.'

'Colin was right. However,' Jago looked apologetic, 'this is a long story. You are sure you wish to hear it?'

'Yes,' said Peter firmly.

'Good,' Jago chuckled. 'It's bad luck for Mark he chose today to visit. I'm afraid where Lance is concerned it is just possible I might have to drag his majesty in. So, let us see how it goes. After the war Lance returned to England, but he hankered for the life of action again, he later told me.'

'The army?'

'No. I never quite knew how it came about, but when I next caught up with him he was on the Allied Commission to hunt down art works gone missing after the war. You wouldn't believe the chaos that the end of the war brought with it. Here one has an image of VE Day and smiling faces, but the wider picture has vanished. Men were coming home long after the war, especially from Asia and the Far East, struggling to cope with severed relationships and to pick up old careers or begin new ones. In France and the other occupied countries displaced men dribbled back from forced-labour and concentration camps, trudging hundreds of miles only to find no home or family left. In this human tragedy, art took a back seat for a while, but as life gradually settled down there was a thieves' paradise of stolen, faked and forged works of art. The Allied Commission began to find that it wasn't just looted art that they had to deal with. Their investigations revealed a whole industry of faking, notably of course Han van Meegeren, who produced such magnificent Vermeers that even after his exposure some experts refused to accept their origin.'

'Was Lance still involved in this line up to his death?' Georgia asked. This was a fertile area, if he had indeed been murdered.

'Yes. He loved it. It gave a taste of danger, but had a worthwhile purpose. He was a great talker was Lance. People trusted him.'

'With reason?'

'Indeed. To Lance it was the game, the chase, not the money involved. Nevertheless he liked the good life, so I've no doubt he was well paid. Obviously he was no longer employed by the Commission by then, but he had plenty of other lucrative avenues open. His yacht alone was proof of that. He was deeply interested in works of art for their own sake, whereas – ' his eye wandered to the books at his side – 'it is history that interested me. Thus we were chalk and cheese, as I said.'

'So this job could well have given someone reason to want to kill him,' Peter said, echoing Georgia's thoughts.

'I agree. There was big money at stake, big for the 1950s at least. There were gangs who operated in stolen and faked art all over Western Europe with links to the Eastern bloc. They would certainly not have allowed Lance to stand in their way if he was foolish enough to cross them.'

'Were you still close to him at the time of his death?' Georgia asked.

'Certainly I was. As you know, I owned Badon House for a few years and so I paid the odd visit to England too, but it was mostly in Paris that I met Lance. Not long before he died he told me there were exciting developments in our joint passion. I was to await more news shortly. I never received it.'

'King Arthur?' Georgia asked with dread, just as Peter chimed in hopefully with: 'Could that have had anything to do with his death?'

'In the hypothetical case of murder, it's entirely possible. The prize was immense. It was the remains of Sir Gawain, King Arthur's nephew.'

Jago looked from one to the other and grinned. He had obviously read her thoughts correctly, for he added: 'I can see you are thinking that this is some Piltdown Man scam. An archaeological booby trap for the unwary.'

'Something like that,' Georgia admitted. This jump from fine art back into fantasy was quite a leap. The fact that Peter's antennae were clearly waving furiously did not escape her.

'You can be forgiven for thinking so,' Jago admitted. 'However, Gawain's bones were not all that was at stake, though they were my own chief interest. For others, including Lance, there was something far more enticing.'

'And that was?' Peter asked, when Jago paused.

'King Arthur's golden goblet.'

Georgia's first reaction was to laugh, but she managed to repress it. A golden goblet? This had to be a joke. Unfortunately, as she could see, Peter was taking this as seriously as Jago and therefore she should at least pay lip service.

'You mean,' she said solemnly, 'the Holy Grail itself.' Not *again*!

'No. Very definitely not,' Jago answered to her relief. 'We are talking the *historical* Arthur here, not the medieval creation. I refer to the goblet he held to the lips of the dying Sir Gawain, the cup that Lance and I were – are, in my case – so sure was buried with his body.'

Georgia rapidly ran through all she could remember of the stories of King Arthur, but nothing rang a bell, and she could see that even Peter was at a loss. Jago had probably intended this, because he chuckled.

'You're wondering whether I'm raving mad, or merely an enthusiast on a hiding to nothing.

I am neither.'

Mark chose that moment to enter the room with a laden tray, and had obviously overheard the last part of the conversation.

'I seem to have arrived at the right time,' he said, putting it down on the coffee table and dispensing tea and rather nice-looking macaroons. 'You'll need to fortify yourselves against the onslaught of the round table.'

'This,' his father said firmly, 'is merely a story about Sir Gawain and King Arthur.'

'Do you hear a bee buzzing, Georgia?' Mark asked with resignation.

'A bee?' She was slow on the uptake, because Mark grinned.

'He refers to the one in my bonnet, I'm afraid,' Jago chuckled, although Georgia sensed tension in the air. 'My own pet theory. I imagine we all have one in some area or another. Henry VII killed the Princes in the Tower, Queen Elizabeth I was a man, and so on. We cherish our bees, and feed them from time to time, patiently waiting for confirmation that we are right. I have long held such a bee, and it amused Lance greatly to feed it whenever he could although, as I have explained, he partly shared it.'

'Where does the bee stem from?' Peter asked.

'Dover,' Jago answered.

Georgia remembered Luke's mention of Dover at the wedding, and, hardly to her surprise, Peter already knew about it.

40

'You mean the story in Malory's *Morte D'Arthur* that Gawain was buried in the church within the Dover Castle precincts?' he said eagerly.

'Quite,' Mark confirmed drily. 'A fact so well established that not a word can be found in print or script to confirm it, save in the fanciful ramblings of a gentleman confined to prison for rape and violence. Fortunately he had an exceptionally good prison library to hand. Come off it, Dad. Face the truth. It's a pretty story, that's all.'

'I'll explain, shall I?' Jago said pleasantly, waving this aside. 'It is Lance's role that interests you, of course, Peter, so I'll begin there. He saw his job as a crusade to keep the art world pure: Lance Venyon versus Forgers of the World, rather as it had been in the SAS, the small band of brothers fighting the many. Every fake or forgery unmasked was a victory for his cause. That's why when he told me about some hitherto unknown oils by Dante Gabriel Rossetti in his King Arthur series, I took it seriously. Rossetti's pen-and-ink drawings and planned frescos on King Arthur are well known, but oil paintings are fewer. In the 1950s the Pre-Raphaelites were less highly regarded than they are now, which made it unlikely that the ones Lance had heard about were fakes, although it was still possible. Lance was sure of their provenance, however. In those days the tests for detection were not so developed as they are today, and a lot depended on provenance, expert opinion and the power of talk. Lance understood that well, which gave him an advantage in tracking art works down. He also knew every trick in the trade about faking provenance. He had to, in his job.'

'You never told me about all this,' Mark said, frowning.

'Didn't I?' Jago looked surprised. 'I suppose because Arthur isn't a subject dear to your heart.'

'Art and fakes are,' Mark replied. 'It's my job, after all.' He turned to Peter and Georgia. 'I'm in insurance and look after the art side. What happened to these paintings, Dad?'

'I offered to buy them, sight unseen, but they disappeared before I could do so. Lance told me the Benizi Brothers were involved, and I knew that that meant my chances were nil. They were serious as well as shady operators.'

'Doesn't that suggest that the paintings were fakes?' Georgia couldn't see where this was leading. It seemed a long way from golden goblets.

'Possibly but more likely the contrary. For some years rumours had been spreading through the Arthurian world, by which I mean not only historians and Camelot devotees but those who seek historical artefacts in the hope of proving Arthur's existence. The rumours concerned not only the existence of this golden goblet, as if that weren't enough, but scripts confirming the story. Naturally Lance and I were excited, since this could confirm my theory and probably pinpoint the place where the bones of Sir Gawain could be found.'

'Here we go,' Mark muttered. 'Buzzing-bee time.'

'Fact, Mark, fact,' Jago said patiently. 'Even you can't deny that there was a tradition long before Malory's time that King Arthur had connections with Dover Castle. There is still a hall named after him, and until relatively modern times a gateway. The present hall dates only from the thirteenth century, but Dugdale's *Monasticon* quotes a source stating that King Arthur himself had built a hall in AD 469 and set aside a chamber for Guinevere. Be reasonable, Mark.' Jago turned to his son. 'Even if one does not accept as fact that Arthur himself had a historical connection with Dover, it most certainly suggests that the name of Arthur was not suddenly invented to throw glory on the monarch of the day. Even Lance agreed this was a tenable thesis.'

'It's a long way from that to where you're going,' Mark said sharply. He now seemed to be deliberately needling his father, Georgia thought. Was there a subtext here she wasn't catching?

'Mark's opinion is about to come into its own,' Jago graciously conceded. 'We shall shortly come to the legend, which does *not* mean that it contains no fact. Malory's *Morte*

43

D'Arthur relates that Mordred, Arthur's enemy, seized the opportunity when Arthur was overseas to crown himself king at Canterbury and help himself to Guinevere too. When he heard the news, Arthur came rushing back across the Channel with his forces, including Sir Gawain, to save the day for England, not to mention his wife. Mordred marched to Dover Cliff to stop him landing and a battle took place. Gawain was injured, a former wound reopened, and after the battle he was found in a ship near to death.

'When Arthur reached him, Gawain asked him to oversee his burial. Arthur buried him in the chapel of Dover Castle, which would have been the early Christian church preceding the present St Mary-in-the-Castle. In vengeance Arthur pursued Mordred's retreating forces and a fierce battle took place on Barendoune, now Barham Downs. Arthur won, Mordred was defeated, and a return match agreed which was to take place in the West Country. The battle was duly fought, and Arthur and Mordred slain. Arthur was taken to Glastonbury where he was buried. Or,' Jago added, 'if you believe the Wymdown tradition, he sleeps in a cave on the North Downs, where he will come again in the hour of England's need.'

'How much of this do you believe?' Georgia asked cautiously.

'I believe some truth lies in it, and Lance agreed with me, when the rumours about the

44

goblet began to circulate. It was believed to be the cup with which Gawain was given the last rites, and which was later held to his lips by King Arthur.'

'On what evidence?' Peter asked.

'There were rumours of old scripts that confirmed it, and that John Ruskin, the nineteenth-century art critic and antiquarian, knew of the goblet. Then came one of the paintings mentioned. Rossetti had depicted King Arthur actually holding the goblet to Gawain's lips as he lay dying in the ship. With the evidence of Sir Gawain's skull—'

'If you believe that—' Mark began.

'I do,' Jago said firmly. 'Just as I believe that Arthur himself existed, whether he be one person or an amalgam of various leaders over a longer period. Caxton, the fifteenth-century printer of the *Morte D'Arthur*, states that the skull of Sir Gawain was still shown to visitors to the church with the marks of the wound that had killed him clearly visible. Henry VIII's antiquarian John Leland recorded in the following century that he saw the bones of Sir Gawain. At some point later, however, they disappeared. Fact, fact, fact.'

Jago glanced from Peter to Georgia, who hoped her disbelief wasn't written clearly on her face as on her brain.

'I grant you,' Jago continued, apparently not a whit deterred, 'that it cannot be proved that the skull *was* that of Sir Gawain and not any old skull introduced by an unscrupulous chaplain at St Mary-in-the-Castle to fundraise for his church. That was the attitude Lance pretended to take, since he liked to tease me, but he confessed that if he genuinely thought there was nothing in the story he wouldn't even be discussing it with me. Lance was particularly fond of another Dover legend about the Lady of Farthingloe, a manor belonging to Dover Priory, who was greatly in love with Gawain and he with her. In this legend Gawain was killed on the battlefield and in searching for him the poor lady discovered his head and took it to the priory canons, from whose ranks the chaplains at St Mary's were chosen. Hence the appearance of only the skull at St Mary-in-the-Castle.'

'But there's no proof since you said the *bones*, including the skull presumably, had disappeared,' Georgia pointed out.

'Quite.' Jago gave her an approving nod. 'But this was 1534. Leland reported all his findings on his commissioned Grand Tour of England to the King, who eagerly noted, no doubt, all the interesting items he'd like for himself.'

'The Dissolution of the Monasteries,' Georgia exclaimed. At last she saw where this was leading.

'Indeed. The exact status of St Mary-in-the-Castle is uncertain. It seems to have had a degree of independence and was responsible to Canterbury, rather than to the priory. The three chaplains charged with looking after St Mary and its relics were undoubtedly aware that the King's men were marching down the Canterbury road towards them with their booty bags to fill. What would you do if you were in their place?'

'Hide the valuables.' Peter gave the obvious answer.

'In the 1860s there was heavy restoration work at St Mary-in-the-Castle,' Jago continued. 'The church had been in ruins for years, and while they were digging to study the original foundations they came across...'

As Jago paused, Georgia longed to reply: 'King Arthur, who leapt up crying, "Is it time?"'

'A lead coffin,' Jago concluded.

'With bones?' she asked.

'Empty,' Jago said deflatingly, 'which could confirm our story. We are agreed that these relics would have been taken to a safe place, but a heavy coffin would have been an impediment for the fleeing chaplains.'

Jago seemed to be entering the land of crazy logic in offering a negative as proof, otherwise it would be all too easy to go with the flow and conclude that this was a tenable thesis, Georgia thought.

'The priory in Dover, their first natural choice,' Jago continued, 'had been quick to list all its valuables and cede the priory to the crown. Compliance was its response to the dissolution order, so no relics would be safe there. The next choice for the chaplains would be to take them to a smaller religious site that the King's men had already sacked, in other words one on the road from Canterbury, roughly where the A2 runs.'

No prizes for guessing this one. 'Such as Wymdown,' Georgia said.

'Where else? It is near the old Roman road, and would seem a good choice since it had much in common with St Mary-in-the-Castle. There is evidence of an early church predating the Anglo-Saxon one, and the church is still named St Alban's, after the British saint who was martyred by the Romans when they clamped down on Christianity. When the Romans became more tolerant in the fourth century, temples were built in memory of the sacred martyrs. St Mary-in-the-Castle could be one, Wymdown another.'

'Tell them, Dad,' Mark said, as Jago came to another impressive halt. 'Beware, you two, the Great Theory nears its climax.'

'Mark is a cynic,' Jago said with dignity. 'At first Lance thought I was up the pole,' he admitted. 'I don't think the phrase is used now, but it was a mild expression for being a loony of the first order. I firmly believed that Gawain's remains and the gold goblet were buried near Badon House, in a field adjoining the churchyard.'

Harry Potter, here we come, Georgia thought. And where was Lance Venyon in all this?

'Why there?' Peter asked, looking all too ready to set off straightaway on a treasure hunt, she noted with foreboding.

'Because Badon House used to be a lodging house for monks collecting tithes, it could therefore have been a place of refuge when the chaplains at the castle church were under threat. I bought both Badon House and the relevant field in 1959, as soon as I was convinced in my own mind of my thesis. Such large houses were going for a song then. Lance and Mary were living in Barham, and later moved to Wymdown on the Woolage Green road, and so they could keep an eye on the house for me. I came over occasionally to examine the ground to work out where the site could be. Lance naturally took a great interest.'

'Looking for the golden goblet?' Georgia asked, grateful Lance was back on the scene.

Jago laughed. 'Yes, although in those days gold objects were automatically treasure trove for the crown, so if you are harbouring thoughts that greed was Lance's motive or a motive for his death, you are wrong. In any case,' he said wryly, 'I found nothing – which is why I'm sharing this information with you today. Wherever that goblet is it isn't in that field. I covered every inch of it with a metal detector, and dug too, but it produced nothing.'

'Except a few old coins and bottle tops,' his son put in sourly.

'So what did you conclude?'

'That my theory was wrong, so far as the burial site was concerned. And yet I couldn't quite believe it. So although I sold the house, I still, crazily enough, own the field.' He pulled a face. 'An old man's fantasy.' Another pause, then a grin. 'Or so I thought once.'

'Are you implying it might still be there?' Georgia asked incredulously.

'No, but it is interesting that for some time now the story of the goblet has been circulating once again.'

'How?' Peter asked curiously. 'Is there new evidence?'

Jago frowned. 'Not to my knowledge, but who knows how such things begin? It's mentioned between enthusiasts over the Internet, at archaeological meetings and so on. Sometimes it's a joke, sometimes treated very seriously indeed. New evidence would hardly be revealed, since any historian would naturally want the glory of discovering the hoard all to himself.'

'That would have been so in Lance's time too,' Peter pointed out. 'A powerful motive for murder.'

Jago smiled. 'Indeed, and that is why – ' a glance at Mark – 'I have inflicted this long tale on you. Gold represents the ultimate Grail of worldly possession, and not only in monetary terms. Nevertheless, however greedy we collectors are for fame, it's a far cry from that to pushing my poor friend off a yacht. Conspiracy theories, Mr Marsh, flourish with hindsight, and so, you must find, do those of murder. Lance was my dear friend, and I too find it difficult to grapple with the fact that a simple accident caused his death. But it did, and I still mourn his loss.'

'A wasted day so far as work is concerned,' Georgia observed, as they drove back to Haden Shaw, 'even though Lance Venyon seems to have been an interesting guy. Nevertheless Jago didn't believe he'd been murdered, and he should know. And before you say this King Arthur link should be followed up, remember that there's no evidence that this golden goblet ever existed, let alone that it's alive and well and living deep in the Kentish earth.'

'It's not all been a waste of time,' Peter said complacently. 'He's a nice old boy and Lance's best friend. And if nothing else it showed us that both art and King Arthur can arouse strong feelings. Even the way Mark reacted shows that.'

'True, but where does that take us?'

'Even best friends can fall out over passionate beliefs.'

'You mean when Jago found there was nothing buried there, he blamed Lance for encouraging him, jumped into Lance's yacht, and once out at sea, pushed him off it.'

'Stranger things have happened.'

'Nonsense. There's not even a sniff of a suspicious death.'

51

'What about Sir Gawain's?'

'Ha, ha,' Georgia retorted crossly. 'We're not running a round-table service ourselves, prepared to right the wrongs done to Gawain's bones.'

'Seriously, Georgia, I think we should look into Lance Venyon's death further, including the lovelies of yesteryear. Let's do the job thoroughly. Gwen said Venetia Wain's daughter still lives in Wymdown. Why not book an overnight stay at Badon House to check into it and perhaps talk to Venyon's daughter again?'

'And if that leads nowhere, we can write Lance Venyon *and* King Arthur's cup off?' One of them had to take a firm stance or they'd be wandering around Camelot for ever.

Peter hesitated. 'Probably.' He gave her a beaming smile.

Badon House gave not the slightest sniff of buried secrets when she arrived there two days later. Nor did Wymdown. Maureen Jones, Venetia Wain's daughter, was out and so was Elaine Holt, so Georgia had spent the afternoon gazing at Lance and Mary Venyon's former home in the hope it might tell her something about its former occupants. Its Georgian windows and neatly trimmed lawn and borders blandly stared back at her, however, telling her nothing at all. Nor had the foundations of Badon House, which she had explored on her return. All the cellar now contained was Terry's wine and a large number of pipes and spiders.

Just as she was prepared to write the visit off on work grounds and enjoy chatting to Gwen, Terry came home with good news. 'You might catch Maureen in the church about seven-thirty,' Terry told her. 'I bumped into her this afternoon and she mentioned that she does the flowers on Friday evenings.'

'Can I ask her about her mother's former lovers?'

Gwen laughed. 'Peter would do just that. Go carefully would be my vote, knowing Maureen. By way of introduction, there's an old fresco on the north wall you can enthuse about.' Gwen elected to delay supper until her return, and so after a drink and nibbles, Georgia set off down the footpath to Wymdown church. The sun had almost vanished for the day, and the minute she entered the churchyard it felt chilly. She could see no lights in the church and was uneasily conscious of her solitariness. 'And no birds sing.' This churchyard reminded her of the Keats' poem. Here, time seemed temporarily suspended in a still heaviness, and she hurried through it to the church entrance, only to find it locked. The bird she was after had already flown, and frustrated she turned to go back to Badon House. She was beginning to understand why Jago was so keen on his theory. It was spooky enough here to imagine King Arthur tossing and turning beneath every gravestone.

Gwen had told her that the field Jago must own was not the one through which the footpath ran, but the one that stretched from the end of Badon House's garden down to the church-yard's side. It lay on Georgia's right at present, and looked too rocky and too much at an incline to be ploughed. That must be good from the archaeological viewpoint. She caught herself, impatiently aware that she was beginning to take Jago's theory as valid, even though he had given up on this field. She decided she would get back to Badon House as quickly as she could.

Nevertheless she lingered in the churchyard, not quite sure why she did so. It was easy to imagine that there was a bear in every bush. She could see plenty of such bushes on the far side where several large gravestones were clustered. A paper bag was sticking out from behind the one on the left. Perhaps this was where the local drug deals were done, debts paid, goods handed over. It was a remote enough place for it.

Automatically she began to walk over to pick up the rubbish, feeling increasingly ill at ease. This churchyard, or at least this corner of it, was distinctly creepy, far in excess of that generated by its prime purpose. It hadn't seem-ed creepy to her the other day, but perhaps this only proved how subjective one's feelings could be—

Something seemed to catch her by the throat. *That wasn't a paper bag.* It was a hand. A still hand.

She found herself running towards it, as if to

dismiss all thoughts of what it might be by disproving them as quickly as possible. She must be mistaken. The splashes on it were mud, the hand—

—*was* a hand. It belonged to a body that didn't move. Couldn't move. The sightless eyes of the dead man stared upwards, his clothes soaked with dried blood. She forced herself to touch the wrist to be sure of what was obvious. It felt cold, and the block of ice inside her that had momentarily stopped all thoughts unfroze. She gagged as the bile rose in her throat and with trembling hands delved into her bag for her mobile phone.

Three

A crime scene. She was standing in a crime scene. Georgia tried fiercely to concentrate on de-personalizing what was on the ground before her as she shivered in the dim light. In the distance the evening sun still shone, but in this tree-shrouded place it had long gone, leaving nothing but her and a dead body. It was that of a young man, with a shock of dark hair, and he had been shot. That was all too clear from the blood on his anorak, obviously from the entry wound in his chest, and judging by its appearance death had occurred not long ago. There was no gun to be seen.

While they had been sipping their drinks inside Badon House, Terry had gone outside to fetch something and had returned with a comment that the only thing that disturbed their peace at Badon House was the occasional potshot at a rabbit or fox. Had he recently heard a shot, perhaps *this* one? Out here, with woods and open fields around, it was unlikely that anyone would hear or care. The night has a thousand eyes: she remembered the poem she'd learned at primary school, but here they would all be closed. There would be a thousand ways for a murderer to escape.

No birds were singing. This was May, the time for their spring song, yet there was no sound at all, save her breathing in the heavy silence of evening. The fresh damp smell of dew contrasted strongly with the ugliness and tragedy of the corpse so near to her. She tried to force herself to concentrate on the crime scene, to notice details to help the police, but all she could do was stare blindly around her, her thoughts a jumble. This corner of the graveyard was more than eerie; it had a darkness and a sinister quality as though even the sun was scared to enter it. Nonsense, she told herself. Pure gothic fantasy. She knew she was wrong, however. Long after this crime had been solved, the place would still smell like this.

At last she heard the welcome sound of the siren growing nearer. Along the lane to the church only rabbits and foxes would have to clear the way, yet its shrillness had never seemed so welcome. With police arrival she would have company, and after giving her statement she could leave. Eventually, that is. She knew it would take time.

Georgia's fingers curled over her mobile. She could ring Luke, but what for? A cry for support? Surely she should be able to cope on her own. She'd ring him after the ordeal was over.

Then, thankfully, she saw lights, as the police car drew up.

'Here,' she called, as doors slammed and flashlights pin-pricked their way through the churchyard. She resisted her impulse to run towards them in the interests of not wanting to add unnecessary footprints to the scene. She had longed to call DCI Mike Gilroy, Peter's former sergeant in his police career. With luck this might just be within his area, but she had reluctantly decided not to. This death was nothing to do with Marsh & Daughter, and she should go through the right channels.

'Miss Marsh?' the elder of the two DCs asked.

Once upon a time, a fatherly Dixon of Dock Green might have patted her on the shoulder murmuring, 'There, there. You leave all this to me.' No longer. The steely eyes of this young policeman spoke of efficiency and impersonality. There were merits in both approaches, and Georgia braced herself to appreciate the only one she was offered.

'Yes,' she replied.

'DC Stewart, and – ' he indicated his female colleague – 'DC Jenkins.' The girl nodded, already on her radio summoning the team.

It would begin now. The machine was set in motion. Georgia felt her racing heart slowly calming down, now that the action was out of her hands. She retreated, while they conferred. She'd heard it all before, even seen some of it from a distance when Peter was a DI himself, and since then during Marsh & Daughter investigations. She had been an outsider then, however. Now she was a part of the investigation. She had found the body and as first on the scene would be automatically suspect until proven innocent. There would be a hunt for the gun when the SOCOs got here; they might think she had removed it. She thought of this with some surprise, uneasy at the thought, as though it linked her to the body, giving her responsibility towards it.

'Are you all right?' DC Jenkins asked, coming over to her. As a Dixon, she wasn't doing badly after all.

'I think so.'

She wasn't. With tension relaxing, Georgia could feel herself swaying, and the DC led her to a dilapidated bench where she could put her head between her knees. It helped a little, especially when the DC volunteered to get some water from the car. Luke, I really should call Luke, she thought dully. And Gwen. Yet by doing so she would seem to be admitting her own weakness. She was supposed to be a professional crime investigator, not to faint at the sight of blood and death. It was more than that causing this, however. It was the atmosphere here, over and above the effects of the time of day and the gloom of the bushes. In this corner of the churchyard there was evil; perhaps from the murder that had just taken place, but perhaps for longer. Unbidden, Jago Priest's story of the chaplains' burial of their treasure came back to her. She could imagine this churchyard, probably much smaller then if it existed at all, and the chaplains passing through it, silent, dark figures in the night, fleeing from their enemies. The field where Jago – and Lance Venyon – had so fondly believed the remains of Sir Gawain to be buried was only thirty yards away.

There was no darkness any longer. The team was arriving and the first floodlight immediately illuminated the scene, white-suited figures were taking control, stepping plates laid ready to avoid disturbing footprints, tent erected, video cameras, and tape. Georgia was far enough away for the inner-cordon tape to exclude her, so she remained where she was, an isolated observer. And then came salvation.

'What on earth are you doing here, Georgia?'

Mike Gilroy asked kindly, sitting down at her side. 'This got anything to do with you and Peter, has it?'

'Is this your case?' she asked him stupidly. She didn't need the answer, she was just overwhelmingly grateful for his presence.

'Yes. I heard your name, so I decided to poke my nose in. Unless of course...'

He didn't need to continue. She understood. 'Unless I'm involved in it. And the answer's no. I just found him.' The use of 'him' was important. It would be so easy to think of the body as 'it', an impersonal object now that life had been taken away.

'Alone in the churchyard in the evening? Walking a dog, were you, Georgia?' Mike prompted her.

She supposed it must sound strange. 'Peter's sister Gwen lives up there—' She waved in the direction of Badon House. 'I'm staying with them overnight. Not a case, or not one yet, to be more precise. They sent me here to meet someone who was doing the church flowers. No sign of her when I arrived.'

'Which was when?'

Of course. He needed every detail. This wasn't just a chat between her and Mike. She was a witness like any other.

'I came down the footpath from Badon House and got here at about seven-thirty. The church was already locked up, and in darkness. I was going away again when I saw something

60

poking out behind the gravestone. I thought it was litter, so I came to pick it up.'

That sounded not only weak, but imbecilic. But how could logic explain all the hundred and one things she and anyone else might do without any apparent reason or judgement – and usually without finding a dead body at the end of the mission?

'Did you touch him? Touch anything else? Gun?'

'No gun. I touched his hand, and then tried for a pulse. I've never been too good at that. I couldn't find one.' How stupid. Of course she couldn't. He was dead.

Mike nodded as though she'd said the most natural thing in the world. 'We'll take fingerprints, and DNA and firearm-residue swabs from you. That should clear you.'

'I hope so,' she managed to joke, although it didn't emerge like one.

'Who was it you expected to find in the church?'

The crime tent was up now, and figures were moving purposefully in and out. The outer-cordon tape was being strung round, and white-clad figures would begin to crawl over the ground like giant slugs, devouring every possible clue in their allotted path.

'I'll be back,' Mike said, as he was summoned away by the pathologist. 'Don't move.'

No problem. She couldn't, much as she wanted to be away from this place. It was ten minutes before Mike returned.

'Do you know who he was?' she asked.

'No. Do you know Wymdown, Georgia? He's probably local. No sign of car keys or credit cards.'

She shook her head. 'I've only been here once. To a wedding two weeks ago. Peter's sister Gwen.'

'Did you see anything at all as you walked through on the way to the church? Did you have any sense that you weren't alone? Did you hear anything?'

'Nothing. Certainly not a shot. Not even a bird.'

'Nothing was changed on this scene while you were checking the body? You're sure you touched nothing else?'

'Yes. I knelt down on the ground, then retreated to make the call. I wanted to see a woman called Maureen Jones in the church to ask her about her mother, Venetia Wain. She was a long-distance sailor—'

'Taking it up, are you?'

'No again.' Georgia managed a smile, conscious he was trying to help her. 'Peter wanted to check something out.'

Mike groaned. 'This case that isn't one yet. Have you two been stirring up enough trouble for it to have any conceivable connection with this?'

'No stirrings at all,' she replied firmly. 'It's only an idea which will probably come to nothing, and even Peter acknowledges that. And it has nothing to do with this death.'

'You're sure you've never seen this poor chap before?' Mike indicated the corpse, now thankfully shrouded from her view.

'Yes. He's a stranger to me.'

'I've seen him,' volunteered a SOCO, who had arrived with some slip shoes for Georgia while they took prints of her shoes. 'In a pub.'

'Helpful,' commented Mike mildly.

'This pub,' was the hasty reply. 'Wymdown. He was a barman in the Green Man.'

'Name?'

'Pass, sir. Sandy, I think I heard someone call him.'

'Georgia!' She could hear Terry's shout in the distance, and realized he was being barred from entry into the crime scene.

She looked at Mike, who nodded. 'You can go. You will stay overnight, though? We'll need a statement tomorrow.' Arrangements made, she made her way back to the churchyard gate, gave her name to the PC on guard for his clipboard, and fell into Gwen's arms. She'd always been such a comforting aunt, especially during Georgia's childhood tantrums, and a quarter of a century later she still was.

'You gave us a fright, Georgia,' Terry said anxiously. 'All those police sirens. We thought it was you.'

She was appalled. That hadn't even occurred to her, and she was immediately remorseful.

'Only a witness. The police want me to make a statement tomorrow, Gwen, so I'll be hanging around for a while.'

'Stay tomorrow night too,' Gwen said immediately. 'Terry's rung Luke.'

More trouble, Georgia thought. She should have rung him, but she didn't care now. All she wanted was to be away from here and back in the haven of Badon House. And then she remembered Terry's reference to pot-shots, and had to force herself to ask him about them.

He looked surprised. 'It could have been in this direction – let me think. It was while I was fetching the torch from the car. Sevenish, maybe.'

'We should tell them.' Georgia's heart sank. She saw Gwen's glance at Terry.

'Not we. Me,' he said firmly. 'You and Gwen get back to the house.'

Luke arrived almost as soon as they reached it. 'There was no need—' she began, as she opened the door to him.

She saw a mixture of emotions cross his face from anger to relief, as he came in. 'I would say there was every need.' He gave her a long hug, then said grimly, 'Never, never, leave me out again.'

'I won't,' she promised. Why had she, she wondered. It had seemed important at the time, but now only stupid and selfish, and she was overwhelmingly glad to see him. Mike would have rung his wife to say he was on a case. Why on earth hadn't she rung Luke?

She couldn't wrestle with this now. She was too tired, and now hungry, she realized. It was well past nine o'clock, and Gwen's dinner was busy spoiling in the oven. It tasted good nevertheless, after first Terry and then the food itself arrived. No one mentioned the body, and it was some time before she realized they must be longing to know its identity. She would, in their shoes, and so she told them.

'But we knew him,' Gwen exclaimed in dismay. 'You know, Terry, that young exotic-looking young man who didn't understand what bitter was when he first came. You had to explain beers to him.'

'Yes. Wouldn't trust him further than I can—'

'Terry!' Gwen said warningly, and he laughed.

'Throw a dart,' he finished. 'But I'm sorry he's dead. Drugs? Gang fight?'

'In Wymdown?' Georgia asked incredulously. Surely this village was picture-postcard territory. 'Do you have gangs here?'

'Sure. Nowhere's immune now. Still, the churchyard seems a bit out of the way; it's normally a punch-up behind the pub. My money's on drugs. Perfect place. Sure you didn't hear a car, Georgia?'

'No.' That wasn't so surprising, since if the shot Terry had heard had been from the churchyard the murderer, if in a car or on foot, would have left well before her arrival. But where was Maureen Jones? She could only recently have left – unless she failed to turn up, of course. And, it occurred to her, the fact that it was a regular job for her rather put the kybosh on its being a drugs rendezvous. Poor timing, if it had been.

She had just finished helping Gwen with the washing-up when Mike arrived. He looked tired, and Gwen quickly made him some cocoa, when he turned down the offer of coffee. 'Have you finished now?' Georgia asked.

'For today at least. The SOCOs haven't, of course. They'll be here for another day or two. I thought you'd like to know that Sandy from the pub was in fact Sandro Daks, born in Estonia to an Estonian family, and now living in Budapest. He was over here to do an art course of some kind at Canterbury and doing pub work to help out. This was his evening off.'

'Had the pub any ideas on why he could have been killed?'

'No, but that's nothing unusual. We'll know more after the autopsy. No obvious signs of injection so far, anyway. No rumours of drugs at the pub, but that's not surprising either.'

'And none in the village, so far as I know,' Terry put in defensively. 'He was a nice lad, even if he did have an eye for the main chance.'

'A wicked smile,' Gwen said reflectively.

'Wicked as in evil?' Georgia asked.

'No. Wicked as in I wish I was forty-odd

years younger, but I'm glad I'm not. The sort one falls for at seventeen.'

'This,' Terry joked, 'is our honeymoon. I feel seventeen again. By the way, Georgia, what happened about Maureen?'

'She wasn't there. Everything in darkness.' Georgia had forgotten they didn't know, and she quickly remedied this. 'I still need to see her,' she finished. Her own mission still had to be completed, regardless of what had happened tonight.

'So,' Mike pointed out gently, 'do we. And *we* come first, Georgia.'

'Do you have to stay another night?' Luke asked later as she hopped into Gwen and Terry's guest bed. 'I'll have to get back tomorrow morning. Saturday or not, this week the oast house calls.'

Georgia hesitated, but this was Luke, whom she loved, so she should give some explanation. 'I'd like to stay here rather longer, go to the pub perhaps.'

'There's a good pub in Haden Shaw.'

No help for it. The real reason was necessary. 'It seems like running away from Sandro Daks' body if I leave too soon,' she confessed.

'In that case,' Luke said practically, 'it's a good job you'll have a warm one next to you tonight to remind you of what you're missing.'

Georgia laughed. 'I'm in complete agreement.' After all it was only one more day and after that not only Sandro Daks, but Lance Venyon, King Arthur, and the rest of the round table could surely be laid to rest for good.

Rest, it appeared, was denied to her, however. Sleep did not come easily.

'Are you awake?' she heard Luke whisper later that night.

'Yes. I can't sleep properly for nightmares.'

'Worrying about Sandro Daks?'

'About death and Sandro Daks.' The nightmare that rolled round her head taking her over, threatening, retreated as she framed it into words.

'It comes with the territory,' he murmured, turning over to hold her tightly.

'What territory?'

'Your job. Peter's job. Even my job.'

'Don't good things happen in it too?'

'You know they do. They just get crowded out once in a while, and need to be hunted down again to make themselves felt.'

They did, and his hands and body assured her of it, first gently, then possessively until pleasure took over mind; eventually mind rejoined it to reassure her that Luke was right. Given its chance, the positive always won. It was merely that in today's world it usually had to play the waiting game.

Next morning, while waiting for Luke to finish in the shower, she found herself at the window, looking over the garden to the field that Jago

Priest had so intensively scoured for traces of King Arthur. She would surely soon be free of golden goblets and Lance Venyon; she could return to Medlars and the project file, which now appeared not frustrating but as a treat in store. Peering to the right, she could see figures moving around the churchyard, early though it was. In the lane the mobile incident van would be set up, and that thought returned last night's horror to her in full force. That too would be over today, so far as her role was concerned. She would give a formal statement and that would be that, except for perhaps giving evidence at an inquest or trial. Her duty to Sandro Daks was nearly over, she told herself. She only had Maureen Jones to think about, whom she hoped she could meet some time during the day – and with luck Elaine too. Then she could take Terry and Gwen to dinner at the pub tonight ...

Yes, and better, she could have lunch there herself. She might learn more by being on her own. Not even Mike, she told herself, could prevent her from taking a pub lunch in the Green Man. Then she caught her own faulty logic. So her duty to Sandro Daks was nearly over, was it? Why then was she intent on going to the Green Man? Because of Sandro himself? Just because she had found his body? No, she realized with dismal certainty, it was because of that churchyard and more particularly that corner of it. The rank smell of evil stemming from it made it seem almost as if Sandro Daks had wandered into it by chance, rather than caused it by his death. And *that* was why she felt the need to rid her mind of it, to convince herself that she had been mistaken – if that were possible.

For a weekday lunchtime the pub was surprisingly packed with customers; then she realized that it was the obvious place for the village to gather for discussion about the crime, especially since the pub was the heart of the tragedy.

Should she join in and establish her street cred as the person who found the body? Georgia decided against it. She was a stranger. Everyone would clam up, glad of a chance to see her as Public Scapegoat No. 1, instead of one of their own. Instead Georgia ordered some food and waited. She seemed to be the only one eating, which suggested whoever brought her order to her might have more time to chat than the bar staff. She was rewarded when her ploughman's arrived courtesy of a good-looking, if sulky, young girl who peered at her unenthusiastically from behind a dark screen of hair falling over her face.

'Thank you.' Georgia waved aside the proffered extra chunk of bread in the interests of an opening gambit. 'I'm not that hungry, not after last night—'

'Last night?' The girl stared at her as though she were bragging about an orgy.

'I'm the person who found Sandro's body.'

'You?' A suspicious look.

'I'm sorry,' Georgia said sincerely. 'It's always a shock when death strikes so close, no matter whether you're close to the person or not.'

'Everyone liked Sandy. He was fun. We had the police here this morning and last night.'

'It was a terrible thing,' Georgia mused.

'He was shot, wasn't he? Did you see it happen?'

A touch of the ghoul was appearing, and it was a hopeful sign that she was at least asking questions. Georgia expanded on what she had seen and not seen. 'Were you his girlfriend?'

'In a way, see?'

Georgia thought she did. The girl who announced herself as Karen would have liked to have been Sandro's girlfriend was her translation of this reply.

'He'd been here eight months. He liked Wymdown, he said.' Karen managed to make it sound as though she were the entire reason for this. As, for all Georgia knew, she was.

'Did he live in the pub?'

'Rented a room somewhere.'

'Was he a clubber? Wymdown seems a quiet place for a student of his age.'

'Nah. He liked sketching and that. He went clubbing in Canterbury or Dover.'

'Did he have a car?'

'If you can call it that. A beat-up old wreck.

71

Yeah. What you interested for?' Karen asked belatedly.

'I don't know,' Georgia replied truthfully. 'I suppose it's because I found him. I felt I needed to know more. Were you working here when he arrived?'

'Yes.' This seemed to encourage her to open up. 'I thought he was gorgeous, but Tom, my boyfriend, said he'd wallop me if I went out with him.' Some pride here, Georgia thought. A century of women's rights had apparently passed Wymdown unnoticed. '"What's he here for, if not you?" Tom asked,' Karen continued. 'So I said he's got family here, he says, wants to look them up.'

'Family?' Georgia picked up. 'From Hungary?'

'Or friends. Dunno. He was asking after someone called Lance Vennon or something like that.'

'Venyon,' Georgia corrected automatically, in shock at this innocent thunderbolt.

'Whatever.'

Karen disappeared leaving Georgia looking bleakly at her ploughman's. It seemed she was not going to be able to wipe Wymdown and King Arthur from her mind as quickly as she'd hoped. Peter would never let this vanish into thin air now that even Georgia had to admit there were questions here to be answered. Lance was linked not only with her bête noire, King Arthur, but worse, with a corpse that she

72

herself had discovered.

After she had imparted this news to Peter on her mobile, he announced that he was coming over. *Now* – in case she was in any doubt. 'We'll have to tell Mike,' he added.

'Of course.' Georgia did not relish the thought of it, though. Mike would not be pleased that his case, picked up through personal concern for her, might have become caught up in one of the Marshes' whimsies, as he called them – generally, she conceded, when he was exceptionally irritated.

She was right, but he'd calmed down by the time he arrived at Badon House. 'I suppose I can't blame you,' he said grudgingly, after she'd explained exactly where they were, or weren't, with Lance Venyon.

'No,' Georgia agreed. How could she possibly have guessed that Sandro Daks had known about Lance Venyon? 'Unfortunately,' she continued, 'Karen, the girl at the pub, doesn't seem to have enquired any further about Lance. She wasn't sure whether he was family or friend.'

'You said Lance Venyon died in 1961. That's a long time to remember someone without having any news,' Mike commented.

'Estonia, where the Daks family stemmed from originally, was part of the Soviet Union until it split away in 1990,' Peter pointed out. 'It wasn't too easy to conduct correspondence and there was no chance of travelling to the West out of the Eastern bloc.'

'That's true,' Mike granted. 'So tell me who I need to speak to about Daks' connection with Lance Venyon?'

'His daughter Elaine. Jago Priest, our main contact, was a friend not family. Do you,' Peter asked, politely for him, since when he normally addressed Mike it was still as DI to sergeant, 'have other lines of enquiry?'

Mike looked at him contemplatively for a few moments, as if making him wait. Then: 'It depends,' he said.

'On what?' Georgia asked.

'On whether this Venyon is a Marsh & Daughter case, or still one of your little hunches.'

When did a hunch become a case, Georgia wondered. Usually when facts began to support it. Marsh & Daughter's cases usually sprang from unresolved crimes that had left their mark on the place where they were committed, as tenprints (in police jargon) on time.

Mike didn't go in for atmosphere, or even hunches. No tenprints on time had yet made any appearance so far as Lance Venyon was concerned – unless he was connected with the corner of the churchyard. No, that was too tenuous, Georgia thought uneasily. Unless of course that was where his grave was? Stop, she told her racing mind. There is nothing, but *nothing*, to suggest anything unresolved about Lance Venyon.

Except his name, her mind retaliated. Spoken

by a young man who was now dead.

She could tell that even Peter was stuck to answer Mike's question, which he confirmed by his eventual reply: 'We don't yet know.'

'My call, then. I'll go with you. The reason that brought Daks to this village is a tenable line of enquiry, which means that Venyon could be too. Now for fact. You tell me Lance Venyon died in 1961 as the result of a yachting accident. We can check that. It's too far back for anyone still active in the force to remember, unless we're very lucky, and I doubt if any files remain, even if there were any in the first place. You said the family believes he was murdered. That's no evidence, of course, but interesting.'

'The wife is dead, so we're only going by what the daughter and grandson tell us, and Jago Priest doesn't agree with the murder thesis,' Georgia explained to Mike.

'Airy-fairy, so far, then?'

'That's our privilege,' Peter rejoined. 'You know we leave any airy-fairyness on our part behind when we take up a case,' and when Mike reluctantly nodded, added, 'Then Georgia and I will take on the Lance Venyon case. OK by you, Georgia?'

'It breaks our rules...' she began, then stopped. What she couldn't voice was her trepidation at the thought of a murderer of today strolling towards them arm in arm with Lance Venyon, especially with King Arthur grinning in the background. It was a formidable prospect. Then she remembered Sandro Daks, who had been a young man in his early twenties but was now dead. A lost life. She owed it to him to see what this was all about. 'It could all be coincidence,' she ended hopefully.

'I don't believe in coincidence,' Peter said flatly, 'until it's proved to be one.'

'You're right. Let's go ahead,' she agreed.

Peter visibly relaxed. 'Good,' he said briskly. 'What are the other lines of enquiry, Mike?'

'Mine,' Mike replied warningly. 'You keep strictly to 1961 and Lance Venyon's death.'

'And if he clashes with today?'

'You know the rules. You're on to me quicker than broadband.'

'Of course.'

'Sandro Daks lodged with a Mrs Saxon on a farm on the outskirts of the village. We've been over his room for next-of-kin details in Budapest. He used the attic for painting.'

'Karen at the Green Man said he did landscape sketches,' Georgia observed. 'That's unusual for an art student today, isn't it?'

'Maybe not this one. We spoke to his tutor this morning. He was a talented pupil, but he didn't specialize. He was a first-class copyist, and as for his own work he did line drawings, landscapes, portraits – you name it, he painted it. He earned money by sketching local sites for tourists.'

'How did he sell them? In the street?'

'One step up. Through a gallery and small

craft shops. In particular a gallery in Dover, so we discovered from his room. We're going to check it out. It's run by a Roy Cook.'

Well, well. Husband of the famous Kelly whom Georgia remembered from Gwen and Terry's wedding. She also remembered her instant limpet-like attachment to Colin. Had she applied her claws to Sandro too?

'...girlfriend in Canterbury,' Mike was saying, 'according to his mates, and one in Dover too.'

Just like Lance Venyon, Georgia thought. At least King Arthur never flaunted his floozies.

Four

'You really think King Arthur's involved in this?' Luke was gracious enough not to laugh. Indeed he had immediately put his publisher's hat on when she began to talk about Lance Venyon, and so mirth would have been out of place.

'I can't quite believe in a rumoured golden goblet being a serious motive for murder, but I suppose Arthur himself could have provided one through those paintings. Or some other art theft could be involved in it.'

Georgia was conscious that she was breaking

the 'rules' by chatting about work while setting the table for dinner. They'd been living together for less than six months, and such 'rules' and 'vetoes' took time to be established. Medlars, however, was a relaxed home to live in, and it was all too easy to forget that in talking to her partner, she was also talking to her publisher. The only fixed 'rule' so far was that Luke's oast-house office was his kingdom alone, and she entered it only on Marsh & Daughter business. Seeing Luke leave for the thirty-yard walk to the oast house was like bidding farewell to King Arthur galloping off for Camelot. She couldn't blame Luke, since she and Peter had their own ivory towers. Haden Shaw was only a mile or two from Medlars, but it felt much more once she was working in Peter's office there or her own.

Luke frowned. 'You mean Venyon could have been on the track of some shady deal that went wrong?'

'That's one theory. Another is that a girlfriend bumped him off, or even his wife, but we haven't made any progress on that front yet.'

'And the death of Sandro D might have been connected with it?'

'Only by an enormous jump. All we have is a coincidence waiting to be turned into evidence.'

'The snag is,' Luke said, watching her drain the spaghetti, 'that if there is a link you can't write it as a Marsh & Daughter case while the police are investigating the Daks death or if a trial is pending.'

'You're right.' Trust Luke to hit the weak point, which Peter had been reluctant to face. 'But we'll take the risk when and if it comes.'

'Georgia...' he began tentatively.

She knew what he was going to say, and would make it easy for him. 'You can't sign the book up with that proviso hanging over it.'

'Not without safeguards.'

'No contract or no money?' she asked practically. Now the question was raised, she might as well get it answered.

He put his arm round her. 'I do love doing business with you, Georgia. The answer to that is no money and a get-out clause on both sides, if you want a contract now.'

'I do love doing business with you, Luke. So generous.'

'But still in business, you note.' He looked anxious, though. 'You don't mind, do you, Georgia?'

'No. We foresaw it.' Well, it was almost true. Peter had been blithely hoping for the best, of course. 'But Peter is stuck on this one at present.'

'And you?'

'I feel duty-bound and getting warmer,' she acknowledged. 'It has an odd attraction in that Venyon's working life and character are intriguing even if there's no evidence of murder so far. But I must admit it's hard to see how we could ever make a credible case for it if he was simply pushed off the boat.'

'Please don't name a living murderer, that's all I beg of you.'

Georgia finished her last set of notes, printed them out for Peter – he liked it that way, even though as they shared a computer system he could easily read it on screen or print it out himself. 'Days of feudal grandeur of having secretaries,' she regularly mocked him, but he simply agreed with her, so teasing him was no fun.

She left her own small house in Haden Shaw guiltily. It always seemed to be looking at her reproachfully for neglecting it. She still kept her office here, and put up occasional visitors, since Medlars was only being 'sorted out' little by little. Most of her time was spent in Peter's office next door, although her own house provided valuable thinking and writing space.

'I've been studying the newspaper reports of the death and later inquest again,' Peter greeted her glumly. 'Not much to go on, are they?'

She agreed. Two weeks had passed, but all their endeavours had produced were two short reports of the inquest in local newspapers, one in the *Dover Herald*, the other in the *Canterbury Express*, together with one of the memorial service six months after Lance's disappearance and one of the funeral. Apart from a list of principal mourners at the funeral, in which the only recognizable names were Mary Venyon and Jago and Jennifer Priest, it told them little. The yacht had been a classic all-wood eighteen-foot Hillyard, and Lance had sailed from Hythe at seven in the morning on 14 September 1961. His car was found parked on the seafront. His wife had said he had left in the mid-afternoon of the day before to meet someone, intending to stay in Hythe overnight on the boat and go sailing the next day – she didn't know whether it was alone or with someone. The boat had been found drifting about four miles off the French coast the following day with the dinghy still on board.

The inquest reports, still closed to the public, had been available to Mike, but had given little relevant information on the body that they didn't already know from Jago, save that there was no indication from the remains of how Lance had died. Due to their poor condition, the remaining organs, which to some extent had been protected by adipocere, having been in the water so long, revealed nothing that could indicate the cause of death, such as the presence of water in the lungs.

'Leading to an open verdict,' Peter had said gloomily, 'and the obvious assumption that it was an accident, especially since the dinghy was still on board.'

What was interesting was Mike's revelation, having seen what police records there still were, that Mary Venyon had clearly been a thorn in the police's side, with her constant demands to view every possible body washed up.

'Which could be a sign of how distraught she was,' Peter had pointed out, 'or the contrary.'

'A guilty conscience? Scared that the body might display signs of her attack on him. After all, why didn't she create a stink at the time if she thought it was murder?' Georgia said.

'Perhaps she did, and they told her politely to go away,' Peter said fairly.

'What about the yacht? Could she have found something on it when it was recovered that made her suspicious that it was murder, such as signs that two people had been on board?'

'Again, why not tell the police?' Peter replied. 'We're getting nowhere fast on this, even on the Daks front. Mike has spoken to Kenyon's daughter, but she couldn't help over Daks. She knew of no family connection and had never spoken to him herself or been approached by him. She did give Mike a family tree proving the Venyons are all Brits, no East European connections so far as he could see. So where now? Do we press on for evidence of murder? And if so where?'

Georgia decided she should come clean. 'There's the churchyard,' she said flatly. 'The fingerprints on time were shrieking at me.'

'Of course. You'd just seen a murdered body there.'

'Give me credit, Peter,' she said patiently. 'It went beyond that.'

'As far as Lance Venyon?'

'Suppose that's where his grave is?' she blurted out. So far as she recalled, Luke hadn't told her at Gwen's wedding exactly where the grave was. 'I was in too much of a state to look at whose gravestones they were when I found Sandro.'

Peter looked taken aback, but he rallied. 'Suppose you check that out before I get excited and wheel myself over there.'

'In the hope that King Arthur is calling faintly from the hills?' she managed to joke. 'Where are you in the hour of his need?'

'He's probably hoping he won't be accused of murdering Lance Venyon,' Peter said caustically. 'You leave King Arthur to me.'

'Have you put him on Suspects Anonymous?'

'Do not, I tell you do not, speak lightly of Charlie's modus operandi.'

It had been her cousin who had invented the software designed to digest all evidence and spit it out in visible form with all its clashes and contradictions. As with so many contributions from the computer world, Suspects Anonymous was helpful within limits. The footslogging soldiers still had their part to play.

Maureen Jones was hardly welcoming when Georgia at last managed to arrange a meeting for Wednesday – this time at her home, which was a cottage on the green facing the pub. At least this was a tangible line to follow up. All too tangible. Georgia could picture Maureen's lean angular form at the head of a crusaders' army holding her own particular banner of uprightness and holiness aloft. She wondered how her affable and informal aunt was faring in this village if all its matriarchs were so rigid and unbending. Even Maureen's garden proclaimed a military approach to life. Despite the rain, the flowers were not allowed to spread in the usual May joyousness of spring, but were neatly trimmed and kept to their own patch of ground. No sprawling by the troops stationed here.

'I have explained already to the police that I did not feel well that evening,' Maureen explained stiffly, 'and so decided to do my flower duty early the following morning. I did so with some difficulty owing to various police impediments.'

Georgia made sympathetic noises, although they were more for the police than Maureen. Any thoughts the police might have about her involvement with the murder would surely be conquered at one blow when faced with the Mighty Maureen herself.

'I expect Gwen explained it was I who found the body when I came to look for you,' Georgia began, 'although it wasn't about the murder that I wanted to see you today.'

'Indeed? Gwen implied it was when she rang this morning.' Her tone suggested that Gwen would be hearing about this.

'Only indirectly,' Georgia amended. 'When

84

Sandro Daks came to the village he mentioned that he wanted to see a Lance Venyon, who in fact had died in 1961. My father and I are investigating that death, and I understand that Lance was a friend of your mother's.'

'I've heard of him, of course, but not through my mother.' The reply was very firm. 'She has never referred to him so far as I recall. She hasn't lived in the village for a great many years.'

This was hopeful. 'She's still alive?' Georgia asked.

'Yes. She is not in good health.'

Keep away, in other words. Maureen's tone made it clear that Georgia hadn't a hope of meeting her.

'I would of course travel to see her, but if she doesn't want me to contact her then I quite understand,' Georgia said warmly. 'I'd be so grateful if you could ask her, however.' She made her request sound entirely reasonable.

'Very well.' It was ungracious, but at least a concession.

'Thank you,' Georgia said smoothly, handing over her business card. It seemed to be her bad luck always to be running into the guardians of those who didn't want or need to be guarded. With any luck Venetia Wain might prove one of them. Unless, of course, Lance Venyon's former lover had something to hide.

Just as she rose to go, the doorbell rang, and Maureen went to answer it. To Georgia's pleased surprise it was Elaine Holt, and she decided to take instant advantage. Today Elaine looked less matronly than in her mauve wedding outfit, but her black trousers, blouse and jacket still suggested this was a lady of firm opinions – a suitable chum for Maureen.

'You were responsible for that delicious food at Gwen and Terry's wedding.' Answer that, Mrs Gorgon, she thought to herself.

To her guilt, the Gorgon proved far from being one the moment her face broke into beaming – and, it seemed, genuine – appreciation.

'You're Georgia Marsh, aren't you? I had a long chat with your father. Lots of fun. Remember, Maureen? We both talked to him.'

A good start, but where to go from here? Maureen was still clearly edging her out, but to her relief Elaine detained her. 'Colin told me he'd been spilling the beans on the family skeletons to you.'

'Only one, and not hidden in any closet,' Georgia replied.

'I never paid much attention to it. I hardly recall my father, being only a toddler when he died, and so it didn't upset me. The police asked me about my father, too – thanks to you, I imagine.'

She didn't seem to mind, fortunately. 'My father used to work with DCI Gilroy in his police-career days, and still does consulting work for them,' Georgia explained. True

86

enough, even if not quite so officially as this sounded.

'I remember someone did come to the village years and years ago, asking for my father. It was just after we moved here, so it would have been about 1990 or so. My mother talked to him. Good-looking chap, foreign, that's why I remember him.'

'Do sit down,' Maureen suggested. It was a lukewarm invitation to Georgia at least, but even so the atmosphere was warmer, and she accepted. After all, Maureen wouldn't want to miss out on gossip as juicy as this. Georgia reproved herself. If she went on this way she'd be turning into a village matriarch herself.

'My father wasn't the sort to have an accident, so my mother argued,' Elaine told her, settling herself on the sofa. 'He was careful on the boat, so she said. He'd learned to take care of himself because of his job, and perhaps he had need to.'

'There was no private motive for anyone to want him dead, enmities with friends, for instance?' Georgia asked as delicately as she could. She could hardly ask if one of Lance's mistresses might have had reason to kill him.

'No,' Elaine said firmly. 'Nor is there a question of suicide. My father and mother were very happy together, so my mother told me. They had different lifestyles, but they dovetailed. My mother was content pottering in the garden, my father loved Wymdown, but also needed the

87

buzz of dashing all over Europe.'

'In search of stolen art works,' Georgia said.

'You know about that?' Elaine looked surprised. 'Did the police tell you?'

'No, Jago Priest.'

'My godfather. Of course. A great chap. I love him to bits. A great support after my mother died in 1995. He told me a great deal about my father's war days.'

'Anything to suggest any reason for murder there?' If Elaine loved Jago to bits she was hardly likely to see him in the role of murderer, Georgia reasoned.

'None that I can think of. Jago might have some ideas. My mother is less likely to have known. We went to live in Dorset shortly after my father's death, where my grandparents lived.'

'What brought you back to Kent? You must have been too young to remember much about it.'

'I was. Pure coincidence brought me here. Pete – that's my ex – took a job in Canterbury and saw a house out on the Barfrestone Road that we liked. Now I live at the top end of the village.'

'Nice and close,' Maureen commented warmly.

It was also a coincidence, Georgia thought, seeing the obvious friendship between the two (which made her think more kindly of Maureen). There was after all a tenuous connection between their two families: Maureen's mother Venetia Wain and Elaine's father had allegedly been lovers.

'Why do you think your mother believed that Lance was murdered? I'm still not clear,' Georgia said.

'I don't blame you. It's pretty hazy,' Elaine replied. 'My mother first told me when I was about twelve, and as a child you embed your first impressions so firmly that any misconceptions are less likely to be chucked away. So far as I recall, the basis of the argument was that he was off to meet someone that afternoon, and it must have been important because Mum said he was very het up about it.'

'Excited or afraid, did you gather?'

'From the way Mother talked about him, I didn't get the impression my father was ever afraid. Derring-do and tally-ho were his approach – or at least,' she added frankly, 'how my mother chose to remember him.'

'The inquest report didn't mention any visitors coming forward. Did they later?'

'Apparently not. Ma was still on about it to the day of her death. Not an obsession, but a niggle, if you know what I mean. She had an idea it was someone from his working life since he'd said he was on an exciting case. But then if it was a rival in his affections she would say that.'

'Any mention of which case?' Georgia asked, hoping for a mention of the Pre-Raphaelites.

'Not that I recall.'

New tack needed. 'There were quite a few people at the funeral – would you know who they were if we sent you a copy of the report?'

'I might. You could try me. My father had a lot of friends, so my mother said. Everyone liked him. Except – before you say it – his murderer, if any.'

'Jago Priest was his closest friend?'

'No idea. He was the best man at their wedding, and I can't remember my mother talking about anyone else by name. I don't think my mother cared for Jago, but that was natural if my father was close to him. She didn't care for any of my boyfriends either – mind you, she was right over Pete. Anyway, send me the list, and I'll do my best.'

'I know you gave the police family details, but would you have any objection if we advertised for former friends and work contacts of your father? In the press obviously and on our website.'

Their website, as well as Suspects Anonymous, was hosted by her cousin Charlie and the 'Can you help' information page was an idea so obvious that they had kicked themselves for overlooking it. It had been going for about six months now, and had produced one or two good results to add to their files. Although an excellent tool, it had nevertheless taken much discussion as to whether such prior heralding of their areas of interest might cause as much harm as good by alerting interested parties before they'd decided on taking a case. She'd agreed with Peter to risk it, but with sufficient variety of names and subjects that the main subject of current interest would be partly masked. So far as Lance Venyon was concerned, it could surely do no harm at all.

Elaine didn't take long to consider the matter. 'Go ahead. I'm far enough away from it not to be upset at raking up the past and my children won't care. There's no other close family to consider. He was an only child and his parents died when I was a child. Contact petered out with the rest of the family soon after his death. I can give you some old addresses, but I doubt if they would help you or the police. My mother implied he more or less wiped the soil of his native Hampshire off his feet when he went off to war, and after it he began a new life.'

'Just one more thing,' Georgia asked. 'How do you feel about the fact that if there is a crime uncovered there could be a book about it?' She was aware of Maureen stiffening.

'It depends on what you find,' Elaine replied briskly. 'If he was murdered, I'd want my children to know the truth, and I'd like to myself after all this. So dig away, by all means.'

'Although it strikes me, Georgia,' Maureen put in sweetly, 'that you may be digging without success.'

Was that a hope or a threat? Georgia wondered.

* * *

The crime scene in the churchyard had been wound up by now, and Georgia found herself once more alone there. This time it was broad daylight, however, not evening; the sun was out and birdsong very audible. There was a world of difference from her last visit. So had her impression then been entirely subjective? She retraced her steps of that night, stopping where she had first seen that glimpse of white. She walked towards the dark corner again, just as tense as before. All traces of where the body had lain and the crime scene were gone, although the trampled-down grass and mud around betrayed how busy this place had recently been. There was nothing save the quiet and peace of country churchyards, as she began her search for Lance Venyon's grave.

Almost immediately she knew she had been mistaken. It *was* still here, that sense of darkness and horror. The mere fact that she was in a hurry to leave suggested that. She felt her heart racing again. The sun now seemed to have a false brilliance, as though doing its best to bring light into an area that had chosen to remain dark. Hurriedly, she began to check the gravestones: Edward Robinson, died 1959. Beloved father and husband. Josephine, wife of Robert Jones, died 1960. Alan Peters, 1958. This was the gravestone across which Sandro's body had lain, but it was clear of blood now. All the gravestones around showed signs of erosion by

92

weather, save for one or two that were clearly regularly tended. With a mixture of relief and disappointment, she could see no sign of one for Lance Venyon.

'Can I help you?'

She jumped as a voice came from behind her and whisked round quickly. It was the vicar or curate, she presumed, as a dog-collared young man strolled up to her. It hadn't been he who officiated at the wedding, and she didn't recognize him. She smiled, relieved to have company.

'I'm looking for Lance Venyon's grave.'

'Wrong place, I'm afraid. I believe it's over here.' He led the way to the far side of the churchyard, pointed it out and tactfully retreated. This grave was well tended, and every word on the stone was readable. Lance Venyon's dates: 1922 to 1961. 'Beloved husband of Mary, father of Elaine. With the Eternal Father.' Next to it was Mary's grave.

Whatever this corner of the churchyard reeked of, it wasn't Lance crying out for justice. It was both a relief and disturbing. If not Lance who set up these vibes, who or what was it? She played with the notion that it was Sir Gawain, but dismissed the fantastical thought impatiently. It was just the weirdness of this place that gave her crazy ideas.

'Are we downhearted?' Peter asked after she had reported to him the following day.

'Frustrated,' she conceded.

'No reason for that. We have a sporting chance.'

'Maybe, but what's the *game*?'

'A Sudoku puzzle, perhaps. Some facts known, others to be sought with their help.'

'One graded diabolical, if so,' she grumbled.

'We have a link in Sandro.'

'A weak one, with just a girl's fleeting memory of a fleeting remark.'

'Nil desperandum, daughter. Mike told me Sandro's father Leonardo has been over here, breathing down their necks. He couldn't offer anything in the way of explanation over Lance Venyon.'

'How do you interpret that as helpful?'

'Don't snarl, darling. Sandro is a descendant of the grandpop who knew Lance, and so Leonardo is too.'

'So what? He knows nothing.'

'According to Leonardo, Sandro was a tearaway, a law unto himself. All Leonardo claimed to know was that Lance Venyon was an old acquaintance of his father. His father had died in 1988, expressing a wish that Leonardo would look Lance up if travelling to the West ever became possible; he had duly come to England as soon as the Iron Curtain lifted, and they had moved to Budapest from Estonia. He found out that Lance was dead, but doesn't recall ever mentioning this to Sandro, although he could have been mistaken. That would fit with the fact that when Sandro found out Lance was dead he didn't make any effort to track down Venyon's living family. Anyway, Mike isn't pursuing the Venyon line any longer.'

'And this is good news?' At least Elaine's mother's mysterious visitor was probably explained. It had been Leonardo.

'Yes. It could clear Sandro out of the picture so that we can concentrate on Lance. It does seem unlikely that Leonardo is anything to do with a family involved in art theft in the 1950s. Mike has checked him out; he's as respectable as they come. A university lecturer in Hungary since he moved there, son of a retired teacher and dressmaker.'

Georgia thought about this. 'All we *know* is that Sandro didn't talk to Elaine. We don't know he didn't make other enquiries, such as meeting Jago. After all, how did Leonardo find out in 1990 that Lance was dead?'

'From the village and Mary Venyon herself, perhaps.'

'In which case he might well have spoken to Jago Priest and so might Sandro, if his mission was other than mere courtesy.'

'Jago would still have been in France in 1990, but it's possible Sandro spoke to him.'

'About what?'

'Suppose he came about those paintings? Maybe his grandfather was an Arthurian fan.'

'A tenable theory, but sheer speculation,' Peter whipped back smartly. 'Which is why

Mike's concentrating his attention not on Lance but on Sandro's working and love lives.'

'Are they both focused on this Dover art gallery?'

'Quite possibly. Kelly Cook was apparently distraught to hear about Sandro's death, and even more so to hear that he had another lady friend in Canterbury. Her husband was equally upset, presumably because of his working partnership with Sandro.'

'So they're in the frame—' That was something at any rate. She had quizzed Gwen and Terry over their acquaintanceship with Kelly. It turned out that Kelly used to work with Terry before her marriage to Roy. Gwen thought she was a laugh, but Georgia wasn't so sure. Vampires were a laugh only until they sank their fangs in.

'Georgia,' Peter interrupted, 'Lance Venyon is our target, and we need him in our sights, not Daks.'

'Even though Lance hasn't left one single fingerprint on time that we can be sure of?'

'He's leaving mental tenprints at least. They won't go away.'

'I agree.' She gave in. 'Silly, isn't it?'

'Not at all. We still have two people who actually knew Lance, apart from the vicar, who we can provisionally assume is a disinterested party. That's two figures to fill in on our Sudoku puzzle. One is Venetia Wain, an unknown quantity as yet. The other is Jago Priest, who looms large in my thoughts. Both have passable motives that might reward investigation. Now that Daks is tiptoeing out of the picture, it's time to offer Jago a pub lunch on Saturday.'

It was a larger group than expected. Jago would be delighted, he had told Peter on the telephone, although his daughter Cindy and Sam were visiting him this weekend.

'I told him the more the merrier,' Peter had said.

'On the grounds that tongues run away in informal chat more readily than in formal interview?' Georgia asked.

'How well you know me.'

'Then we'll invite Luke too. Three of us, three of them.'

'Excellent. He can take care of the drinks and food while we talk.'

This was a role that fell rather often to Luke in such circumstances, and Georgia had felt a rare tug of loyalties. By luck, it was warm enough to sit in the pub garden and the Priest family was already present when they arrived. Cindy, with a mop of dark hair and lively face, was a surprise, having nothing of Mark's caution – at least superficially. She was obviously younger by several years, but seemed to spring from a different generation. There was no Mr Cindy, it seemed, but there was Sam – who proved to be her daughter, not son.

'So confusing,' Peter muttered as he manoeuvred his chair into place.

'Don't be a fuddy-duddy,' Georgia hissed at him. She took Sam for a student from her orange spiky hair and general fashion mode of jeans, bare midriff, bangles and scarves, but it turned out that she was twenty-two and that she and her mother ran a craft shop in Canterbury. Both ladies seemed to have plenty of the get up and go quality but in different ways. Cindy would be the businesswoman, Georgia suspected, while Sam did the pushing.

'So what's this about Pops' old chum being bumped off?' Cindy asked, once food had been chosen and Luke had obediently disappeared to order it. He rather liked the silent partner role in such circumstances, he had reassured Georgia, because he could take a back seat and sum up situations objectively rather than concentrating on his own contribution.

'The jury's still out as to whether he was,' Georgia replied. 'So we've come back for further direction from the judge.'

'I'm honoured,' Jago chuckled. 'But I still don't buy the idea that Lance was murdered.'

'What was so interesting about this Lance apart from the fact that he knew Prester?' Sam gave her grandfather an affectionate squeeze of the hand.

'Prester?' Peter looked enquiringly at Jago.

'Sam's pet name for me. After Prester John, I fear,' Jago replied ruefully. 'Sam is a tease, as well as my firmest supporter where my theories on the historical Arthur are concerned. Prester John as you no doubt know was a twelfth-century fantasy about an eastern emperor who kept the then known world engaged in a quest to find him for four hundred years or so.'

'Like King Arthur and the Grail,' Sam said straight-faced, 'only Prester John was more fun. Just fancy, it was probably one monk who set up a scam that had the West thinking it had this all-singing all-powerful all-dancing mighty potentate in the East to defend Christianity for the righteous against the naughty old Saracens. He was richer than Croesus, more powerful than Charlemagne, seventy-two kings worshipped at his feet, all the jewels of Ind—'

'I think we've got the picture, Sam,' Jago said gently. 'Sam, you see, has this notion that it was the excitement over the quest to find Prester John that in the twelfth century obscured the historical King Arthur by reviving the king through a quest for the Holy Grail.'

'Reviving?' Cindy snorted. 'Creating him, more like.'

'Nonsense, Mum,' Sam flashed back. 'Arthur was *real*. Prester was a joke, but Arthur's something different.'

'Bosh,' her mother retorted.

'Why can't you see Grandpops has to be right?'

Georgia felt like waving a flag to call a truce over King Arthur, but decided it would be more diplomatic to retreat and help Luke with the drinks. By the time she came back with her tray, she was relieved to find that the discussion had moved on. Peter was talking about Sandro Daks.

'What's he got to do with this?' Cindy asked sharply.

'Did you know him?' Georgia asked in surprise.

'Yeah.' Sam answered for her. 'We both did. He did work for us in Canterbury. He was murdered, but what's it got to do with you?' She was the suspicious one of the two, Georgia could see, and also protective of her mother, for all her combative stance. A point in her favour.

'A double interest. I found his body—'

'My dear Georgia. I'm sorry to hear that,' Jago said. 'An appalling shock for you.'

'It was. And another shock to find out later that he had some slight connection with Lance Venyon.'

'What was that?' Jago asked, frowning.

Georgia explained, conscious that all three Priests had their eyes firmly fixed on her. 'We wondered if he came to see you, Jago, since he didn't get in touch with Elaine. Someone might have told him you were his best friend. His father Leonardo might also have contacted you in 1990, although I think you were still in France then.'

'I don't recall a Leonardo Daks at all.' Jago thought for a moment. 'I was working in Toulouse by then, so I would have been difficult to track down. I believe Sandro might have telephoned me some months ago, however. I didn't recognize the name because I don't think he gave it to me. He asked if I knew Lance's whereabouts, I explained he was dead. I didn't want to refer him to Elaine for obvious reasons. He seemed quite satisfied and that was that.'

'He didn't explain why he was interested?'

'Yes, he did. He said he was anxious to trace a painting with which Lance had been connected. That was why I saw danger signals. Knowing Lance's line of work, I could have been speaking to the Mafia or some descendant of the Benizi Brothers, or worse an unscrupulous Arthurian collector in search of the goblet. I assured him that Lance was dead, referred him to Wymdown churchyard for confirmation, and told him that his family had moved away and I'd lost contact. I heard no more. International art thieves are not my speciality, I fear.'

Georgia thought this through. 'It's unlikely the Benizi Brothers would be so determined to track Lance down after so long.'

'Don't be too sure,' Jago said. 'I told you the rumours about the golden goblet had begun again. There are several blogs devoted to it.'

'Suppose the painting Sandro mentioned *was* the Rossetti of Gawain and Arthur,' Peter suggested. 'What made Lance so sure about the provenance?'

'Because it had been held by the same family

who had bought it from Rossetti in the 1850s. What Lance could not be sure of was whether the goblet was genuine or whether it was Rossetti's imagination at work. But he was on the brink of tracking down the scripts and other evidence to confirm its existence and reveal its whereabouts. That was the exciting news I was eager to hear when news came of his death.'

'By Gad, the jewels of Prester John,' breathed Sam, open-eyed.

'You jest, young lady,' Jago said amiably.

She giggled. 'I'm with you all the way, Grandpops.'

'Maybe this painting with the goblet was the reason for Sandro's death,' Cindy put in quietly. 'It all goes back to this Lance Venyon.'

'Nah,' snorted Sam. 'Have a go at the Cook's Tart for the reason. He told the old witch she was a joke.'

Could Sam or even Cindy have been Sandro's Canterbury girlfriend? Georgia wondered. Not Cindy, she thought. She looked too businesslike to take up with such a young toy boy. 'What about her husband?' she asked.

'You mean this lad was having it off with him too?' Jago asked innocently.

Sam turned on him. 'No joke, Prester. Sandro was all right, till the tart started poking her butt in.'

'Would Roy Cook have had any reason to kill him?' Peter persisted. 'Apart from Sandro being his wife's bit on the side?'

'It's possible,' Cindy said. 'Sandro painted for the tourist trade and we weren't his only outlet.'

'Could he have been mixed up with any illegal art trade?' Georgia asked.

Cindy looked at her in amused scorn. 'He'd hardly tell us, would he? Ask Mark. Art scams are his department.'

Of course. Georgia remembered that Mark worked on art claims for an insurance company.

'He's what one might call a modern equivalent of Lance, only more static and rather more formal,' Jago explained. 'It was more gripping in the old days.'

'Yeah,' Sam laughed. 'Men with hats pulled over their eyes. Me Big Spy, you evil monster threatening civilization as we want it. Anyway, Sandro wasn't like that. His real love was painting nudes.'

Jago fixed her with an eagle eye. 'Sam? Not you, I trust.'

'What of it? He stuck a new face on me each time.'

'Another blank wall?' Georgia asked Peter as they drove away. 'Or do we have a gate this time? If Lance was on the verge of some exciting discovery, whether over the goblet or the Rossettis, or both, the possibility remains that Sandro's grandfather was involved too.'

'Let's say some rubble has been cleared from our path,' Peter replied. 'What do you make of Jago now?'

'A nice guy, good at fielding balls and throwing them back. Nothing leads us on.'

'I disagree. I have a feeling the next signpost points towards Paris.'

Five

In the late spring Paris always flaunted herself at her most beautiful, Georgia thought. Here on the outskirts, it was so green that it seemed impossible that the grey of the city was only a metro ride away. Madame la Contessa d'Orvona lived in a Vincennes mansion overlooking the huge public park and chateau, and with any luck was Lance Venyon's former lover Madeleine. If only Luke had been able to come too. He loved Paris, whereas Peter never travelled to France. From his perspective, it was the country that chose to harbour his treacherous wife Elena – albeit she was in the Dordogne several hundred miles from here. Luke could not spare the time from work, however. Even Eurostar's speedy travel wasn't inducement enough for him to tear himself away, and so she had decided on a quick day trip, even though that had involved getting up at the crack of dawn to join the train at Ashford.

The chance of meeting the Countess Madeleine had been too good to turn down, especially coming so hard on the heels of Peter's prognostication that Paris might be their next stop in the hunt. There was no word yet from Venetia Wain, and Madeleine's had been the only hopeful reply to their advertisement on their website. She had known Lance Venyon, her message stated baldly, and Marsh & Daughter were welcome to visit her.

'Go,' Peter had said promptly. 'I've plenty to do here.' That was true. Elaine had studied the list of named guests at the funeral, but it had rung no other bells for her than the distant relations she had mentioned. Nevertheless these all had to be followed up with the help of the old address book Elaine produced for them. Georgia also suspected he intended to have a session tracking down blogs on King Arthur.

The small formal garden between this mansion and the broad tree-lined avenue outside spoke of money in itself, Georgia thought, judging from the architecturally arranged trees and shrubs growing through a pebble base. It was impressive, yet not off-putting, perhaps because the statuary around was equally well chosen. Soft weathered-stone classical statues seemed part of the garden rather than objects deposited there for themselves alone. It occurred to her that this was probably because they were genuine antiques rather than garden-centre offerings. Nevertheless the latter seemed to have their place too. Dotted around she could see friendly stone frogs, a heron by a small water cascade, and a stone cat regarding them thoughtfully from the shade of a bush.

What, she wondered, would she find once she was inside the house itself?

For starters, it was a maid – if a cheerful bustling middle-aged lady could answer to that description.

'Bonjour, madame. Entrez, s'il vous plaît.'

Georgia was then escorted through an entrance hall which was a cross between the Louvre and an antiques fair. Pictures, furniture, china jostled together for the eye's attention. She didn't have time to take them all in before she was shown into the room where Madame la Contessa awaited her.

Once again she was taken aback. This was no ageing floozie sighing for the bohemian 1950s. The countess was tall, well-built and except for exquisite tailoring of her suit could have attended morning service in an English country church without attracting any notice for non-conformity. Even so, it was she rather than the Aladdin's cave she was standing in who attract-ed the attention. Despite her obvious years – mid to late seventies? – her eyes and move-ments were lively as she came forward to greet Georgia.

'It is good of you to come all this way, madame.' Her voice was deep, almost husky, and that too had life in it.

Despite the French formality of the greeting, Georgia was now in no doubt of Madeleine's origins. She had falsely assumed the countess was French since Lance had met her in Paris, but she wasn't. Her walk alone proved that.

'You're British, madame?' she asked.

'I am. I haven't lived there for many a long year, but I still think kindly of it, and visit when I can. Do sit down, please.'

'I don't think London could rival this.' As she sat in the elegant armchair, Georgia glanced at the glories surrounding her, and did a double take. Surely that was an original Degas painting? And the long-case clock must date back to the eighteenth century. She had to tear herself away from further gaping at the wonders around her, but Madeleine looked amused.

'One of the advantages, or some might say disadvantages, of being married to an antiques expert.'

So that explained it. 'Is that how you met Lance Venyon?' Georgia asked.

Madeleine didn't answer directly. 'Tell me what your interest is in Lance, Miss Marsh. Your website reveals a great range of subjects, but your books are apparently all about murders. I notice you've just published one stemming from the Second World War.'

'That's correct.'

'Is Lance concerned in your current case? You realize he died in 1961?'

'Yes. There's a possibility that he was

murdered, and we're looking into it to see whether there's any evidence to support it.' She had Madeleine's full attention now. 'Could you believe that?' she continued.

'Easily,' Madeleine replied calmly.

'Even though he is thought to have died in a boating accident with no suggestion that we can yet find to the contrary?'

'Yes.'

Georgia quickly debated where to take it from here. She didn't want to leap in baldly by asking who Madeleine thought the murderer might be, and laying one's cards on the table could often be an advantage. 'Most of our cases are about murders that have gone unsolved or where injustice has occurred,' she told the countess. 'Lance doesn't come into that category yet. What does seem irrefutable is that he led a risky working life in a shady world, and there might well be fertile ground for the allegations to turn into evidence if we could get closer to that.'

'A shady world,' Madeleine repeated thoughtfully. 'Could you explain that?'

This conversation wasn't going well, Georgia realized. Madeleine was quietly taking control of it. Nevertheless it was early yet and although she'd made a bad choice of words herself, the situation might be redeemed. 'His job, we're told, was to chase up stolen and faked art works in Europe.'

'Stolen? You mean by the occupying forces

during the Second World War? I don't know how long the Allied Commission to track down such works was active, but it's true that Lance was still involved in that kind of work by the mid-50s when I met him.'

'Art thefts were really coming into fashion by then,' Georgia agreed.

'And that's all you think Lance was doing?' Odd phrasing, since 'doing' was ambiguous. Georgia decided not to press the point. 'Yes. Did you know Jago Priest, Lance's friend?'

'I did.' The shortness of the reply and her body language suggested she was not a fan.

'He thinks Lance's line of work might have included art forgeries as well as theft.'

'Thinks? Jago's still alive?' Madeleine asked sharply. She looked surprised, then said, 'By forgeries you mean paintings intended to deceive by confusion with the original, rather than fakes of a style to gull the unwary.'

'I don't know,' Georgia confessed, aware that she was being forced on to the defensive.

'It's quite possible,' Madeleine continued, her composure regained. 'As no doubt you know, the Allied Commission's work produced interesting byways.'

Georgia seized her chance to take the battle into the opponent's camp, which seemed well defended. 'There was apparently one gang in particular whose trail Lance was hotly following about the time he died. The Benizi Brothers were his target.'

'Or he theirs, from the way your thesis is running,' Madeleine commented lightly.

'It follows,' Georgia agreed. 'Did Lance talk about his job when you knew him?'

'Sometimes he would make reference to a particular case. If I ever asked specifically whom he worked for, he didn't tell me. With Lance one laughed and joked, one made merry. He was there or he was not. In those days we did not sit down for serious career talks. Let's say he usually – not always – had plenty of money, and it was hardly polite to ask whence it came.

'I met him about 1954 in Paris,' Madeleine continued. 'My parents were both British, but my mother had been in the SOE during the war, and my father was a Francophile. When postwar Britain became too gloomy they moved to France, and I moved with them. I was twenty-three by then, so I lived in an apartment of my own. That's rather a splendid word for the nest of servants' rooms usually found at the very top of the grand houses in central Paris. Mine was in the boulevard de Courcelles. I looked out of my attic window on to the rooftops of Paris – what a sight. All the mountains and valleys of the world could not compete. Such life, such colour, such sadness. Paris was mine. I was a secretary in the Louvre, and every day I drank up what Paris had to offer. I met Lance in the museum one day, and it went on from there. Where to, you might ask.'

She cast an amused glance at Georgia, who was indeed thinking just that. 'But I would not reply,' she continued, 'since it is not relevant. For some time I had a spare room in my apartment and Lance became in effect a lodger. He travelled all over Europe, sometimes he talked of it, sometimes he did not. It was understood. And of course when he married in 1957 he would return to his Kentish home for weeks at a time.'

'Was he still doing this in 1961?' Georgia asked hopefully.

'No. I had met my husband and had been married two years by then. I last saw Lance a few months before his death.'

At last Georgia felt that she was being offered a key, if not an open door, to Lance Venyon. It was her job to turn it. 'Even if he didn't talk much about his job, you must have formed an impression of your own. Was he a private investigator, for instance, specializing in art crime?'

'*Art* crime?' A male voice, and dear heaven, one she knew. Her whole stomach seemed to turn over as dizziness hit her and she had to struggle for control. The door to the room, which had been ajar, was now fully open – and in walked trouble. 'What *are* you up to, Georgia?'

It was Zac.

Zac, her ex-husband, looking just the same as when she'd last seen him in prison twelve years ago to tell him that she was filing for divorce. Zac, the most incompetent con man one could imagine, Zac, who specialized in art and antiques – if specialized was the right word where he was concerned. Zac, with his infuriating lopsided grin, the floppy mop of dark hair and beguiling look of innocence.

'What the hell are you doing here?' she asked wearily. So many scenarios were whizzing through her head that she felt physically faint. This came of turning keys into unknown territory, but the last thing she had expected was Zac to be lurking behind the door. The last and most scariest thing is one's own past rearing up.

'I did tell you to keep away, Zac.' Madeleine sounded furious.

'Sorry, Maddy. I couldn't resist seeing Georgia again.' He was grinning at her, damn him.

What on earth *was* this set-up? Did this woman *know* she was harbouring a con man, Georgia wondered wildly. Was Madeleine a con artist too? Was Zac her toy boy? Surely to goodness he couldn't be her husband? She'd said he was an antiques expert. Zac obviously was too young to have been her first husband, but maybe he was the second? Madeleine looked far too sensible, but she wouldn't put it past Zac. Forty years' age difference would mean nothing if Zac took the fancy into his mind. If only Luke were here – no, thank goodness he wasn't. He'd pick up her confusion right away, and guess the reason. Old memories were stirring all too vividly within her.

'I must apologize, Georgia,' Madeleine said briskly, abandoning formality. 'Zac is a colleague of my husband's, and friend of my son's. It is a complete coincidence and an unfortunate one that he is here at the moment.'

So at least the toy-boy theory was out of the way. But did this absent husband *know* what he was letting loose in his house of priceless treasures?

'In case you are wondering...' Zac had his little-boy look on and unfortunately Georgia knew it could be a genuine one. The trouble with Zac was to decide (since he could never decide himself) where make-believe began and sincerity abruptly ended. 'Maddy does know about my nefarious past.'

'Fortunately,' Madeleine said gravely, 'my husband doesn't need Zac's advice on wine.'

Georgia laughed. Zac's downfall had been over a particularly inept scam in this department.

Regardless of his lack of welcome, Zac threw himself down in the armchair next to Georgia, and it was all she could do to stop herself from edging away. Zac was good at body language. It went with his trade. Space invader, mind invader, was Zac. And now he was settling in, she realized to her horror.

'I'm sure you'll understand, madame,' she said to Madeleine firmly, 'that I can't speak freely in front of Zac and as I don't have long before I have to leave for my return train—'

'But I can help you,' Zac interrupted. He wore his hurt look now. (She remembered that one well: 'What do you mean, *stole*?')

The worst of all situations, and she had to turn the tables. 'What about?' she asked stonily.

'Madeleine said you were coming to talk about Lance Venyon.'

And she had thought his offer to help was the worst. It wasn't, this was. Left to herself, she'd get up and walk away, but she wasn't alone in this. There was Peter to consider, and she was a professional. They'd agreed to take on this case. She plunged on, conscious that Madeleine was deliberately leaving the stage to her.

'You weren't born till the late 1960s,' she told Zac flatly. 'You can't have met him.'

'Of course not.' Indignation at being mis-judged oozed from him. She knew all his expressions. 'But I've moved in his world long enough, and he's not forgotten. And I have contacts.'

Sure he had, all of them either doing stir or temporarily out planning the next disaster. Despite herself, however, she had wanted to hear more.

Zac obviously hadn't missed her sudden interest. 'There's a lot of talk in the cafes I hang out in in Paris, just as there was in the 1950s, only now it's done in cyberspace too. Lance was mixed up with some golden cup mysteri-ously supposed to be buried in Kent, like that

114

one they found a year or two back. This one wasn't Bronze Age. It was—'

'Fifth or early sixth century. King Arthur's goblet,' Georgia finished for him resignedly. Trust Zac still to be sailing in the good ship *Fantasy*.

Zac looked disappointed. 'You know.'

'A little.' She decided it might be wise to backtrack. How odd, though, that she could even be talking to Zac on a normal basis.

'Of course the Arthurian buffs have been getting excited.'

That was Zac. Trust him to convey the impression that he moved in the midst of powerful groups with his ears flapping. 'What do they collect?' she asked. 'Bits of the Round Table?'

'Scripts, old books, archaeological finds, some specialize in the medieval resurgence of interest, some in the Anglo-Saxon historical side. The Arthurian world is vast, ranging from the ultra-respectable Arthurian Society to those who live in a Camelot of their own.'

Georgia was momentarily silenced. Did Zac really know his stuff over this? It would be the first time ever, if so.

'Zac's right,' Madeleine said. 'There are whispers, and what's more I do remember Lance burbling on about it in the 1950s.'

If Madeleine was in on this, then grudgingly Georgia was prepared to admit she might be wrong about Zac on this occasion. Had he got this from Jago, Georgia wondered, or did he

115

have independent sources? It had to be the latter, because Jago would see through Zac in a minute. In any case, she reminded herself, Jago's researches had led him to the wrong place.

The wrong place? She caught her mistake. So she thought there was a *right* place, did she? This was ludicrous. Any minute now and Zac would vanish into thin air like the nightmare he was, and take King Arthur with him.

'Hang on, Zac,' she said. 'Rumours start somewhere. Any idea where the current ones did?'

He shrugged. 'Not a clue. How could I? There's a blog devoted to it, though.'

'Yes, I've heard that.'

'Not meant for every Tom, Dick and Harry,' Zac continued, 'or all the treasure hunters in the world would be out there with their metal detectors. Only the cognoscenti. You have to know their blog codes. The golden cup – or goblet as you call it – is referred to as Prester John, King Arthur is the Crusader, and Gawain is Indiana.'

'You *are* joking, Zac.'

'I am not.' Great dignity here.

'Prester John was a hoax.'

'Precisely,' Zac was triumphant. 'To fool the uninitiated.'

'More than you can do.'

She was instantly ashamed of herself for this childish retort, but nothing could have brought back her early disastrous marriage more clearly. A union of ill-matched kids, Peter had grumpily called it when they married, and, sure enough, he'd been right. It had ended up with his having to arrest his own son-in-law for fraud.

'Sorry,' she muttered. 'And thanks. How do I get on to the blog?'

'Dunno.'

She closed her eyes in disbelief. 'Do you think—' Talk about entering the maze one more time. Nothing, but nothing, with Zac was ever concrete. Anyway, Sam's pet name for Jago was Prester John too, which suggested he contributed to the blog, and Google would no doubt oblige anyway, now she had the code words.

She made a determined effort to try again. 'Do you think Lance seriously thought he was going to find this goblet, Madeleine? Or was it Arthurian paintings he was after, as Jago said?' She stopped abruptly. It was all too easy to chat in front of Zac. It was when he was silent that he could be at his most dangerous.

'I have a vague recollection, but too vague to rely on. Why not ask Jago? He was the King Arthur fan par excellence.'

'Perhaps he did Lance in,' Zac suggested helpfully. 'Would he have had a motive?'

'Who knows with that man,' Madeleine said.

'Why should he?' Georgia asked. 'He'd be interested in keeping Lance alive if he was on the trail of the King Arthur goblet. After

117

Lance's death his own efforts came to nothing.'

'Poor Jago.' Madeleine laughed for the first time. 'I almost feel sorry for him.'

'Depends where he looked,' Zac said casually. 'There's sacks of Anglo-Saxon stuff dug up in Kent. Woodnesborough near where the Ringlemere Cup was found has always had a legend that a golden statue of the Norse god Woden was hidden nearby. Suppose the Ringlemere cup really was Arthur's. Even if it was Bronze Age, it could have been a family treasure.'

Georgia laughed. 'According to Jago, Arthur's goblet and Gawain's remains were in Dover Castle church until the sixteenth century, and only then rehoused. Rather too late to start a legend about Woden. In any case a gold statue is a far cry from a cup.'

'Gold has a mysterious power over men,' Zac pointed out.

And especially over him, Georgia thought, wondering why he was trying to impress with this solemn pronouncement. Change of subject, she decided. 'Did Lance talk about his private life?' she asked Madeleine. 'His wife died some years ago, and his daughter knows nothing of her father save what her mother had told her – which wasn't much help to us.'

Madeleine shook her head. 'I suppose he must have done so from time to time. Lance was – well, rather like Zac. He came and he went. I remember him as a...'

A con man? Georgia nearly asked, but bit it

back – which was just as well as Madeleine continued: 'In that we never actually knew what he was up to. A fresh idea every minute.'

'Nevertheless you're sure that his job was to pursue *real* objects whether stolen or faked. In other words, not hunting objects as a collector. He wouldn't chase fantasies because of an inner dream?' Georgia asked.

'How do you know the goblet's a fantasy, Georgia?' Zac enquired.

She rounded on him. 'You mean you know there is a real goblet, Zac?'

'Maybe.'

'If you know, why not tell us?'

'I like to keep you guessing. You owe me that.'

The phrase 'takes your breath away' came to mind. Georgia could hardly speak with irritation. *Owe* him? Owe him what? Five years before, subconscious doubts and fears rose to the surface with the certainty that he was lying and all the beautiful objects that passed through their small terraced house were the result of cons. She'd defended him fiercely when Peter had first broken the news to her. She'd spent four years of alternate bliss and bedlam. Four years of blind adoration blasted into shock and disillusion. Four years of sexual bliss blinding her to the truth – even the memory stirred her as she thought of it. So she *wouldn't*. She'd think of Luke. Whose image for the first time ever failed to come to her rescue. She was on her own.

'Of course,' she replied mildly, which she was delighted to see disconcerted Zac. With luck he'd try to please her now, by offering a little titbit. Sure enough.

'I met a chap whose father had known Lance in the 1950s. I think he'd seen the goblet,' Zac offered.

'Pull the other one, Zac.' So even Madeleine found this hard to take, to Georgia's relief.

'All right, then,' Zac backtracked, 'maybe he hadn't. But the story going round the cafes is that Lance Venyon knew where it was.'

'Jago Priest also thought he knew where it was. Only it wasn't,' Georgia pointed out.

'Is that right?' Zac looked interested. 'Where did he dig?'

'Near Woodnesborough as it happens,' Georgia lied through her teeth. That was the trouble with Zac. He reduced you to his level.

Zac laughed. 'Is this Jago Priest any relation to Mark?'

'His father, probably,' Georgia said cautiously. 'Do you know Mark?'

'Yeah. A bit. He moves in the same world.'

'The underworld?'

Zac gave her a pained look, just as another male entrant arrived, and no prizes for guessing who this was.

'Signora Marsh, *ciao*, Zac, Magdalena...'

'My husband,' Madeleine said, as the short plump bustling elderly man with twinkling eyes

120

came over to kiss her. 'You're back early, *caro*.'

'I could not miss our English visitor.' He looked more like Danny DeVito than a Hollywood Italian count and Georgia warmed to him at once. 'Zac, you are keeping our guest entertained?' he asked.

'Very,' Zac said lazily, shooting Georgia a glance.

'Unfortunately,' Madeleine said tranquilly, 'I discovered after you left this morning, darling, that our poor guest was once married to Zac.'

The count laughed delightedly. 'So, we are one big happy family. As for me, I am too lazy for divorce, even if Papa allowed it. And Magdalena—'

'Is too old for change,' his wife supplied.

This was a madhouse, Georgia decided. A stalwart English lady in her mid seventies, a mad Italian count roughly the same age, and her own former husband all rattling around in a palace of antiques. And incidentally whose antiques were they?

'We were talking about Lance Venyon and King Arthur, darling,' Madeleine said. 'And, guess what, Jago Priest is still alive and well,' she added brightly. 'And Zac has been contributing.'

A glance between husband and wife as though they had Zac's measure, which was a good sign. 'Do you remember Lance?' she asked the count.

'Of course. Who could not? The crazy

Englishman who terrorized Europe to track down beautiful artworks.'

'We're looking for any hints that might explain his death in 1961,' Georgia explained. 'His wife thought he might have been murdered, and his working life might have provided reason for that.'

'*Si, signora.*'

'Do you,' she asked in desperation, since he didn't seem disposed to continue, 'know of any cases he was working on in the late 1950s? He got very close to one gang, the Benizi Brothers.'

He beamed. 'I know. I was an antiques and art dealer. Lance came in one day to ask if I have stolen goods. What, me? I said. No. Lance then tells me what he is looking for. I ask people about them, and give him what help I can.'

No mention of King Arthur yet, Georgia noticed. She would have to prompt him. 'Jago said Lance was excited about some hitherto unknown Pre-Raphaelite paintings.'

'There I can help,' the count said grandly. 'Then we all have luncheon.'

'That's very kind,' she began, appalled at the idea of extending her exposure to Zac yet longer, 'but—'

'Wait till you see the garden, Georgia,' Zac said enthusiastically. 'We'll be eating out there.'

She glanced at Madeleine, who nodded. It seemed Georgia had no choice, and as she had to eat lunch somewhere, she agreed. 'I'd like that very much.' Well, part of it, she amended to herself.

'Now I have something to show you,' the count said. 'Come with me, Mrs Georgia.'

'Darling,' Madeleine began. 'Surely not—'

'*Cara*,' he interrupted firmly. Another glance and Madeleine rose quickly to join Georgia and her husband.

As Georgia wondered what on earth this was about, she followed obediently in her host's bustling wake. Madeleine took her arm, and Zac brought up the rear like an enthusiastic puppy. Naturally. He never liked losing touch with things, including wives.

Where was she going to find 'the something', she wondered, as the count led the way upstairs, with his entourage behind. The first storey of the house, and so far as she could see the second too, seemed to be understudying the Quai d'Orsay art museum, if the stairwell was anything to judge by. Paintings hung on pale lemon-painted walls, antique furniture on the landing gleamed with years of polish. The count flung open an ornately white-and-gilt-ornamented door and ushered her in.

'Our bedroom,' he announced. 'Magdalena and I make children here.'

'Not so many nowadays,' Madeleine commented gravely.

The joke stopped Georgia from fully taking in her surroundings, but when she did she found herself in an austerely elegant ivory-painted room, with pale green shutters and bed linen, and minimal light furniture. There was only one painting in the room, on the wall facing the bed, and her attention was straightaway riveted on it. It was Pre-Raphaelite, and depicted an obviously dying knight on what looked like the deck of a ship. In the distant background were cliffs and a familiar-looking castle, other knights clustered round, and kneeling at the dying knight's side was —

'King Arthur,' she blurted out in shock. 'It must be Gawain and Arthur.'

'And the golden goblet,' Zac added smugly.

She looked at it first in disbelief, and then in admiration. She knew some of Rossetti's work, though not specifically the Arthur drawings, and could see that this was a fine painting. It was not as heavily romanticized as some of his work, but full of passion and yet at the same time peace. As with his *Arthur's Tomb* the figures were sharply defined, almost angular, but here the eyes were not focused on the other knights or even on Gawain, but on a golden goblet. King Arthur was holding it at Gawain's lips, and it was so positioned that it became the focal point. Small, gold, ornamented but not heavily, it shone out, demanding the viewer's attention.

'Dante Gabriel Rossetti, Italian artist,' the count joked. 'This is what you seek, Mrs Georgia.'

'The painting Lance Venyon discovered?'

'*Si*,' agreed the count.

'The painting that the Benizi Gang was after?'

'Yes,' he agreed again.

'But how—?'

'I should formally introduce my husband,' Madeleine said softly behind her in a sudden inexplicable chill.

'I do it myself, *cara*. How do you do, Mrs Georgia. I am,' the count said proudly, 'Antonio Benizi.'

Six

The rear garden of the house had far less formality than the front. Here bushes, grass, winding paths and arbours lived together with no apparent design. A terrace under an awning ran the width of the house and on it was a table laid for four. It looked instantly attractive. Georgia was still getting over the shock of learning who the Count of Orvona was, made easier by the fact that Antonio had waved aside an apology. She suppressed an image of Luke at his desk, sandwich at his side. Nevertheless she wondered how she was going to explain today away to him. Omit all mention of Zac?

Confess? But what to? Being the victim of circumstance or to the lurch of excitement that she was trying to ignore? She'd think about that later, she decided. At present she had enough to cope with in seeing Zac's grinning face across the table. With Antonio and Madeleine at the two ends, it made an intimate setting that was all too familiar. At least Zac wouldn't be crass enough to say, 'How like old times,' but she had her retort ready in case he did. Instead, she asked him politely:

'Have you known Madeleine and Antonio long?'

'Five or six years. I met Roberto, their son, much earlier, probably while we were still married, Georgia.'

Trust him to slip that in, she thought crossly, with its implication of an ongoing link between them.

'I turn up now and again to ask Antonio's advice,' Zac continued.

Antonio (Georgia already thought of him that way) looked pleased, as though it were the greatest honour in the world to be giving advice to a con man. As a gang leader himself – *if* he was – she supposed that was natural. It was hard to believe that this was all happening. Even her sense of chill in the bedroom had vanished. One thought of villains creeping along dark alleyways, plotting in secret hide-aways, not having lunch on a terrace in the sunshine. Madeleine had an old cotton sunhat on, Antonio's shining bald head was equally well shielded, and Zac didn't care. Nor did she, aware that she was beginning to relax.

What did Zac ask Antonio's advice on, she wondered. Whatever it was, it was unlikely to be legal.

'Zac asks me about art,' Antonio explained, 'and the wicked things that men do for it. I am an old man, so it is most flattering.'

'Information is all Lance came for?'

'Of course,' Antonio replied. 'What else? This gang story, Georgia,' he added seriously, 'Jago has it wrong. Very wrong, but then he would. He did not like us, and we did not like him. Perhaps he killed Lance.'

Georgia was taken back, and obviously seeing this, Madeleine leapt into the breach.

'Darling, just because we don't like Jago that doesn't make him a murderer.'

Antonio shrugged. 'He loved King Arthur. He was very interested in gold goblets. If Lance was in his way, Jago could kill.'

'He was very affable to us,' Georgia said defensively, 'but of course he's much older now. In his younger days he might have been very different.'

Antonio, having made his point, became the happy host again. 'We not like him because of Jennifer.'

'His wife?' Georgia's interest quickened. Was she the forgotten factor in the story?

'Jennifer was my friend when I first came to

Paris,' Madeleine explained. 'We shared the flat in the boulevard de Courcelles and I stayed on when she married Jago in 1956. She'd known him a long while, and he badgered her into marrying him. I didn't think she would be happy. Jennifer was a lovely woman, both to look at and in her nature.' She shrugged. 'That's foolish. How can one describe a friend when they are, or were, part of you? Is she still alive?'

'Jago told me she died two years ago.'

'I'm sad to hear that.' Madeleine was clearly upset. 'Antonio and I married three years later, and Lance took over my flat until we moved to Rome in late 1960. I lost touch with Jennifer after Lance's death.'

'The marriage seems to have worked out, at least from what Jago says.'

'He would say that,' Madeleine said wryly. 'Lance had been passionately in love with her, of course, and she with him, so I never understood why she married Jago. Lance married Mary a year later, so I suppose all was well.'

Lance had been Madeleine's part-time lodger for four years then, between 1956 and 1960. She wondered again how close Madeleine had been to him. It *was* relevant, regardless of what Madeleine had said earlier. Nevertheless Georgia reproved herself for her prurient mind. The two had been close, whether as friends or lovers. Did it matter? Yes, because a possible theory then arose of whether Jennifer had been preferred over her.

'I liked Lance very much. Dear friend,' Antonio announced. 'My brother and I have chain of antique stores, Rome, Vienna, Paris, London. Easy for Jago to think of us as a gang, but we are honest traders. Always, we were that. Many good things came from the East then, so Vienna was well placed. We go there to live after we leave Rome.'

'Were antiques smuggled out when Eastern Europe was still in the Communist bloc?'

'We not see it as smuggling,' he replied blandly. 'No contact between East and West then. Lance knew the Benizis had their ears to ground, but that we know what is right, and what is wrong. The Benizi Brothers believe there is more money in being on right side. Too much danger in being bad. But – your glass empty, Georgia.' He reached over to remedy this.

'But,' she prompted him.

'But you must know bad side too. I knew good men, I knew bad men, and they both trusted me.'

'It sounds a difficult line to walk,' she observed frankly. 'And,' she reasoned, 'if the bad men trusted you, what help could you give Lance? You couldn't tell him anything without betraying the bad men. You'd soon be a dead man.'

Antonio laughed delightedly. 'You have a clever wife, Zac. Ah, sorrel soup.' He kissed his fingers to signify his pleasure. 'Made in heaven, like marriage. It looks good, yes?'

'It does,' she agreed wholeheartedly. Nothing so reassuring and comforting as a whole tureen of soup and large chunks of bread to accompany it.

'I am good too, am I not, Magdalena?'

'A paragon of virtue,' his wife agreed. 'That's why Lance liked your advice.'

'*Si*,' Antonio agreed. 'He often came to me about stolen pictures. I told him whether he had any chance of getting them back or not. I tell him whether it was a private theft for ransom or whether it has gone to a collection. I tell him how much value it had on market. All this and I do not betray the bad men.'

'Lance was a good man? Never bad?' Georgia was conscious that she was slipping into this framework very easily.

'Good, yes, but just a little of bad,' Antonio replied.

How to get to the bottom of this? She decided it could only be by plunging in headlong. 'That painting you kindly showed me...' she began, deliberately hesitantly.

'Ah yes, Mr Rossetti's.'

'Was it in your possession when Lance discovered it? Were you the family,' she said, treading on eggshells, 'that had owned it since 1855?'

'No, no.' Antonio shook his head vigorously. 'It was not owned by Big Bad Benizi gang. Lance brought it to me to ask if I thought it genuine. Is it fake? It has good provenance, he told me. In 1855 Rossetti's lady friend Lizzie Siddal came to Paris, but spent too much money. So Rossetti painted a picture quickly, sold it and brought money to her here. He was very pleased, because the poet Mr Robert Browning was in Paris too so Rossetti have a friend here. He stayed with Lizzie ten days, but she was not well and kept to her room. He needed more money for his lovely lady, so he painted another picture. He used the studio of the artist Purvis de Chavanne, later very famous but not then. He had an atelier to teach students, and he let Rossetti paint his picture there in return for lessons to pupils. The picture was the death of Sir Gawain, and very good. He sold it to a cafe in Pigalle to get money for Lizzie. Rossetti was very fond of King Arthur. He painted his *Arthur's Tomb* watercolour that year, the *Lady of Shalott* drawing the following year, and designs for Oxford Union. Busy man, and greedy lady. A sad story, because the poor lady died young.'

Antonio had tears in his eyes. 'I ask Lance to buy the painting of Gawain for me,' he continued. 'I liked it. Also, I heard rumours in Paris about the goblet in the picture being real, so I asked Lance about them. He said he had heard them too. So if painting was genuine, Rossetti must have known about the goblet story.'

'Do *you* believe the painting is genuine? Have you had it tested?'

'No. For Magdalena I break my own rules,' Antonio declared. 'She liked the painting too, and there were not so many tests in 1959, as there are today. Also, I did not want to know. When insurers come, I tell them it is a true painting and so pay more than I need. But I am happy to do that, because Magdalena and I believe it true, and so it *is* true.'

'Did the rumours circulating about the goblet in the 1950s *begin* with this painting? Lance was waiting for some news to tell Jago about it, when he died.'

'Lance said they began before, *then* he find painting. Rossetti knew the goblet was real – Lance was sure of that.'

'How? Is this something to do with Ruskin and old scripts?' Georgia was getting more and more intrigued.

'*Si.* Rossetti was a great *amico* of John Ruskin, who as you know was very important man in art world. He live in London, south of the big river Thames, and Rossetti go to visit him often. Ruskin was a big collector maps and texts. In the year Rossetti went to Paris, Mr Ruskin visit Deal to study harbours, so he could easily have visited Dover too, which is very near. In Dover at that time there were many historians and collectors, and Lance told me there was a letter from Ruskin to Rossetti telling him he had been given a scrap of old manuscript about goblet, and where it was buried.'

'Where was that?' Georgia almost croaked. This must certainly have been the news Jago had been waiting for. The script written by the chaplains of St Mary-in-the-Castle as a record, which had later been lost.

Antonio chuckled. 'I'm sorry, Mrs Georgia. Lance did not have either the letter or the script. He looked for them both for me and for Jago; he looked for two years but then he died.'

'Oh.' Anti-climax. The end of the story missing. The trail cold. Unless of course Lance *had* found them...

Antonio was watching her. 'You have some of this nice pasta, Georgia. It will cheer you up.'

He was right, and as pasta replaced the soup tureen, and red wine flowed, the afternoon began to take on a surreal quality. The Benizi Gang faded across a distant horizon together with any leads it might have to Lance Venyon. Instead she, a retired antiques dealer, his wife and Zac were having a friendly lunch in the sunshine in what seemed an Eden of delight. If there was a serpent amongst them, he was keeping his fangs to himself. Or were they just hidden, ready to strike? One never knew with serpents.

She tried to focus on the fact that she had to leave shortly, that she still hadn't heard much about why Zac was here, and that she had let down her own guard in discussing the Venyon case. Well done, Georgia, she congratulated herself. All she had achieved, once again, was a discussion on King Arthur.

'Remember that Manet of mine, Georgia,' Zac was prattling. 'I kept it under the bed because it was so beautiful I wanted to feel I owned it.'

She remembered it all too well, but it was a step too far on Zac's part to mention it, since it forced her once more to recall all the other lovely things 'of his' in their home, that Zac had assured her were trifling gifts from clients. In those days she didn't know a Ming from a Minton but she was wiser now. Although, if she were so clever, what on earth was she doing here, she wondered. She toyed with the notion that the entire King Arthur story was a red herring to divert them from the truth about Lance Venyon.

'So you're a PI now, Georgia,' Zac said idly, 'Bulldog Drummond, Philip Marlowe and good old Sherlock all in one.'

'Hardly a PI,' she said mildly. 'Peter and I write books for a living.'

'Any time you want my input,' Zac offered generously, 'you have only to ask.'

'How good of you,' she replied warmly, secure in the knowledge that sarcasm always passed Zac by. 'About what?'

'This Venyon fellow.'

As so often in the past, she'd walked right back into it. 'Do you know anything about him, other than the rumours about the goblet?'

'Not much.' He gave her a disarming smile.

134

It didn't succeed. 'Then I'll hold on a while before taking advantage of your offer,' she replied. Like when hell freezes, she thought savagely. Still, it had given her an opening to return to Antonio on the question of Lance.

'If you believe Lance could have been murdered, both the painting and the goblet could have been reasons for it.'

Antonio chuckled. 'You think I killed him because of that painting? That I stole this Ruskin letter and script?'

Damn. That wine had not been a good idea, and she was covered in confusion. 'I didn't mean to imply—'

'I forgive you. We wicked Benizi Brothers go in with our guns going pop, pop, pop. This is how we live every day, don't we, Magdalena?'

'Of course.' Madeleine laughed. 'And I don't blame Georgia for believing it.'

The sticky moment had passed. 'Do you know who Lance bought the picture from?' Georgia asked hastily.

'He say it came from the Milot family,' Antonio replied promptly. 'They owned it from the time Rossetti painted it. The family ran the cafe in the Place Pigalle, and kept the picture. When the Milots became rich, they bought a chateau near Orléans and there Lance found the painting.'

'Did he tell you he thought it was genuine, as Jago recalls?'

'Jago wrong. Lance was not sure at first. We

both thought there would be a big market for it if the rumours about the goblet were true, whether the painting was fake or genuine. So I asked Lance to buy it. You know King Arthur was a French king?'

'I didn't.' Once more Georgia was taken off guard.

Madeleine laughed. 'The Grail story originated in Europe, so naturally the French would like to think him French. Historically, as Jago would confirm, one theory of Arthur is that he was actually a king of Brittany, or more particularly of the British colony in the peninsula. He was called Riothamus, and popped over with his troops to give the Britons a hand in fighting off the Saxons.'

'Is that included in Jago's thesis?' Georgia asked. It didn't ring a bell, but would fit his story well.

'Probably, since he was lecturing in Paris at the time, and was getting very excited over Gawain's bones. I don't think Lance ever showed him the paintings. He was—'

'Eh, Magdalena,' Antonio interrupted chidingly. 'You bore our guests with talk of Arthur.'

'And you also, Antonio,' she shot back.

'Only because, *cara*, Lance brought Arthur to me.'

Jago described Madeleine as temperamental, Georgia remembered, and for a moment she had seen a brief suggestion of it. 'So didn't Lance want Jago to see the Rossetti?' she asked, to break the pause that followed. Had she mis-heard, or had Madeleine referred to paintings in the plural, just as Jago had?

'I think not,' Madeleine replied promptly. 'Lance said he wanted to find the Ruskin evidence before he got Jago too excited over the painting. We and Lance were at one over Jago. We refused to accept balderdash from him about King Arthur.'

'So neither of you believed in the golden goblet?' Georgia's head began to spin in earnest. 'And yet you bought the painting.'

'Caught you, Magdalena,' Antonio chortled.

'I did believe in it. I still do,' Madeleine replied calmly. 'As much as I believe in the golden statue of Woden. All legends have a basis of truth, so Jago could be right. Lance doubted it, but nevertheless he brought that picture to show us, just in case.'

The story was circling back again, and Georgia knew she had to break through it. 'Everyone seems a cog in the story of Lance Venyon, not a principal, so who would want to murder him?'

'Perhaps,' Madeleine pointed out gently, 'no one did. The fact that Antonio and I could believe it happened doesn't make it a fact.'

'That's what my father and I have to sort out,' Georgia said ruefully. She decided to take a risk. 'Would anyone else have known about Lance's work? Venetia Wain, for example.'

Madeleine stiffened, as only an affronted

Englishwoman can. False step, Georgia realized – or perhaps not. 'Venetia was the sort of woman who would claim to know everything and in fact understand nothing,' Madeleine declared.

Antonio laughed delightedly. 'Magdalena not like Venetia. Me, I love her.'

'Nonsense,' Madeleine replied calmly.

'So quiet, so sweet, so—'

'Catlike,' his wife finished for him. 'In Lance's Garden of Eden that Eve didn't need a serpent to tell her how to cause trouble.'

'Trouble for Lance or for others?' Georgia had nearly said rivals, but fortunately caught herself in time.

'The same thing. For Mary, certainly.'

'Could Mary have thought Venetia murdered Lance?'

Madeleine shot her a glance and Antonio was frowning, unusually for him. 'I can't say. I hardly knew Mary,' Madeleine said at last. 'And she's no longer alive, you say.'

No, Georgia thought with resignation, and yet Mary was the only reason that she was sitting here today. If Lance's murder was fantasy on Mary's part, then there was no case to answer. Apart from the mysterious and probably innocent visitor he was meeting that afternoon, there wasn't an atom of evidence that Lance had died other than by accident. The creepy atmosphere in the churchyard bore no connection to him, and even if Gawain himself lay buried deep beneath its ground, there was little Marsh & Daughter could do to avenge his death.

And then she saw Zac was about to speak. Trouble?

'Exciting life you lead, Georgia.'

'A thrill a minute,' she cautiously agreed.

'What about current crimes? Have you heard the big story about the art thefts in Kent?'

She racked her brains in vain. 'No.'

'That's what I'm working on,' Zac said nonchalantly, one arm hooked over the back of his chair. 'There's a scam in progress. The latest thing is not merely stealing the originals, but replacing them with copies so good they'll never be questioned. There's a break-in, one or two minor originals are pinched but left unreplaced so that it looks convincing but the real aim is the switch of the major paintings.'

'How do they get exposed as copies?' she asked.

'Tests, Georgia dear. At any point suspicion could arise, and then the tests are made. That brings an insurance problem because it can't be proved *when* the switch was made. It could be years later the query arises. Sometimes, like Antonio, the owners don't care if it's fake or genuine and keep it anyway, but sometimes they're extremely narked.'

'Naturally enough. How is the job planned?'

'Sometimes with some insider help, but usually through scouts passing information.'

'But if they go to the trouble of breaking in,

why not take all the originals?'

Zac looked at her pityingly. 'Elementary, my darling. It buys time to get the hot stuff away and sold before the news hits the hot list. If they're unlucky of course they switch paintings only to find the original was a fake too.'

She wouldn't mind betting that Zac himself had fallen foul of that. 'How do the copyists get to know the picture so well that they can copy it to that standard?'

'Preparation, preparation, preparation in tracking down who has pictures famous enough to be in good reproduction, somewhere. If it's a house or museum open to the public one browses round, first with one's Aunt Agatha, secondly with one's squalling kids, thirdly in a tourist group; that gives an indication of the true colours and condition of the painting, and then the reproductions kick in as guides.'

'And how did you get drawn into this?'

'Believe it or not, Georgia, because I was a suspect.'

She began to laugh. Then he looked so indignant that she couldn't stop. 'I do believe it.'

'It's not a joke,' he replied crossly. 'I was questioned by the Art and Antiques Unit in the Specialist Crime Directorate, part of the Metropolitan Police, on the grounds I was the inside man. I do valuations for insurance companies and auction houses.'

'You mean you're living in Kent?' she asked,

aghast.

'Sussex.'

Relief, close though Sussex was. 'Did they arrest you?'

'Naturally I was able to prove my innocence.'

'That's a change.'

'I offered to help them, to keep my nose to the ground.'

'Does it sniff anything?'

'Of course. You don't believe me, do you?' He put his mysterious look on. 'Well – and this goes no further, you understand – the centre of suspicion is a chap called Roy Cook.'

'In Dover?' She was jolted out of her afternoon stupor. This was getting very close to home.

'Do you know him?'

'Of him,' she said guardedly. 'I met his wife.'

'You know darling Kelly? Well, well, what a small world.'

'I've met her, but your secret's safe with me. How are the Cooks linked to the thefts?'

'I've a theory, not yet proven, that he's the organizer or at least a high-up operator. I'm pretty certain he arranges the painting of the copies.'

Mike's words came back to her with sickening clarity: 'He's an excellent copyist, his tutor said.'

'By Sandro Daks?' she asked warily.

He looked impressed. But then Zac was good at that. 'Yes, the poor chap who was murdered.

Did you know him?'

'No.' She swallowed. 'I found his body.'

'My poor Georgia,' he exclaimed. 'I'm sorry. What a shock. It had occurred to me,' he added, nose almost visibly twitching, 'that his death could be something to do with the thefts.'

What on earth was she doing discussing this with Zac? Ten to one it hadn't occurred to him until she put her big foot in it by mentioning Sandro. 'Could he have been one of Cook's copyists? I know Cook sold his tourist drawings.'

'I'm sure he was. I met Sandro once. Didn't take to him. Bit of a chancer, I'd say.'

'Pots calling kettles black, Zac?'

'I'm never underhand,' he said, with dignity.

No. That was the trouble. He just forgot to mention things. He steamed ahead without thinking round or through a problem. That was why he was so incompetent. If the Arts and Antiques Unit was using him its success ratings would seriously decline.

'Are you interested in the Daks case, Georgia?' Zac continued casually.

She recognized this move. 'To some extent.'

'Because you found the body? That would be just like you.'

Trust him to guess. 'No. Because he told someone he wanted to find Lance Venyon.'

It was a risky comment but even so she hadn't bargained on the response. There was an instant stillness at the table, and it wasn't caused by

142

Zac. As in the Benizi bedroom she had that same feeling that something was going on here from which she was excluded. Madeleine and Antonio said nothing, looking at her with politely bland expressions. It was Zac who broke the silence.

'That's a coincidence, isn't it?' he said brightly.

Seven

'You're pulling my leg.' Peter stared at her in amazement – and she could hardly blame him. She'd kept the news about Zac until last. More important (for Marsh & Daughter) was to tell Peter who the Count and Countess of Orvona were, and even more importantly that they, as Mary Venyon, believed that Lance could have been murdered. Then, as casually as possible, she had told him about Zac.

'Do I look as if I'm joking?' she asked flatly. 'It was Zac. And he hadn't changed.'

'That sounds credible.' Peter grimaced. 'What doesn't is that you're still relatively sane about it. Tell me all.'

She did – nearly all, at any rate. She kept to herself the frisson that seeing Zac had given her. It had almost disappeared overnight in the

143

normality of relating some of the day's events to Luke plus a night's sleep. 'Do I accept Zac's kind invitation to introduce me to Roy Cook and Co. in Dover?'

'Dover,' Peter repeated thoughtfully, and she could see exactly where this was leading.

'No,' she said firmly. 'Not Dover Castle on a nostalgia trip in the steps of King Arthur. This would be a visit to a twenty-first-century art gallery.'

'Bound up with a crime, if Zac is to be believed. Do I have to remind you all this could be his fantasy? It's only because we know about the Daks connection that you're taking it seriously.'

'There's only one way to find out,' Georgia said. 'We should hand the lead over to Mike in case it's new to him.'

'You think Zac would want to take Mike rather than you?'

Caught off guard, she laughed. 'You'd be surprised. Zac claims he sometimes works with the goodies, the Art and Antiques Unit of the Met. He tells me that as a former suspect in these art thefts, so he had some claim to credibility.'

'Knowing Zac, he's probably lying over that too.' Peter hesitated. 'It's your business, Georgia, but is Luke going to clap his hands in joy at the idea of your going on little jaunts with Zac?'

'I doubt it.' Knowing Luke he'd clam up, not

try to stop her going. He was too fair for that, especially if it was work-related. Nevertheless he wouldn't like it one little bit. That was a given; what was not a given was how she herself would feel about it. If she were honest and stopped trying to dismiss the thought, she had found being with Zac all too easy, despite every hackle in her body being raised in self-defence. It was hackles, wasn't it? Nothing else. No refiring of old embers, no lingering wish for yesteryear?

'And so?' he asked.

'I'd go if Mike agreed.'

'I'm glad you remembered this is Mike's case. What if I came too?' he threw in casually.

Clever, she thought. 'Is this a test, father dear?'

'It is.'

'Then yes, come by all means. Or take my place.'

'Neat, Georgia. I'll ring Mike. Let Zac stew for a while; we've other fish to fry.'

'What breed of fish?'

'You helped catch them,' he pointed out. 'You ought to know. Firstly, Venetia Wain is in our sights. She rang me, and we're going to the seaside next week. Won't that be nice?'

'Splendid. Madeleine is cagey about her, per-haps naturally if she feels proprietorial over Lance's favours. Antonio is cagey too. Could be something there, especially since they aren't fans of Jago either?'

145

'Why not, I wonder?'

'Largely because he married Jennifer, I suspect,' Georgia said. 'She was Madeleine's flatmate.'

'Ah. Even more interesting. That has some ballast with it.'

Georgia groaned. 'In the shape of King Arthur galloping in with hidden treasure stories and paintings? Incidentally Madeleine, like Jago, referred to paintings in the plural, but all they discussed was the one I saw.'

'You did well in getting them to show it to you.'

'It was more that they decided to show me,' she said fairly.

'Why should they do that?'

'Because it might have been the reason that Lance was killed. And,' she continued crossly, 'here we go again. Every time we follow a lead about Lance Venyon it lands up with King Arthur. I know this pleases you, but nevertheless it could be just a wild-goose chase to deflect us from the *people* involved. Like Venetia Wain.'

'Has it occurred to you that the reason for King Arthur's frequent appearance is that he really was the cause of Lance Venyon's death? I had a merry time on the Internet yesterday, with one blog in particular. Jago was right. Theories are buzzing to and fro like hornets, and just as potentially dangerous. I suspect that Jago is working under the not very complicated codename of Badon because his current hobby horse is the Battle of Badon Hill, Arthur's big battle – if we assume he is Gildas's Ambrosius Aurelianus, who routed the enemy Saxons, and gave peace to the land for many years. Although Malory's story of Arthur's fight with Mordred on Barham Downs doesn't describe a decisive battle, Jago is convinced that it was here that the historical – if I might use that word – Battle of Badon took place rather than in the many other sites in the British Isles suggested for it. Jago is convinced Badon is simply a word-of-mouth mishearing, a contraction of Barham Down. The theory has a few dating problems, to put it mildly, but Jago has an answer to them all.'

'Which is?'

'If you've a day or two to spare, I'll tell you.'

'Most kind of you. I take it Barham was a Saxon or Anglo-Saxon word, not Celtic?'

'Yes. Jago eagerly points out that the Saxon for bear was *bera*, and the name Arthur, originally Irish, also means bear. The snag, which Jago's opponents point out with relish, is that the Saxons would be unlikely to name a hill after the chap who slaughtered their mates.'

'What about the goblet?'

'Whispers, whispers. Some think it's somewhere on Barham Down, and nothing to do with Gawain. Others that it's at Richborough or Eastry.'

'But it is thought to exist?'

'The consensus is yes,' Peter said cautiously.

'Based on what?' she whipped back.

'Don't be fierce, Georgia,' he replied mildly. 'There are references to Ruskin, for instance...'

'Yes, Antonio mentioned that too.'

'Antonio? You do seem to have struck up an accord.'

'I can still tell a hawk from a handsaw,' she replied, nettled at this implication.

'I'm not sure Hamlet could, in fact.'

'In any case,' she continued firmly, 'that's only one line. We gave it precedence because we began the investigation with Jago – whose passion is King Arthur. We're not getting to the man himself, where Lance is concerned. It's time to move on.'

'And Sandro Daks?'

'The only link we have is that Lance was a friend of his grandfather's. Like most young men, he took this so seriously he didn't even bother to contact Lance's daughter.'

As Margaret came in Peter scented an ally in his indispensable carer. 'What's your view of King Arthur?'

'Richard Harris,' she said briefly. 'In *Camelot*. And lunch is in half an hour.' She removed the coffee cups and disappeared.

'There you are, you see,' Georgia declared. 'Arthur's a dead duck historically. Only survives on celluloid.'

'And in the passions of men, Georgia.'

* * *

148

The seaside proved to be further away than the Kentish coast. Venetia Wain lived on the outskirts of Bognor Regis in Sussex, and when on the following Wednesday Georgia drove there with Peter it took them past familiar territory, as they had visited the air museum at Tangmere during their last case to meet former Spitfire pilots. Aldwick, where Venetia lived, was where George V had famously stayed with his Bognor-loving wife Queen Mary, despite uttering the famous royal words of 'Bugger Bognor'. His Majesty had hardly been staying in the worst part of town here, Georgia thought, as she drove along the Aldwick road after leaving the Bognor promenade. The sea could lift one's spirits even on a dull day such as this, especially in a town getting ready for the holiday season. Unfortunately it had displayed little of its Regency splendour, but here and there she had had glimpses of a more gracious past.

Venetia lived on a newish estate, in a pleasant yellow-brick home with lattice windows, and from the size of the garden alone it spoke of a leisured retirement – though that was probably an illusion in today's world.

A ring at the doorbell brought instant response from a barking dog, which was rapidly silenced with a firm, 'Quiet, Falstaff,' from within. The door was opened by a small wiry lady of about eighty, and a collie's head was poking suspiciously round its owner's legs.

'Let's sort out the wheelchair,' she said

briskly after greeting them, and summing the situation up. 'Round the back, I think.'

Peter had said that Venetia had simply brushed this issue aside on the telephone with a casual 'we'll manage'. 'That could mean anything,' he had forecast gloomily, 'from a long flight of steps to a privy at the end of the garden.' In this case, fortunately, it merely meant entering through large French windows at the rear of the house and a ground-floor bathroom.

'I'd move in tomorrow,' Peter said gratefully.

'Delighted.' Venetia disappeared into the kitchen, leaving Falstaff to entertain them, and returned with a medley of coffee cups in a variety of different chinas and colours. 'Now,' she said, seating herself in an upright chair, 'you want to talk about my old lover Lance. Not so old when I met him, of course.'

Georgia was relieved. So far no sign of the serpent, even if she could believe in the Eve. Venetia must have been stunning when younger. 'I was wondering how we would broach the subject. Your daughter explained that you weren't very well, so we didn't want to spring it on you.'

Venetia waved this aside. 'Maureen says that to everyone. Some people are such bores. They want to ask frightfully technical questions about sailing, and I've long since put all that out of my mind. Or else they want to probe what my innermost thoughts might have been out there alone on the ocean. Most of the time it was what to have for supper.'

'Do you still sail?' Peter asked.

'As a passenger only. I've a dog to think of.'

'You take him with you?' Georgia misunderstood.

Venetia laughed. 'Hardly. He prefers the smells of dry land. What's your interest in Lance and me? I've looked at your website, but I'd like to hear it from you.'

'His wife' – Peter launched into the by now familiar words – 'didn't believe that Lance's death was an accident. She thought he was murdered.'

'Of course he was.'

Venetia's reply, even more assured than Madeleine's, flabbergasted Georgia and she could see that Peter was equally taken aback, so much so that Venetia looked astonished. 'Well, presumably you do too or you wouldn't be here.'

'We were expecting a blank look of surprise,' Georgia confessed. 'That's what the response often is. Especially as in this case we haven't yet come up with firm evidence of murder.'

'Surely even the murderer would be surprised,' Venetia said drily. 'It's well over forty years ago. He or she would assume it over and done with. Have one of my scones – they're as hard as ship's biscuits, but no weevils, I assure you.'

This procedure took some time, but allowed them a respite to readjust, especially since the scones were delicious. 'Why are you so sure he

151

was murdered?' Peter asked.

'Lance wasn't the type to have an accident by falling overboard. He loved life too much to let it cheat him that way. He never drank when he sailed, he was never much of a drinker anyway. He obeyed the rules of the water, which I suppose was odd as he never obeyed any on land.'

'Such as?' Peter enquired politely.

'Marriage for a start,' Venetia said cheerfully. 'He led Mary a worm's life – I can't say dog's, since Falstaff finds his rather good. I know I contributed to Mary's worm's life but if it hadn't been me it would have been someone else, and anyway there were several someone elses.'

'You mean he wasn't serious about you – I'm sorry,' Georgia apologized belatedly when Venetia didn't answer.

'I take no offence,' Venetia said at last. 'I was thinking how to define serious. Yes, Lance was serious. I was serious too. I loved the damned man for a while, but it was serious between us within given boundaries. We both knew we were too similar for a marriage to work between us; he was already married to Mary and saw no need to alter the situation. I was married too, with a husband I didn't much love, but with a child that I did.'

'It must have been difficult for you,' Georgia said.

Venetia looked amused. 'Not at all. I was

away sailing for weeks at a time, and Lance was travelling. We met abroad, we met in England, but seldom in Wymdown, except socially. Then we were all the best of friends. It worked splendidly, especially as I'm pretty sure both our spouses knew anyway, and chose for their own reasons to ignore it.'

'Have you any ideas as to who murdered him and why?'

'I could have done, for a start,' she said cheerfully. 'You'll have to decide whether I did. A nice puzzle for you. We could have a murder weekend, and write your book for you.'

'We'd need a little evidence,' Peter pointed out.

'Signed confession, that sort of thing?'

Whether or not Venetia was a suspect, she was certainly an eccentric. 'That would be a start,' Georgia said, 'but I'd hate to be sued on the grounds that it was false.'

'Very well. Let us be earnest.' Venetia pulled a face. 'I could have killed Lance, believe me. I had reason to. I was in Wymdown when he died. We had arranged to meet on the 13th in Hythe, the day before he vanished.'

'You were actually in Hythe that day?' Peter asked.

'I should have been. I had a call from him just before I set out, telling me something had come up. He sounded flustered, which was most unlike Lance. He said he couldn't make it after all.'

'Did you take that to mean he wasn't going himself or that he didn't want to meet you?'

'Whatever I took it to be, he clearly meant the latter.'

'Mary Venyon testified at the inquest that he was expecting to meet someone that afternoon, presumably in Hythe. Was that you?'

'I wouldn't know. We'd arranged to meet at sixish, have a meal and sleep on board, perhaps go sailing the next day.'

'He didn't mention another visitor before you? I'm meeting X at three so you come at six – that sort of thing?'

Venetia regarded him with an amused eye. 'It's a long time ago, but I'm sure I'd have remembered something as obvious as that – I'd even have told the police. As it was, I knew nothing, and I was off the hook to get over the shock by myself. That was tough, especially when the boat was found. Of course if I'd pushed him off it, it wouldn't have been a shock,' she added straight-faced.

'True. Did you have any reason to kill him?'

'Oh yes,' was her casual admission.

'And that was?' Peter took this in his stride.

'Patience. I'll tell you, but first you must understand what Lance was like. I once told him somewhat savagely that he was like the sea. I'd call him Father Neptune from time to time, to which he replied that I was Mother Carey. She looks after the souls of drowned sailors, doesn't she? Daft, the things you call each other when you're in love. Lance claimed I'd have a job with his soul, and he was right. He could be kind and thoughtful, a good lover on a calm blue-skied day, with just the occasional swish of waves lapping on the beach, but there were times when one couldn't predict him at all. The tide was out. I could never reach where he was then, nor did I want to. There were times when the tide was racing in, when he was all set to go haring off on a project, sweeping all before him, not caring what wreckage he caused. There were times when he was as buoyant as the Dead Sea, supporting you by the sheer force of his personality. But there were also the times when he'd let you sink like a stone without a moment's hesitation. And there were the stormy times, bad weather ahead. Batten down the hatches. Stay in harbour. Anchor where you can. Lance is heading this way.'

'Which mood was he in at the time he disappeared?'

'I saw him the day before he left for Hythe. I'd say the mood was stay in harbour. Storm rapidly approaching.'

'From which direction? Did he give any idea?'

'No, but he'd been preoccupied for some days. I'd see his car nipping up the hill on the Barfrestone Road. Jago Priest had bought Badon House—' She glanced at them. 'You've heard of him?' When Georgia nodded, she continued, 'Mary and Lance kept an eye on the place for him, arranged for work to be done and so forth. It wasn't unusual to see one or other of them nipping up there, but I noticed Lance going that way several times, usually alone or with Mary, but once with a young man.'

'Do you know who that was?' Peter asked.

'Oddly enough, I did ask him casually about it, and he said his name was Michael. Nothing more, and the mood was definitely storm brewing. Silly, isn't it, the details one remembers?'

'Perhaps you remember it because something struck you as odd about it, and maybe that was only because Lance was indicating bad weather ahead.'

'No. More likely retreating into the place I couldn't reach. Far-distant lands.' She hesitated. 'In fact, we'd met in Canterbury by chance on the 12th, had a flaming row and he broke it off. I twitted him about being Jago's caretaker, or some such mild joke. He went ballistic. Accused me of spying on him, trying to possess him. As if I'd want him lock, stock and barrel. No way. He told me whatever feelings he had for me were over. It was getting too hot. He hardly bothered to be polite, which was unlike him. The Lance I thought I knew had vanished for good.'

'You said he was changeable. Why did you think this was different?' Georgia asked. This was beginning to add up. When she had told Zac that she knew about his antics, he too had just changed. No attempt to hide and, for the moment, a brief one, he had been stripped of all pretences.

'I did say that,' Venetia agreed. 'This time I knew there would be no coming back. You learn that at sea too. Rules are OK, but it's the fine-tuning that gets you to know the sea and quick reactions that keep you alive. It was the same in my private life. I knew I needed to react quickly, so I broke it off.'

'You said that he did,' Peter reminded her.

'Did I? Perhaps it was mutual. Let's just say that by 13 September 1961, the day before Lance disappeared, we were not in a state of harmony, and the phone call finished it. That meeting we had arranged in Hythe was simply for me to pick up some of my possessions that I'd left on the boat.' She paused. 'Believe it or not, I still find it painful to recall the shock of Lance's turnaround.'

'But you were not only going to meet him' – Georgia was puzzled – 'but stay overnight and go sailing.'

Venetia grimaced. 'Yes. We'd already made the arrangement and given the appropriate excuses to our spouses. After the break-up, there were still things to discuss, some of my possessions were in his boat and vice versa. So we thought we might as well meet and get it over with, though I doubt if I could have stayed over as planned. Too much emotion. Then came the phone call *cancelling* it.'

'So what did you do?'

'I acted like any irrational woman. I went to see Mary, of course.' She raised an eyebrow. 'I can see that shocks you.'

'Let's say surprises,' Georgia amended.

'Do you always behave with dignity in such situations?' Venetia looked from Peter to Georgia.

Youch. Georgia thought of Peter when her mother Elena had walked out, of herself and Zac, and couldn't answer yes. Even so she wondered whether she would openly admit it as Venetia had. Perhaps when she was eighty she would be able to look back objectively and do so, although she doubted it. 'No. I have lapses,' she confessed. Peter said nothing.

Venetia nodded. 'I had a lapse that afternoon, and I've never regretted it. Tell me, what do you know about Mary? Quiet, stay-at-home, the devoted wife Lance could always come back to?'

'Yes,' Georgia agreed.

'A stereotype, and people are rarely that, save superficially. Mary was all those things. She was also devious, spiteful and ruthless. Her life centred on one person: Lance. Not even – though this is not for the record – on her daughter. That changed after his death, save that his memory became sacrosanct. While he was alive, nothing got in the way of her determination to retain Lance for herself. Not even Lance could break that steely grip. She used a

158

long chain but a very strongly forged one. Mary knew about me, I'm sure, just as she knew about his other affairs. I was different because I was on her home patch. I'm sure it was she who decided that it was time my husband knew – not that he cared.'

'Was it she who persuaded Lance to end the affair?'

'I wish I could say yes, but I can't. She didn't like me, and was wary of my influence, but it suited her. It gave Lance a thrill of excitement in his home village that she couldn't provide, and I suspect that she feared that this time if it came to a battle she'd lose him, if not by divorce, then emotionally.'

'For the same reason she tolerated his friendship with Jago Priest?'

'Yes. What happened to that dry old stick? I met him once when he owned Badon House. We moved away not long after Lance died so I lost track – not that I wanted one.'

'He's alive and well, and no longer particularly dry.'

'Mellowed with age, then. Still living in Paris?'

'No. In England.'

'Good grief. These potty fanatics must keep going because they won't let go of their pet theories. Still banging on about King Arthur, is he?'

Georgia braced herself.

'He is,' Peter said, avoiding her eye. 'King

159

Arthur too is alive and well and living in a cave in Kent, together with his goblet and a few scrolls as an ID card in case he's woken up by the motorway noise. Did Lance talk about him?'

'About King Arthur? I don't remember. He might have. He talked mostly about places, paintings, people, Paris – that was his first love.'

'Did he mention Antonio Benizi?'

'He didn't talk about him that I recall, but I met him and his wife, the famous Madeleine. That was Antonio, wasn't it? Small, Italian, dark-haired, quicksilver brain—'

Georgia thought of Antonio now. Silvered certainly, but how quick? Quick to outwit her? She had come away with nothing tangible save a sight of the painting – and that was by his design.

'Yes, and they knew Jago in Paris too, being Lance's best friend.'

'Best friend?' Venetia looked at them oddly.

'Yes. What's wrong with that?' Georgia was taken by surprise.

Venetia began to laugh. 'Typical of Lance to give that impression – and for Jago to perpetuate it. Lance loathed Jago. No doubt about it.'

Peter shot a startled look at Georgia, and she could see her own shock reflected in his face. So much for knowing Lance the man.

'By loathe, do you mean really hated, or disliked? They were in Paris for some years together and you said that Lance looked after Badon House for Jago.'

'I use words precisely. He loathed him,' Venetia said in answer. 'At least,' she amended, 'during the time he knew me. That would have been from about 1958 to the time of his death. I suppose when they first met there might have been a time that he tolerated him.'

'But why did he hate him?' Jago seemed affable enough, Georgia thought, and he implied that he and Lance were on the best of terms. 'Did Jago do something to offend Lance?'

'One could say that.'

'What on earth was it?'

'He married Jennifer.'

Of course, Georgia thought. She'd been asleep at the switch. Madeleine had said something about that, but surely she had implied such feelings had passed when Lance married Mary.

'Is she still alive?' Venetia continued.

'No. She died two years ago. Is Jennifer important in Lance's story?'

'Was Guinevere to Lancelot?'

'Are you telling us that Lance stayed in love with Jennifer?' Peter asked evenly, as Georgia grappled with the implications.

Venetia nodded. 'And believe me, I should know. That's why he stayed in touch with Jago, his so-called best friend. A great joke, as Lance saw it. Jennifer was the place in his mind that I could never reach.'

'You said Lancelot,' Georgia asked carefully. 'Does that imply they were having an affair after she married Jago?'

'I expect so. Not openly. Like Guinevere, Jennifer knew which side her bread was buttered on. All I know is that the lady had taken up permanent residence in his heart, his mind and his love life. To misquote a now well-known phrase, there were three of us in Lance's and my pillow talk.'

'Could you have made a mistake because of your own feelings for him? Imagined—'

'No, I could not,' Venetia interrupted briskly. 'Firstly, he told me so, secondly, that bitch Madeleine Beaufort told me so and thirdly, the lady herself smugly informed me.'

'You met her?'

'Of course. She made sure of that, and so Lance was eager too. She and Jago had been married for a year or two by then, and had a child. Jago and she, Lance and I and Madeleine and her husband all spent a merry evening at the Café Procop – you know it?'

'I do,' Peter said. The tone of his voice told Georgia he'd been there with Elena.

'Everyone who is anyone from Benjamin Franklin onwards has been there. So of course that's where we went. I was introduced as Lance's girlfriend, regardless of the fact that he was married. Jennifer took my measure, all

162

charm and smiles. I doubt if Jago noticed a thing. He was rabbiting on about King Arthur as usual, Lance was playing us off one against the other and Jennifer continued to sum up the competition. She was beautiful, I grant you that, and did a good line in warm companionship. At the end of the evening, when we left the restaurant, I was alone with her for a few minutes and she dripped her poison in my ear. I think she realized I was of stronger metal than Lance's other flames, so she was reasonably subtle about it. "Do you know Mary?" she trilled, and I said I did but that she need not worry on Mary's behalf about me. There was a pause, then beautifully timed with a beautiful smile, she replied: "I don't." She had the most lovely voice. Deep and husky. She looked like the Pre-Raphaelite paintings with Jane Morris as model. She had the dark eyes and hair, and an oval face so flawless that when she chose it could be entirely expressionless. This displayed her at her most beautiful, but also served to hide her inner feelings. It's my belief there was a block of ice in there, except where Lance was concerned, of course. "Do take care of yourself," she urged me. "Lance is a breaker of hearts." I'd already figured her out, so I replied: "Of yours, you mean." "I think not," she said sweetly, and delivered by that lovely voice it sounded all the more chilling. I knew then I hadn't a hope. Fortunately I didn't want one. As I told you, one doesn't set sail without knowing the rules, and although the rules changed somewhat abruptly when I saw how things were with Jennifer, I was wary from then on.'

'If the attachment was so strong, why did she marry Jago?'

'Lance told me it was a mistake. Jennifer was as much in love with him as he with her, and both were then single. They had one of those stupid rows that everyone has. Lance was an adventurer, he had a fling with Madeleine, Jennifer took the huff and married Jago who was well-off and secure. Lance was not, and I suspect that had something to do with it.'

If Venetia was right, Madeleine was back in the picture. Georgia realized she was going to have to reassess her visit to Paris.

'So you can see if I really wanted to kill Lance, I would have done it there and then in Paris,' Venetia said. 'But I didn't.'

'Others might have had cause. Madeleine or Jago.'

Venetia considered this. 'Perhaps, but hardly likely. Madeleine seemed perfectly happy with rich cuddly Antonio, and Lance jogged along under this pretence of being Jago's best friend, as the only way he could stay in touch with Jennifer without risk.'

'If Jago found out about them, that would have given him reason to kill Lance.' Georgia could see Peter was thinking that way too by the brief nod he gave her.

'If we're talking theoretically, yes,' Venetia

agreed. 'And if Jago could muster enough passion to do it.'

'He had reason enough,' Georgia argued. 'If he planned it carefully, came over from France, met Lance and went to sea with him on the 14th —'

She stopped abruptly, as Venetia laughed outright. 'In a *boat*? I said theoretically. I'm afraid there's a fatal flaw in your theory.'

'Which is?' Georgia asked, taken aback.

'Jago would never set foot on a boat. Absolutely no way,' Venetia said. 'Even if you told him King Arthur and Sir Gawain had anchored just outside Dover Harbour, he'd only stand on the quayside with binoculars.'

'Are you sure?' Peter asked, looking as shell-shocked as Georgia felt.

'Quite, I'm afraid.' Venetia looked at them in amusement. 'I offered to take Jennifer and Jago out in my own Hillyard, but Jennifer looked at me in that superior way of hers. "If only," she sighed, "but Jago hates the water so much that even fishing in a river is barred." Jago looked annoyed, but agreed he was so hydrophobic that he couldn't swim or sail, but fortunately had no desire to.

'No, don't look to Jago,' Venetia continued more soberly. 'Look to Mary. When a worm turns, it can be vicious in real life, particularly if it's a snake in the grass too. As for me in the role of villain, I have no alibi if you want to pursue me. I was with my husband, but he'd lie in his teeth to put me in the frame.'

'If Jago is ruled out, what about Benizi?' Peter asked.

'Possible, if there were a motive. He can't have felt friendly towards Lance if he was aware of the tendresse between his wife and Lance.'

'And Jennifer?'

Venetia smiled. 'How satisfactory that would be – if you could find any reason. Never forget Jennifer.'

And for the first time Georgia glimpsed the serpent in her.

Eight

'Do you believe her?' Georgia watched Peter at his computer clicking on Charlie's Suspects Anonymous program. He'd been unusually quiet on the way home, and it was only now that she realized why. He'd already decided on a reshuffle of his Internet players.

'Unfortunately, yes. This requires major re-thinking.'

'Taking Jago out of the Burglar Bill suspects?'

'Temporary demotion.'

'Putting Venetia in? She seemed willing enough to volunteer.'

'Double bluff?'

'Perhaps. It would be good cover. Let's put her in with reluctance. I liked her.'

'We like Jago too. Did you believe what she told us about his and Lance's relationship?'

'Yes,' Georgia said after reflection, 'although both Jago and she could have been telling the truth. Jago could perfectly well have believed Lance had been his best mate, while all the time Lance was seething away with frustrated passion for his wife and intense dislike for him.' She remembered the elderly lady she'd seen in the photograph in Jago's home and tried hard to equate her with a luscious sexy Guinevere. Trying to strip away the years from images taken years later was always difficult. The past remained a book whose text was difficult to bring alive, needing determination and sympathy to fight one's way into it.

'True, O sage,' Peter agreed. 'Do you mind if I put Zac in as a suspect?'

Georgia was jolted back into an area she preferred to ignore. 'As a joker?' she asked wryly. She had been so deep into her personal reaction to Zac's reappearance that she hadn't considered the possibility that his arrival was no coincidence. And that would mean Madeleine and Antonio had planned the day very carefully indeed, which she couldn't believe.

'Why not? Let's say Zac is a wild card, role as

yet unfathomable. Did you tell Luke that we've decided to go to Dover, Mike willing, and who with?'

This last sentence came out without a pause, intended no doubt to catch her off guard. 'Not yet.' The words to tell him hadn't yet come, nor had the right moment and Luke would be able to deduce her ambivalence simply by the way she spoke. Or was it merely guilt on her part to think that way? Nevertheless it would surely be better to tell him about Paris after she returned from Dover – if they went? There was no point in upsetting him needlessly.

'What about putting Madeleine and Antonio in as suspects?' She had to get away from the subject of Zac.

'You liked Antonio, didn't you?'

'I did.'

'Italian charm?'

'If so, that doesn't mean it's false.'

'Let's agree he's a sweetie-pie. But can't a sweetie-pie also be a criminal?'

'Yes,' she agreed. 'But we don't know *he* is. He claims that he was a trusted bridge between the criminal art fraternity and the honest joes, accepted as such by both.'

'That would seem to be the case. I asked Mike to run some checks after you returned from Paris.'

'You didn't tell me,' she said accusingly.

'You were preoccupied with Zac.'

She opened her mouth to deny this, but

realized that it was all too true.

'Interpol hoped for years to pin the Benizi brothers down to a more criminal role than the one you've described. It failed, but that doesn't mean that the brothers have been forgotten. Far from it. They're still very active in the art and antiques world, and still watched. It's not the same generation as Lance dealt with, and probably not the next, but the one after that. With Russian millionaires thirsty for art treasures the world is currently the Benizi brothers' oyster.'

'Are they informers?'

'They wouldn't have lasted two days if so. No, they're either just what they claim, or fiendishly clever villains.'

'Assuming them the former, they wouldn't be suspects, would they? They're unlikely to have had a personal motive for murdering Lance.'

'Why not? Madeleine can't have been pleased if he was forever mooning over Jennifer during their affair – correction, friendship until proved otherwise, despite what Venetia says.'

'Good point,' she conceded.

'Moreover the Benizis are as strong a link as Jago between today and Paris of the 1950s which means Lance Venyon, so far as we're concerned.'

'They don't like each other, so they would hardly be allies in some conspiracy,' she objected.

'Benizi *says* they don't like each other. So far as the fake angle is concerned,' Peter continued, 'there were plenty around on the Continent last century. Apart from van Meegeren and his Vermeers, there were Otto Wacker and his Van Goghs, Dossena's classical sculptures, Malskat's medieval paintings, to name but a few. There would have been plenty of candidates for any Rossetti fakes, and Benizi would have known that.'

'There wouldn't have been as much of a market for a fake Rossetti as for a Vermeer,' she said obstinately. 'It doesn't make sense. Anyway, Antonio says he doesn't want to know if it's a fake or not.'

'I find that strange considering his former career, from which I doubt if his mind has retired, even if he professes to have done so physically. What seems to me unlikely is that both Lance and Antonio could be moving in circles where the chances of its being fake were so high, and yet neither of them appears to have taken steps to check it.'

'The painting could be genuine,' Georgia said defensively, 'even if the goblet is a figment of Rossetti's imagination.'

'The rumours about the goblet predate the painting,' Peter pointed out to her annoyance. 'And there's no mention of it on the blogs, only references to scripts that might or might not still be around. After all, Dover Priory had a highly regarded library at the time of its dissolution, which disappeared after the priory obediently submitted its catalogue to His Majesty's men.

Some of its treasures turned up later in other libraries; many did not, but weren't necessarily destroyed.'

He grinned at her, furthering her irritation. 'I think we need a clearer timetable,' he continued.

She guessed what might be coming. 'You think I should talk to Antonio again.'

'I've already done so,' Peter said smugly.

'You might have told me,' Georgia exploded, unreasonably perhaps. He was implying that she felt a rapport with the Benizis which blinded her to the fact that they were clearly not coming entirely clean over Lance Venyon.

'I'm telling you now,' Peter rejoined placidly. 'A fresh eye or rather ear was needed. Madeleine answered, and I asked whether Venetia was right about Jago not liking boats or water. She confirmed it without hesitation.'

'She didn't mention it to me,' Georgia said.

'Perhaps you didn't ask her. She sounds to me like a lady who isn't forthcoming unless pushed.'

'It's possible,' Georgia reluctantly agreed. 'What about the sticky relationship between Jago and Lance? Did she confirm that?'

'She didn't answer me. She handed the phone to Antonio.'

'And he said?'

'Ask that nice Mrs Georgia to come to Paris again. We talk. But this time,' Peter added, obviously noting her pleasure at the suggestion,

171

'take some ammunition with you.'

'Against Zac?'

'No.' He gave her a withering glance. 'But find out what he was doing there.'

A typical Monday morning. Despite the fact that June had arrived, the Gare du Nord presented its usual grey face to Georgia as she descended from the Eurostar five days later. She had carefully packed her ammunition. Jennifer, as well as Madeleine and Antonio, would take centre stage in this discussion, together with Venetia. There was one other shot she could fire. Their website had thrown up another contact – a Barry Hoskin whose father, Professor Richard Hoskin, now in his nineties, had known Lance and would be willing to see them, although the phrase 'not in good health' had sounded ominous.

Her journey to meet Antonio and Madeleine proved shorter than she anticipated, because they were waiting to welcome her with beaming faces.

'I didn't expect this treatment,' Georgia greeted them cautiously, somewhat taken aback, as they led the way to their car – complete with chauffeur, of course.

'We make a visit somewhere first, then we have lunch, then we take you to Vincennes,' Antonio announced. What was in store this time, she wondered, aware that the initiative had been swept away from her – no doubt intentionally. Antonio, for all his bonhomie, was the sort of person who never did anything without good reason, and in her case, she realized, that would not be for her company, but to do with Lance Venyon. So much for the 'now we talk'. Control had been taken out of her hands, which was an unwelcome position – as was the rear of this car. She was constantly being thrown against Antonio as they shot along the pavé road straight over minor crossroads at which the driver gave not a blink to right or left.

'Does he race at Le Mans?' she joked.

'No. Nürburgring,' Antonio answered, so seriously that she was inclined to believe him.

She was aware that she was already relaxing in response to the Count and Countess of Orvona's delightfully informal company and that she should be on her guard. Trust Antonio to take her by surprise again, however. When their destination was reached, she saw that they were outside the Louvre. Antonio issued instructions to his madcap driver, they descended, and she followed in the wake of the Benizis as they strode off for the entrance.

They were hardly the only visitors, and it was difficult for Georgia to keep up with her hosts let alone enquire what they were here for. Stealing a painting, perhaps? Swapping a Rubens for a copy rolled up in Antonio's jacket? To look at a Rossetti? Who knew with this pair? She hurried behind them as they took the stairs at the double, and noticed a sign she recognized.

Her heart sank. She had a strong suspicion that was where they were heading, although goodness knew why Antonio and Madeleine would want to show her *La Gioconda*. Georgia had seen the *Mona Lisa* at least three times before, and magnificent though it was, she hadn't planned to spend her precious time here today admiring it. Sure enough, she was right. Antonio and Madeleine were joining the usual crowd surrounding this well-guarded and surprisingly small painting.

Antonio craned over the heads of the crowd. '*Voilà*,' he said. 'You see, Mrs Georgia?'

'I do, but I don't understand.'

'That's just the point,' Madeleine said softly. 'One doesn't.'

'I have a clever wife,' Antonio said. 'Look at this lady. What is she smiling at? Is it at a joke? Is it sadness because she does not like being wife of Francesco del Giacondo? Is it ennui because she does not like this painter Leonardo?'

'There are no answers to that,' was all Georgia could think of to reply.

'*Non*. But there are more questions. Do we look at this lady and ask: are you true, are you fake?'

'No,' Georgia admitted.

'Yet why not?' Antonio said. 'Some say this is a forgery. A copy. There are other *Mona Lisa*s in the world. There was big law case once from American lady who said she had real *Mona Lisa*, but this painting won. Suppose the judgement wrong? Or suppose the real *Mona Lisa* still lives under bed of the men who stole her in 1911? Do we ask that as we look at her smile?'

'No,' she said again, feeling remarkably helpless.

'I tell you why not. Because what we see in this lady is not just what is on the canvas but the soul of the painting. Always there is the soul in every picture. And if soul shines out, we need not ask more. It satisfies everyone.'

'Not everyone,' Madeleine objected, to Georgia's relief, since she had had much the same thought. 'Some want money, and that's where the artist's name is important.'

'Yes, but we – ' Antonio struck himself on the chest – 'you, my Magdalena, you, Georgia and I, Antonio Benizi, we want soul first, then money, and that is good. Come,' he beckoned, 'we will look at the soul of Goya, the soul of *Venus de Milo*. That lady has great soul, even if she have no arms. True?'

'Yes, but—' Georgia broke off, because Antonio was already bustling away on his high-speed tour. This was ridiculous. She began to feel like Alice and the Red Queen, rushing faster, ever faster, to she knew not where. What was all this about? To pave the way for confessing that his 'Rossetti' was a fake? Or that it didn't matter even if it was? Either way, what had it to do with Lance Venyon?

At last Antonio came to a halt. 'That is the end of souls, so now we will see forgers. Then

175

lunch.'

The latter sounded an extremely good idea, and forgers at least struck a more relevant chord with her. Nevertheless it was severely cutting down on the 'now we talk' time she would have with them.

She had no sooner walked out of the Louvre with them than as if by magic the car reappeared, and another high-speed terror drive took place. This time their destination wasn't an art museum but a street hardly a stone's throw from the Champs-Elysées. It was so narrow that the car took up almost the entire width. 'You come back ten minutes,' she heard Antonio instruct his personal Formula One driver. At the rate he drove, Georgia thought, that would give him time to reach Vincennes, have lunch and be back again.

The street resembled those to be found in any large town. Always behind the facade of the broad boulevards were the working people's apartments, grey anonymous exteriors, large old wooden doors, tiny balconies where only pigeons added life. No sun could creep into this narrow road to breathe life into green plants. The trees of the Champs-Elysées seemed a world away from here where every dwelling looked the same and gave no clue to what went on within. Perhaps that was the point – it was ideal for forgers.

'It's been a long time, Antonio,' Madeleine remarked. She still looked the ultra-respectable

Englishwoman, and Georgia couldn't imagine how and where Madeleine could ever have known this place. But then did she know the real Madeleine? According to Venetia Wain, obviously not.

'Yes,' Antonio agreed. 'Which is the number? I forget.'

'Number 13,' his wife replied quietly.

'Of course.'

Number 13 was a few paces along from where they were standing, a door like all the rest with only a brass number on the wall beside it to indicate its individuality.

'Gloomy,' Antonio remarked.

'Are we going in?' Georgia asked.

'No. I do not know who lives here now, but inside once upon a time was the Louvre.'

'*Scusi?*' Georgia thought she had misheard.

'Here were all the paintings of the Louvre, all the precious objects. Here was a palace, all the glories of the world. You have heard of Kranowski?'

'I don't think so.'

'Great artist. Great faker. He had a family business here in the 1950s. He loved the past, did legitimate copies on commission, but preferred making his own. That way he created new great works. Domenico Kranowski was a great friend of mine.'

'Although he was a faker?'

'Is necessary to know fakers and forgers in antiques trade. I study their style, so I recognize them if they try to sell work to me. Domenico knew that. "I never fool you," he tell me. "You are too clever." So I know the Rossetti painting is not his. Kranowski was a lovely man. His father was a faker and his son. Kranowski wanted revenge on a country that did not protect his father. Jewish, you see,' Antonio said matter-of-factly. 'So he became an even better faker than his father, so that he could laugh very hard at all French experts.'

'Was he finally exposed?'

'*Si*. In 1961 and the family disappeared like magic. But it was not I who betray him. No one trust me if I do that.'

She saw what he meant. If Antonio was, as he claimed, a bridge between the legal and illegal art worlds, then he was right – although the bridge claim hardly tallied with Mike's information from Interpol. 'Could Lance have exposed him?' Georgia asked. 'If so, there could be a motive for a revenge killing.'

'No, no. Lance was also great friends with Domenico.'

It all sounded very chummy. 'Even though Lance's job was to track down forgeries and fakes?'

'Not like that at all. The villains not always the fakers. The fakers like their work. The bad men are those who set up con, find buyers, do deals. You heard of Israel Ruchomovski? He was master faker, great artist.'

'I don't think so.'

'He was a gold- and silversmith, over hundred years ago. He loved objects of the past, so fake his own. He was not a bad man, he was a very good man. He created the ancient Persian Tiara of Saitaphernes, a big golden helmet which the Louvre bought. You know what he said when he was praised for this lovely fake? He said, "This not good at all. My sarcophagus is much better." This sarcophagus was on exhibition in Paris as ancient relic and winning much praise. Very funny, eh?'

'Are you suggesting Ruchomovski might have forged the golden goblet?' Georgia asked, confused.

Antonio gave her a charming smile. 'Who knows? But I think not. Fifty years too early. I only point out that there is soul in fakes too. There is soul in the tiara, soul in the sarcophagus. What's in a name, your Shakespeare says. You know the old joke, there are twice as many Monets in the world as Monet ever painted. So now we have lunch, eh? And then we go to look at Gawain painting again. We will look to see if it has soul.'

She had been counting on an informal lunch at Vincennes to shoot off her ammunition, but once again control had been taken out of her hands. In the small Italian restaurant with crowded tables Antonio had chosen, it was impossible to hold a meaningful conversation and Antonio was in good form cracking joke after joke. It was equally impossible to be annoyed. He reluctantly agreed she could pay the bill in return for their hospitality on her last visit, but when she asked the waiter for it, it appeared that there wasn't one. It was apparently an honour for the restaurant to supply them with copious food and drink (on which she went more carefully than last time). Nevertheless she managed to fire one shot in the car on the return to Vincennes.

'Have you seen anything more of Zac?' she asked.

'No, Mrs G.' Antonio chuckled. 'He only came to see me for news of Roberto. He our youngest son, who work in Vienna.'

'A lovely city,' Madeleine immediately replied. 'Have you visited it?'

Georgia hadn't and Madeleine's prompt account of it carefully took the subject away from Zac, and try as she might she couldn't work the conversation back again.

Once in Vincennes, Antonio was intent on rushing her straight up for her date with King Arthur, but he wasn't getting away with this one so easily. She was going to use all her ammunition this time.

'Before I see it again,' she said firmly, 'I have to confess to a problem with it.'

Both Madeleine and Antonio looked surprised. Too surprised?

'If Lance dealt with fakes and you were both so knowledgeable about the world of fakes in Paris, Antonio, how can it be right that you can't tell immediately whether it's a fake or not, only whether it has soul.'

'We do not recognize the style in this case,' Antonio said promptly. 'Even fakers have styles, brushwork, care of detail, use of colours. Chrome yellow is one. In a fake that shows more clearly than in a straight copy. This one very good, and could be Rossetti. We study Rossetti carefully, see no difference. And yet, not quite sure, you know?' He flashed her a beaming smile, but she stood her ground.

'But I still don't understand why Jago wasn't brought in on this?'

Antonio considered this. 'We live in Rome when Lance show us painting, so maybe that M. Jago not see it. We told your papa on the telephone that he is right. Lance did not like Jago because of Jennifer. Jago probably never noticed and thought they were great friends. He was only interested in King Arthur, and thought Lance was too.'

Georgia pounced. *'Thought?* So Lance's interest in Arthur wasn't as genuine as Jago believes?'

'Lance,' Madeleine took over, 'was interested in all sorts of things. He would pick up interests and drop them as new ones came along. Arthur stuck, because Jago was always so obsessed with it.'

'Then why didn't he show him the painting?' Georgia persisted. 'He told him it existed, but apparently Jago never knew it was actually in his hands, otherwise Lance would have been forced to show it to him before bringing it to you in Rome.'

'Why?' Madeleine asked guardedly.

'Because of Jennifer.' Their faces were expressionless as she continued: 'You agreed that Lance still loved Jennifer and vice versa, and that he kept up the relationship with Jago because of that. So he would not have risked being banned from the household through keeping Jago in the dark over something he was so obsessed about. He'd told him about the painting. Why not show it to him too?'

Antonio heaved a sigh. 'This is a clever lady, Madeleine. We tell her, yes?'

Madeleine nodded, watching her husband closely.

'The reason he did not tell Jago he had bought the painting is that he wanted to save it so we could all get a higher price from Jago when he found Mr Ruskin's letter and script proving the goblet really existed. Jennifer agreed. Great joke. So Lance said he loved King Arthur too, and wanted to help him find the goblet.'

'So Jennifer still loved Lance?' Georgia asked.

'She never spoke a word against Jago, but I think she did,' Madeleine replied. 'She sounded devastated when she wrote to tell us of Lance's death. The last time I heard from her she was pregnant again and then we fell out of touch.'

Two shots left but these could easily be dud

bullets. 'Does the name Richard Hoskin meant anything to you?' Georgia asked. 'A professor, who says he knew Lance? Or have you heard of a young man called Michael? He was a visitor not long before Lance died, so Venetia Wain told us.'

She thought she saw a flicker of reaction in Madeleine's expression, but if so it was gone so quickly that she could not be sure.

Antonio shook his head. 'Sorry, Mrs Georgia, many people know Lance.'

'Neither of them?' she asked.

'What lady Venetia tell you bound to be wrong,' Antonio replied briskly. 'Now we see picture. We decide if it true or false. Whether it speak to us like *Mona Lisa*.'

Georgia followed them upstairs and into the bedroom again. The painting impressed her as much as before. This time, she ignored the dying knight and King Arthur, and studied the goblet first. It seemed to glow with a life of its own, its relief just faintly discernible upon it, including something that might conceivably be an animal. It was the whole goblet that drew the attention, though. Both Sir Gawain's and the King's eyes were on it, not, it seemed to suggest, for the gold but for what it symbolized for them. It was, she recognized, the painting's soul.

'True or false, Georgia?' Madeleine asked gently.

'Are you asking me,' she replied hesitantly,

'whether I think this is a fake, perhaps a Kranowski painting? Is this what this is all about?'

'No,' snapped Antonio indignantly. 'I tell you Kranowski did *not* paint this. You tell me what you think. With all my experience I still do not know. Does that goblet exist or not? Is this painting fake? Is the goblet fake? If the painting is genuine, did Rossetti believe the goblet existed? Tell me, please.'

Georgia drew a deep breath. 'It does have soul,' she said. 'And that makes it genuine, but not necessarily a genuine Rossetti.' She took a step into unknown territory. 'What about the other paintings? When I came last time, you referred to paintings in the plural, and so has Jago.'

Instantly she was aware that the atmosphere had changed. Antonio was very still. 'You make mistake, Mrs Georgia,' he said pleasantly. 'You mishear me. Only one painting.'

'Lance might have known about others,' Georgia persisted, interested to see where this might be going. 'Which is why Jago referred to more than one. Perhaps Lance deliberately misled you?'

'No.' Another charming smile. 'You understand? *No.*'

She did. It was a message that cooperation was over and it was time to leave – and to lighten the atmosphere. 'Silly of me.' She shook her head as if at her own stupidity. 'If Rossetti was only in Paris for ten days he couldn't possibly have painted more than one.'

The tension relaxed, as she had hoped, but as she got into the car to be chauffeur-driven to the Gare du Nord they insisted on coming with her. Not, she suspected, through politeness but because they wanted to be sure she left without questions to Mr Formula One. What, however, would those have been? About the paintings? About Roberto? About Lance? Or about Zac?

Nine

Questions span round Georgia's head until it felt like a washing machine, and she longed to hurl them at Peter immediately she returned. Not a good idea, though. They needed to be thoroughly rinsed before she could present them coherently. Moreover Luke would be waiting too, and this time her account of Paris could, thank goodness, be less edited than her previous one. One purpose this had served was to relegate Zac to a compartment of his own in her mind, rather than have him obstinately keep popping up in the Benizi story. Although over that, she was uncomfortably aware, there was still a question mark over his role.

It was therefore not until the following morning that she went to find Peter. Conversation with Luke had been confined to a straight account of the day. He had had supper waiting for her, and once back home Zac had tiptoed out of her thoughts with only the faintest acknowledgement from her.

When she arrived at nine o'clock Peter was not in his office, and there was no sign of Margaret. For a moment she feared that he had had one of his 'turns'. These were becoming less frequent now that the years were passing since Rick's disappearance but nevertheless when they did occur they were violent and terrifying, leaving him shivering at horrors she could not share, but could well imagine. She hurried into the bedroom and was relieved to find it empty. Instead she tracked him down to the garden where she saw him already installed at his working table under the fig tree, Margaret doing her best to persuade him that breakfast was a good idea. It lay on a tray on a trolley at his side.

She shrugged when she saw Georgia. 'You have a go.'

'Ah,' Peter glanced over his shoulder, 'perfect happiness, Georgia. That's what they say.'

'And that's breakfast?' she enquired amicably.

'Sitting under one's own fig tree.'

She agreed there was something in the shape of the fig-tree leaves that seemed to make it a peaceful tree, as well as – in a good summer here – a fruitful one. The pile of books already before Peter, however, suggested that he had a mission in mind rather than a browse.

'No Internet today?' she asked, dropping a kiss on his head.

He waved a hand at the pile. 'Books. What news from afar?'

She scented an opportunity. 'Have your breakfast, and I'll tell you.'

Margaret disappeared inside the house, and Peter actually took Georgia at her word, listening avidly throughout a bowl of muesli and a croissant.

He continued munching for a few minutes after she had finished, and then sighed. 'So let's sum up. The painting has almost certainly got to be a fake. This so-called evidence is far too tenuous.'

'Agreed.'

'Or, of course, the Benizis could be kidding you; they know the painting to be genuine and want to make a killing now that the King Arthur story is getting big again. His cup coming back to meet the saucer, so to speak.'

'Very cute,' she said disapprovingly. 'And though you might be right in theory, I don't see anyone having a plan that would involve waiting forty-odd years to come to fruition.'

'What about cases of wine? Antonio Benizi works in a family business, there's the next generation to think of.'

'I still don't buy it. They are traders. If they knew the painting was genuine, as soon as the

Pre-Raphaelites became popular again they'd have flogged it. What's interesting is what happened to the other paintings, if any. Antonio certainly didn't like my asking about them.'

Peter frowned. 'One lost Rossetti is possibly genuine, two or three make it look rather contrived, don't you think? And aren't we getting off the point, which is Lance Venyon's death?'

'I don't know where the point is any longer,' she said crossly. 'It's like a maze, every dead-end avenue adds to the fog of misdirection.'

'As no doubt Antonio Benizi intends,' Peter observed.

'Possibly,' she conceded, then saw his expression. 'All right, *probably*.'

'How about certainly?'

'If so, so what?'

'That suggests the painting or paintings *are* fake, probably the goblet too, and led to Lance's death.'

'No,' she argued. She wasn't going to accept that she'd been completely hoodwinked by Antonio. 'Even if the painting is fake, the goblet isn't necessarily so. *Aargh*,' she broke off in despair, seeing she was on quicksand now. 'Where now? All roads barred.'

'Nonsense,' Peter said briskly. 'What about gangs for starters?'

'Gangs in the plural? Gents with hats pulled over their eyes?'

'Gangs aren't always villains. We have two of them. The Benizi Brothers, because whichever side of the legal line they tread, they most certainly constitute a gang.'

'And the other?'

'The gang behind the current art thefts, to which we tentatively put the Roy Cook name. There's a remote chance the link between them could still be Lance Venyon.'

'Via Sandro Daks. But *is* it a gang?'

'Ask Mike. He's due here in half an hour. He's had a word with the Metropolitan Police. I hate to point this out, Georgia, but Zac too is a link between the two gangs.'

'Mike must have been thrilled at that idea,' she said hollowly, wrestling with this depressing notion. Mike had known and been wary of Zac almost as much as Peter, and been involved in his arrest.

She was right, although when he arrived, Mike grudgingly admitted, 'For once, Georgia, your ex is telling the truth, though the Met is using him at a low level only. It's only just beginning to unravel the scam. It's been well thought out. Straightforward burglary with one or two nice but hardly earth-shattering pictures pinched. Sigh of relief from the owners, who then don't bother to check their valuable paintings carefully enough. They're the ones for which copies have been substituted. It could take months, even years, for them to come to light. Even if chemical analysis proves them to be forgeries, it would take a devil of a lot of proving that it was due to the burglary, since the path is well and truly grown over.'

'And Zac's role in this?'

'Spying out the possible forgeries. So far they've tracked down a so-called Turner in Elham Castle, a William Etty in a Sussex museum, a Lawrence portrait of a former lord of the manor at Egerton Grange, and a Pre-Raphaelite somewhere. They'd all suffered minor burglaries in the last three years. The Art and Antiques Unit doesn't yet know if all of the forgeries are connected, or whether any of the paintings were copies when they were acquired. It's inclined to the former, though. As with anything else in this field, the style, even in forgeries of others' works, becomes familiar, as do the materials and ageing methods.'

'Which Pre-Raphaelite?' Peter enquired.

'Burne-Jones, I think.'

'King Arthurs?' he asked hopefully.

Mike laughed. 'Getting hung up on the gent, are you, Peter? The answer is no, as far as I recall. Anyway, I've cleared it for you to drop in to Roy Cook's gallery so far as the Met is concerned. Only on the Lance Venyon front, of course. As for me, I'm not too keen, but I suppose I trust you.'

'Is Cook a suspect for Sandro's murder?'

'Close,' he replied. 'And could get closer if he's tied in to the Art and Antiques case. They're pretty sure that Cook is involved in that, either as a runner for the scam or the top brain. No gun's turned up yet for the murder. It was a semi-automatic, fired from about three feet away.'

'Have you questioned Zac?' she asked.

'No. Thankfully, I'm the middleman,' Mike said. 'Anyway, the Met has vetoed your marching in there with Zac at your side. They wanted to veto you too, but agreed that if by chance there was a link to this Lance Venyon it might be better coming from you than us policeman plods.'

Relief. Without Zac, she would have all her antennae pointing towards Roy Cook, rather than wondering what her ex-husband might say next. Zac varied in performance; he could have an intuitive grasp of a situation, or he could plonk the largest foot in the world into it.

'Is it OK for me to go?' Peter asked.

'That's up to you to decide between you,' Mike replied. 'One can look casual, two – particularly with the wheelchair – might look like a deputation.'

After Mike left – rather reluctantly since the garden was cool and pleasant on a hot day – Peter decided Mike was right. He would pass on the Roy Cook front, but he maintained his right to visit the castle, which she willingly conceded. She even agreed to accompany him.

'Any other open paths to Lance Venyon?' she asked.

'Professor Richard Hoskin for one. I was in touch with the son yesterday. His father was a professor of history from 1954 to 1976 at the

University of Hampshire. Wrote several books, naturally; they were about the Anglo-Saxons.'

'Not King Arthur, and how he routed them at the Battle of Badon?'

'No mention of Arthur.'

'Then I can't wait.'

'You'll have to. The appointment's not until Friday. Meanwhile it's back to His Majesty.'

'By time machine?'

'No, by courtesy of Jago Priest. I can't help feeling you're right and that that churchyard is involved in this problem, even though Lance's grave isn't in the corner where you felt that strong atmosphere. Give it another go, will you?'

'Just to stand in that corner?' She was puzzled as well as reluctant.

'No, check out that field as well. Check where they thought that treasure was buried. I've spoken to Jago, and he's deputed daughter Cindy to show you the spot marked X.'

'I can't see that this will achieve anything. Have you been blogging again?' she asked suspiciously.

'No, Georgia, I've been thinking,' he replied with dignity.

'About what?'

'Golden goblets.'

Cindy looked around the Badon House kitchen appreciatively. Georgia had picked her up at the Canterbury Park and Ride and driven her to

Wymdown. Cindy proved knowledgeable about art history and it had been interesting to talk to her on her own. At their previous meeting she had been overshadowed by her ebullient father and her daughter, who was coming to pick her up in their car later after the shop had closed. Today Cindy looked far more the business-woman, with her long smart skirt and blouse, dangly earrings and expertly applied cosmetics. Here was one very cool and confident woman, Georgia thought, who was happy to leave the role of extrovert to Sam and Jago. No business of Cindy's would dare to fail. Nevertheless she seemed pleasant enough and certainly very fond of her father. Gwen and Terry had obviously taken to her, from the way they were chatting over tea and eclairs.

'Dad told me he owned this place once,' Cindy said.

'That's right. Do you share Jago's theories about King Arthur?' Georgia asked.

'Hardly. My interests are strictly factual. What one digs up provides the basis for deduc-tion, not the other way round. Sam is the fanciful one.'

'Just about King Arthur?'

'That among other myths and legends. It's the folklore aspect that attracts her. She does rather good drawings if she sets her mind to it. Horror, chiefly.'

'Of folklore?' Gwen asked curiously. 'What's so horrid about that?'

'Plenty. There's a strain of fear running through it. Like life. The Hooden Horse is pretty scary to a child. The Bogey Man, the Sandman, the Green Man, all nasty things that go bump in the night and come out to grab the unwary.'

Georgia laughed. 'Do you paint too?'

'I take a sketchbook when I travel, but chiefly I buy it and sell it. I've more of an eye for that, so I'm told. Now what exactly are you hoping to find in Dad's beloved field?'

'A golden goblet would be nice, but short of that just the site that your father has ruled out as the location. I'm sure he must have other sites to investigate by now, as I gather he still hopes to find Gawain's bones.' She wouldn't mention the churchyard – that was her own nightmare.

'Ever see a blue moon?' Cindy said caustically. 'I know Arthur's goblet is flavour of the month again at present amongst the bloggers and nutters, but you're right: the site wouldn't be in this field and Pops knows that. He says general attention is firmly focused on Barham Downs at present and that every Arthurian bloodhound is out there in disguise sniffing over every inch.'

'Does your father still do his own sniffing?'

Cindy considered this. 'I suppose he'd like one more bash. Every time I visit him I find him blogging away on the Prester John sites, or crawling over maps, past and present. Now that his first site is ruled out, he's paying more attention to the other early churches, Coldred for instance, since that was linked to Dover Priory. And of course he's interested in the Barham Downs area too.'

'Because of his Battle of Badon theory?' Georgia asked.

'So you've picked that up, have you?' Cindy looked surprised.

'Peter did, from a blog.'

'You are thorough. Or are you getting gold fever yourself?' Cindy wasn't smiling anymore.

'It's safe from me,' Georgia replied lightly. 'Our interest is only in Lance Venyon.'

'I doubt if you'll find him buried in the field,' Cindy retorted drily. 'But let's go and look.'

Georgia was glad she hadn't persuaded Peter to come with her. It was no place for a wheelchair. Quite apart from the narrow gateway, the field shelved more steeply than it had appeared from the churchyard end, and although it was grazed it was otherwise untended. Clumps of nettles and brambles dotted the grass, and the ground was uneven.

'It's down here.' Cindy led the way to the churchyard wall on the far side of the field. 'Pops' theory was that the chaplains needed both a protected spot and one they could easily find again when, as they hoped, the old religion was restored. After all, even in the sixteenth century fields were ploughed and they wouldn't have wanted to risk damage or discovery by third parties.'

Even though the ground was more even here, there seemed to Georgia nothing remarkable about it.

'Pops was convinced that the earlier church preceding the current St Alban's was nearer here, and that its ruins or foundations could well still have been in existence in the sixteenth century when the chaplains lugged the remains of Sir Gawain here. In his dreams, that is. He argued that they would want to avoid the new St Alban's for security reasons and might have picked on the old foundations as giving extra protection. That could have meant roughly here, Pops thought, where we're standing. After he'd found nothing, he had the geophysical survey done. He pounced on every shadow it showed. Zilch. And he was so sure. St Alban's has a lot of Roman tiles and stuff in its construction and that would tally, Pops says, with there having been a lot of rubble around from the earlier church when they built the current one.'

Once again Georgia had an image of a solemn funeral procession of chaplains marching down from their lodgings in Badon House for a formal reburial. Gawain's would be semi-sacred relics, and so there must have been some sort of ceremony, however brief. Even on a sunny summer's day it was possible to believe it happening in this remote spot under its shading trees. Yews lived a long time, and the ones she was looking at could well have seen exactly what happened when the chaplains came. Or, she had to remind herself, *not* seen anything. Jago's thesis had proved wrong. If the bones were anywhere, it wasn't here.

'Pops thought the site would have been here because of the cross. Do you see?' Cindy pointed behind Georgia to the field they had just walked down.

At first she couldn't, but gradually she made out what Cindy meant. There were long hummocks of land on the incline low enough almost to blend into the general unevenness of the ground. Shaped like prehistoric barrows, they crossed each other. 'Pops felt that the remains would have been buried at its foot just here,' Cindy explained.

Georgia could see why Jago had been so taken with the idea, but that was a long way from convincing her. 'Three hundred and fifty years have passed,' she objected. 'The field wouldn't have been the same shape then.'

'Why not?' Cindy asked reasonably. 'In past ages they didn't have a habit of building on every green site available. This would have been grazing ground for years. It's no use for cultivation, and anyway it would have been glebe land belonging to the church. No, if there was any truth in the story at all, it must have seemed a reasonable bet for Pops that it was here.'

'And still your father keeps the field for sentimental reasons.' Now that she was here,

Georgia could appreciate all the more Jago's agony when his years of hope culminated in nothing.

Cindy shrugged. 'Why not? It earns grazing rent; not much it's true, but enough to pay for maintenance. I reckon he'll only sell it if the goblet is actually found on Barham Downs or wherever.'

'Do *you* think that's possible?'

Cindy laughed. 'I told you, I deal in facts. Sam's view is that as there's a consensus, the dratted goblet must exist, and so it's just a question of where. The Ringlemere Cup was found more or less by chance, so maybe this one will be too. We've even had enthusiasts turning up at St Alban's even though Pops has been careful not to draw attention to Wymdown and his exploded theory. Each one blogs away hoping to steal a march on someone else's theory while jealously guarding his or her own.'

'Her own? Not gender-orientated, then?'

'No way. One blogger believes the village of Womenswold holds the goblet, simply because of feminist principles – regardless of the fact that the village's name originally meant forest of the warriors; another that the goblet must be in Wales because Guinevere is a Welsh name, and so on.'

'What about the Kent Archaeological Society? Are they involved?'

'Not to my knowledge. They require solid

evidence, as I do. There's masses of Roman, pre-Roman and early Anglo-Saxon stuff dug up in Kent, especially round here, and even if such a goblet were found it's a big step to its being connected with Arthur. Pops reckons that if it was Arthur's personal goblet then it might be ornamented with his personal bear symbol, so that might help.'

Georgia's mind flashed back to the painting, and the possible animal relief on the goblet, then firmly brought herself back to reality. 'But you're inclined to believe it's all a South Sea Bubble of fantasy?' Even if there had been such ornamentation in the painting, it could provide no evidence without Antonio agreeing to its undergoing modern tests.

'Of course it's probably fantasy,' Cindy agreed. 'But I admit to a tiny doubt. Just suppose it's not. Something has sparked this story off again, and suppose it was hard evidence that did so, not just gold fever.'

Georgia tried to keep the lid on speculation. 'Does the name Richard Hoskin mean anything to you?'

'Not a thing. Should it?'

'He's someone who claims to have known Lance Venyon, and therefore might also have been a friend of your father's. And Lance,' Georgia said firmly, 'is the reason I'm here, though it's hard to remember at times.'

'You still think he was murdered, don't you?' She looked at Georgia curiously.

'There are grounds for it. Did your father have any further thoughts about it?'

'You shook him,' Cindy admitted. 'He doesn't see how the murder could be connected with Sir Gawain and Arthur, though. He'd be more inclined to think one of Lance's ladies pushed him overboard.'

The sudden arrival of Sam prevented Georgia from taking this further.

'Hi, Mum.' Sam was coming through the churchyard gate, her bright auburn hair making a vivid splash of colour among the dark green of the trees and bushes.

'The tour's over,' Cindy called out to her. 'Sir Gawain has ridden off, taking his goblet with him.'

'You shouldn't mock it,' Sam said fiercely. 'It's our roots.'

'Sorry,' Cindy answered peaceably. 'We're just checking the roots of Sir Gawain, if that's OK by you.'

'One look from you, Mum, and any self-respecting legend would wither in its historical bed. She's a cynic, Georgia.' Sam turned to her. 'She doesn't see the point of investigating anything you can't touch. Grandpops is much more sensible.'

'Sensible?' Cindy threw at her. 'Who buys a home the size of Badon House just for a whim?'

'Someone with soul, Mum.'

Soul again. Soul of King Arthur, soul of the

Mona Lisa, soul of the goblet. And it all boiled down to a patch of barren ground, here where Georgia was standing. Why had Peter been so keen that she should check it out?

Georgia could hear Sam and Cindy's argument continuing after they had said their farewells and were returning to the car. She was about to return to the comfort of Gwen's tea and cakes herself, when she remembered with sinking heart Peter's request about the churchyard. The creepiness might have gone by now, she comforted herself as the gate creaked eerily in the stillness, but she changed her mind as she reached the corner where Sandro's body had lain. The atmosphere was just as stultifying as she had found it earlier. Here she had stood that evening, here by this gravestone where she had first seen the hand. And still that coldness persisted, a shiver stemming not from the sun or from the tragedy of Sandro Daks, but from something else. Did this, *could* this, connect to Lance Venyon? She still couldn't see how. She was chasing a will-o'-the-wisp, and it seemed trapped in this corner.

'Peaceful place, isn't it?'

She turned round, half expecting to find the young curate she had met before. Instead it was an old man, whom for the moment she didn't recognize. Then she realized it was the former vicar whom she'd met at the wedding.

'I'm sorry if I startled you,' he said politely. 'I visit my old church from time to time. St

Alban's was my favourite. The nearest to God, perhaps. Are you still hunting for Lance Venyon?' he enquired. 'You asked me about him when we last met.'

'Yes. Sandro Daks, the young man who was murdered, had mentioned that Lance was a friend of his grandfather's. It rang no bells with Elaine Holt, though.'

'Nor with me. I have nevertheless been thinking about Lance quite a lot since you mentioned him. Odd the way some small thing can trigger one's mind into motion, and then it refuses to stop. It has an obliging way of producing items from the back of one's mind.'

'And did it over Lance?' This sounded hopeful.

'It did indeed. Lance and the goblet.'

'King Arthur's?' Did everyone in the world know about it?

'I can see you've heard of it. Lance told me some story about it. So far as I recall, he was helping a friend to track down the cave Arthur's supposed to be buried in, and fully expected to find the goblet too. He was optimistic of a result soon. I was far less optimistic but nevertheless intrigued. After all, it might have meant a relic for St Alban's.'

'You don't remember where he thought the cave was?' Was this a new line or Lance spinning a variation on the real story? The latter, she guessed.

'Alas, no. Dreams always break off at the

vital moment, I'm afraid, and my memory often does the same. I do recall the day Lance left here, however, and this is not by summoning up some false memory. He was in his car, and told me he was off to Hythe – or was it Dover? – to go sailing. I wished them a happy journey, not realizing of course that I'd never see him again.'

'Them?' she picked up, with a quickening sense of excitement. 'He wasn't alone?'

He looked startled. 'Did I say that?' He thought for a moment. 'Of course. That's why I remembered. He had a woman with him.'

'His wife? Venetia Wain?'

'No. I'd have remembered if so. She was a stranger to me.'

'Just how much reliance can we place on the vicar's memory?' Peter asked, when she returned to Haden Shaw.

'Not a lot,' Georgia replied regretfully. 'How can he be so sure of the day?'

Peter looked at her in frustration. 'For the first time I feel at a loss. Venyon keeps slipping away from us. How do we catch hold of him? He's as slippery as an eel. If it wasn't for King Arthur, I'd chuck this one in. And even he's going nowhere. I'd hoped your seeing the actual site might have sparked something off.'

Unexpectedly his pessimistic mood made Georgia more positive. 'Don't give up yet,' she said. 'Question one: do we think there's something odd about Venyon's death?'

'Yes, but I haven't a clue what it is.'

'Question two: do you think there's a link between Antonio Benizi, his painting, Lance, Jago, perhaps Jennifer and the fabled golden goblet?'

'Yes.'

'Question three: and a link with Sandro Daks?'

Peter hesitated. 'Yes.'

'Question four: just because it's difficult do we want to give it up?'

He looked at her gratefully. 'Phrase it more positively.'

'Question four: are we going forward even though it's foggy?'

'Yes.'

Antonio Benizi might, she acknowledged, have led them into a deliberate maze, but even mazes had centres as well as exits. It was finding them that was the problem.

Richard Hoskin lived in the far hinterland of the village of Burwash, nestling in a narrow lane. It was the sort, Georgia thought, that might lead either to a dead end or to a major highway at a moment's notice. This one, she discovered, did not conform. It wound on and on, up hill and down dale until she wondered whether she'd mistaken the way. Just as she began to think this was the case, Hillsview miraculously appeared, at least the plaque by the gateway told her so.

Of the house itself there was no sign. It must be shrouded in trees, which made its name inappropriate.

Its driveway led to a large Victorian mock-gothic home, ugly but comfortable-looking. It was clearly Barry, the son, who opened the door. He must be in his mid-sixties, she estimated, and seemed an unlikely carer for an ageing relative; he was a vigorous, outdoor man, with a bronzed face and athletic build. He exuded welcome, however, for which today she was more than usually grateful.

As soon as they went into the pleasant living room it was clear just why his father needed a carer. Professor Richard Hoskin was sitting in an upright armchair, with vacant eyes, and a pleased expression with which she imagined he greeted all visitors.

'How did you pick up our request for information?' she asked after introductions had been made.

Richard Hoskin continued smiling, and it was Barry who answered cheerily: 'My father uses the Internet, don't you, Dad?'

A vigorous nod from his father, so Alzheimer's had not completely claimed him. 'Lance,' he agreed brightly, which was a hopeful sign.

'You feed the name into Google every so often, don't you, Dad?' Barry prompted. 'Yours was the first site it returned so it excited him,' he explained to Georgia.

Another vigorous nod.

'Was Lance a friend of yours?' Georgia asked him, but nothing came in response.

'I'm afraid I can't help,' Barry said, dashing her hopes. 'I'd never heard the name until I saw Dad typing it one day and asked him about it.'

'What did he reply?'

'He said Arthur.'

Of course. This was squaring the circle yet again. 'Do you know why?' she asked, but Barry shook his head. 'Do you know Jago Priest?' she persevered with the professor.

His eyes shifted and he looked puzzled. First he shook his head, but then nodded.

'A friend of yours?'

A shake of the head as Richard Hoskin lost interest in Jago.

'How do you know Lance Venyon?' she prompted, hoping Jago's name might have helped shift a block.

'Yes.'

This was encouraging at least. 'In the art world?'

'Raphael.'

'Your favourite painter is Raphael?' Another blank. 'Lance specialized in Raphael's paintings?' Nothing. Was Raphael all he could manage of Pre-Raphaelites? She had a sudden hope. 'Lance and Rossetti's paintings of King Arthur?' Nothing. Try another tack. 'You're a professor of history, specializing in the Anglo-Saxon period, so does that include the Arthurian age? King Arthur fought the Saxons.'

Jackpot. This produced an excited gabble of words, between him and Barry, which she couldn't follow. Barry looked at her doubtfully. 'She wouldn't be interested, Dad.'

What was this about, Georgia wondered in frustration. At the moment she'd be interested in *anything*.

'Lance,' the professor said again, making moves to struggle up from the chair. Something was obviously afoot, as Barry went over to help him.

'He wants me to take you to see his special room,' he told her. 'Be warned.'

There was no point in her asking which room and why she should be wary. She'd go with the flow.

'This way.' Barry indicated the French windows, leading into the garden, and she went outside. It was a large garden, and it must have been part of an old farm at one time, because at one side was an old barn, much older than the house, tiled and restored. A garage? she wondered, as she waited for Barry to help his father outside. She'd once gone to see someone she had set down as a dull old stick only to find he had a 1903 Dion Bouton in perfect condition in a similar barn and more classics in the garden, or rather automobilia junkyard. That was Peter's sphere of interest, and so he had been highly annoyed at having missed it.

This garden, however, was spectacularly neat

and well kept. Each flower knew its place, and no weeds had been allowed to block their nourishment. Barry was leading his father straight to the barn, which implied this was the special room, and she followed at their side. Coming in from the sunshine as he opened the door, she could see nothing in the gloom, until Barry switched on the lights.

Not just any lights. Not just any special room. She was transported to Camelot, as a thousand candlelights lit the raised platform at the far end. There was a round table, similar to the ones she had seen in tourist towns, but at this one twelve knights in full armour were sitting. At least it had baulked at the thirty or more knights suggested by Malory. The Siege Perilous had been left empty. An intense light shone on it, creating the impression that Sir Galahad would come racing in with the Grail at any moment. For all their democratic seating arrangements at the Round Table, however, Arthur was clearly marked out as head of the court, and behind him was a simpering Guinevere. Morgana la Fay peeped in on the scene from the rear and Merlin stood as a maître d' to the proceedings at one side of the platform.

Richard Hoskin cooed contentedly to himself as he gazed on his creation, which she enthusiastically admired.

'Lance Venyon?' she then asked him tentatively, wondering how he came into this story. Hoskin nodded, waving a hand towards the sides of the barn, almost invisible in the dim light. Some more juggling by Barry with the light switches, and the stage was darkened, taking Camelot back into fairyland, and the rest of the barn illuminated. Now she was no longer in Hollywood but in a museum. Every wall was covered with ancient swords and helmets, while display cases were filled with pottery, rings, bowls and bronzes. She wandered up and down, half puzzled, half admiring. What had this to do with Venyon? Nothing that she could see, so why was she here?

Another case displayed fragments of parchment in a language she didn't recognize. The original script of *Beowulf*, perhaps? Certainly fragments showing miniature exquisite pictures were of battle scenes, and Viking ships – or, she thought suddenly, of the Battle of Dover? Could they possibly have come from the chaplains' supposedly lost record of the Arthurian story? Another was in a different script, looking somewhat more modern, and with a picture of three monks praying. Or were they the three chaplains of St Mary-in-the-Castle?

'Do you know where all this came from?' she asked Barry, having made the appropriate noises of appreciation to his father.

'I've no idea, I'm afraid.' He looked genuinely apologetic. 'This lot wasn't here when I left for university in 1958; then there was a spell in the army and some years abroad, so I was only really aware of it when I came back after

Mum's death. He said it was part of his work, and Camelot was just his way of having fun. Not being interested in the subject I never questioned it. After all, even after he retired, he still wrote research papers and articles, as well as a book or two.'

'The collection must have some value, from its sheer quantity.'

'Especially to the bloggers.'

Georgia looked at Barry in astonishment. 'He knows about blogging?'

'He's glued to blogs for a considerable part of each day under the code-name Camelot. It beats television hollow.'

Hoskin must be too ill to take much active part now, but the past might still be vivid to him, if only she could reach it.

'Lance Venyon,' she tried again, then with a pause between each name: 'Jago Priest. King Arthur's goblet, Sir Gawain. Rossetti, St Mary-in-the-Castle, Wymdown.' Nothing, so as a last resort she tried 'Raphael' again.

She listened hopefully as another excited babble flowed but all she could make out were the words 'Michelangelo' and 'Lance's hat'. *Hat?* She tried Raphael again, but only received the same reply.

'I'm afraid that looks like it,' Barry said apologetically. 'I'd better close up here.' Georgia took the hint, giving a frustrated look at this wonderland. Whatever secrets it held, if any, were further away than Camelot itself.

Ten

'You'll be delighted to hear that Professor Hoskin is a fan,' Georgia announced. Peter had asked her to call in before returning to Medlars, and she had been happy to do so. She was looking forward to describing the glories of Camelot.

'Good,' Peter replied with relish. 'Tell me more.'

'The bad news is that there's precious little to take us forward. His memory is all but gone, save for odd snatches from the past.'

'Such as? There's many a pearl in a closed oyster.'

Georgia doubted that, but obediently related what little the visit had produced before embarking on Camelot. His reaction to this, plus her description of the museum, was all she could have hoped for, which compensated for her meagre offering in the way of hard information.

'So in fact,' Peter summed up, 'all we know for sure is that the professor admires Raphael and Michelangelo and that Lance had a hat. Well done.'

She laughed. 'Thanks. Luke—'

'Ah yes. Luke. Our publisher, who, it seems, will not be awarding us the most generous contract in the world for this case. Can you do anything about warming him to the potential of this project?'

'I'll try.'

'Then we can consider the possibility that Professor Hoskin did mean the Pre-Raphaelites and not Raphael and that therefore he was somehow involved with Rossetti's painting. More immediately, it's time to visit Dover to discover what you can about Sandro's link with Venyon.'

Visions of Zac hovered uncomfortably near.

Peter was watching her carefully. Spot on as usual. 'Did you tell Luke about your meeting Zac in Paris?'

'No.'

'Foolish of you. Zac rang me today to suggest a date. I told him Mike had vetoed the trip, and he took it with suspicious equanimity. I should tell Luke about his reappearance, if I were you.'

'There's no need. Zac won't be there,' she said mutinously. Trust Zac to ring Peter direct.

Peter sighed. 'Sometimes, Georgia,' he announced, 'dearly as I love you, you can be very trying to live with. Has that occurred to you?'

'Yes. Door closed.'

'Very well. Now that we are temporarily enclosed in our own kingdom let us concentrate on its concerns. I have had a whole day to

212

reflect on them. King Arthur and his goblet. Firstly, your point about the painting having been in the plural when Jago referred to it, but contradicted by Antonio. I have checked. The Benizis have no branch in Vienna. They do in Budapest, and the branch is run by Roberto Benizi.'

Shock waves ran through Georgia. Her error? No, she was sure of that. 'A mistake,' she said defiantly.

'Tut, tut. You can do better than that. Secondly, we need to know more about Jago's wife Jennifer and perhaps about Dover Castle.'

'Dover Castle?' she repeated in bewilderment.

'Seeing the site Jago dug failed to spark off anything helpful, but Dover might. Anyway, I want to go there. You can see Cook alone; we'll meet in the Castle car park. But Jago first.'

'What did you think of Arthur's field?' Jago chuckled, settling into his garden chair. For mid-June, the weather was extremely warm and his garden was a welcome escape from the closeness of the house.

'Cindy was a first-class guide.'

'She's wasted selling arty-crafty stuff. She should be out there digging for victory like Sam,' Jago said.

'Or for Sir Gawain,' Georgia joked.

'If only I was sure of where,' Jago replied. 'The more I think about it, the more I'm convinced that Lance must have got hold of the vital clue as to where those bones lie.'

'You still believe they *are* to be found?'

He looked surprised. 'Of course. A good thesis never dies, it just awaits proof. And proof is always around the next corner. That's what Jennifer used to say. She was a great encourager. Look, have I shown you our wedding photo?' He struggled out of his chair and went inside the house, emerging with a framed photograph.

Jennifer was indeed spectacular, Georgia acknowledged, delighted to be shown this without even having to ask. Even in the formal 1950s fashions, with the pinched waist, and full petticoats and little hat, Jennifer looked as if she, like Helen of Troy, could launch a thousand ships. She stared out at Georgia faintly smiling, enigmatic within the oval perfection of her face. At her side was a much younger Jago. With age he had filled out, was almost bald and had added the beard obviously to compensate for the lack of hair above. Bespectacled and earnest-looking, Jago looked almost nervous of his beautiful wife.

'Was Lance at your wedding?' she asked.

'Certainly. He was our best man.' Jago bustled inside once more and came out with another photo, not framed this time. 'This is my favourite,' he said. 'It was taken after the civil wedding; we had the church service afterwards.'

There was the same perfect face; this time Guinevere was sandwiched between her Arthur and her Lancelot, and the shortest of the three, although the eye went immediately to her. Much the same as Jago, Lance looked the adventurer, challenging the camera, as though he found life a perpetual joke. It fitted with the image that Antonio had painted of him, but, Georgia reflected, if Jennifer had been the love of his life, then in this photograph that could hardly have been the truth. Lance must have been displaying a brave face to the outside world.

'Is Mary Venyon in this photograph?' She peered at the indistinct row standing behind the trio.

'I don't think Lance had even met her then.'

'Or Madeleine?'

'Of course. She was Jennifer's great friend, although I'm afraid that she and I did not get on well.'

'She was one of the two of Lance's lovers you referred to earlier.'

He looked surprised. 'I don't believe I said that. A great friend of his, certainly, but if they slept together it was never mentioned, not even between Jennifer and myself. Venetia Wain was the most serious threat to Mary.'

Apart from Jennifer, Georgia thought. That gorgeous face smiled out at her like Mona Lisa's. She is older than the rocks among which she sits. Someone had once written that of the

Mona Lisa, and it surely applied to Jennifer Priest too. The timeless tug of sex, Eve's power over Adam. 'You didn't tell us that Madeleine married Antonio Benizi,' she said.

'Didn't I?' Jago looked puzzled. 'How could I have forgotten that? I suppose because we lost touch so long ago. I did tell you – didn't I? – that the Benizi Brothers were interested in the Arthur paintings that Lance told me about?'

Paintings in the plural again, she noted. 'Antonio Benizi only recalls one.'

'Does he?' Jago thought for a moment. 'Perhaps he is right, I can't be sure. Mists of time and all that.'

Yet Antonio *was* sure – or was he? And what difference could it possibly make? She needed to move on. 'Antonio and Madeleine Benizi took me to the house where the faker Domenico Kranowski lived with his family. Did you know them?'

From his reaction it obviously rang a bell. 'I didn't know Domenico. I knew *of* him. A talented family.'

'Could he have faked those Arthurian paintings?' She was interested to see if he would come up with the same reply as Benizi.

He did, looking surprised. 'No. Lance would have been on to that right away.'

She decided to say nothing about the painting that hung in the Benizi bedroom. Fitting a jigsaw piece into the wrong place could hinder or ruin the chances of solving the puzzle. Go

216

carefully, she thought. 'Lance must have seen the painting of Gawain, so didn't you ask if you could too?'

'Of course,' he replied promptly. 'But he explained it was a delicate matter. If I, a known Arthurian enthusiast, was seen to be interested it would raise the price immediately and the paintings could well go to the highest bidder – which could not have been me. I did not have the funds either for that or for the script that could have revealed where the goblet lay.'

'Which also, forgive me, could have been faked.'

'Dear me, you are pessimistic.' His eyes twinkled. 'It could, but highly unlikely. Fortunately, the catalogue of the contents of the Dover Priory library survives, disclosing that one of its spheres of interest was early British history, scripts obviously written in earlier times by the monks. One such for instance was called *Histories of the Britons and Early English Kings.* A fire at the priory had destroyed many treasures, and between that and Henry VIII's bloody-mindedness just think what records confirming Arthur's life and presence in Dover might have been lost to the world. Or even still exist somewhere. Who knows? There could well have been a record by the chaplains at St Mary-in-the-Castle containing the Arthur story, the presence of the goblet and exactly what there was in the way of Sir Gawain's remains and possessions. His sword, for example. Perhaps a buckle. There might even have been a disguised clue as to where they intended to take their precious relics if they were ever threatened. Since the church was within the precincts of the King's own property, the chaplains would have felt their loyalties divided. Were they there to serve God or Mammon – the latter being in the form of their lord and master Henry VIII? His Majesty has more to answer for than his matrimonial adventures. If, as I believe, they felt the remains of Gawain were relics of the Church, they could well have consulted the priory, and a written record be made. And the Ruskin letter is similarly probable, given his passion for maps and medieval scripts.'

'In theory, yes,' Georgia said gently. Then, remembering those scraps of parchment in the Sussex Camelot, 'Does the name Richard Hoskin mean anything to you?' she asked.

'Of course,' he replied instantly. 'A notable Anglo-Saxon historian. I have his books somewhere.'

'He is also interested in Arthur and has a great collection of artefacts,' she said. 'You'd enjoy it.'

'I'm sure I would. You've seen it? Met him? Tell me about him.'

He listened attentively while she did so. 'He has Alzheimer's now,' she concluded. 'He is well into his nineties.'

'Poor fellow,' he murmured. 'One must avoid

taking fantasy too seriously.'

'You seem to manage it well,' Georgia pointed out.

Jago chuckled. 'I try to, otherwise I can imagine St Peter greeting me with a belly laugh at the Pearly Gates when he tells me that there was no such person as Arthur. I should argue back, of course. Now, how's that young man you told me about? The one who knew Cindy and Sam. Any advance on finding his murderer?'

'No arrest yet. I hope Sam wasn't too upset by his death?'

'More than she let on, I suspect, but she's dealing with it. She's a lass after my own heart, willing to humour me in crawling over the pros and cons of where Gawain lies, not to mention the goblet. She reminds me of myself when young, eager to sail the seven seas in search of truth.'

'Metaphorically, I presume,' Georgia laughed. 'I'm told you don't like sailing.'

'Correct, Georgia. In real life I stick to dry land. Much safer.'

'Where are you off to?' Luke asked casually.

'Dover,' Georgia replied. Now that Zac was not included in the party, this was easier to answer. All the same she was wary. Usually he didn't enquire about her movements, and she was conscious that Zac had been in her mind all too often in the last week or two. 'Somewhere there's a link between Sandro Daks and Venyon, and that gallery is our last chance for finding out what it is. Besides, how could I deprive Peter of a day with King Arthur?' She was joking, but Luke didn't seem to find it funny. Early morning blues, probably.

Luke shrugged. 'It's your royalties at stake.'

She refrained from pointing out that Marsh & Daughter didn't yet have a contract. She had tried several times to talk to him about Zac, but had backed off. Her feelings about her ex-husband were her own affair, and could only hinder the strong new growth of her relation-ship with Luke since she had moved into Medlars.

As she walked along St Thomas's Road in Dover to find the gallery, she realized how great a hindrance Zac would have been. Muddling today's work with her private life of yesteryear would have been a big mistake.

When she reached it, the Pad and Palette proved, as the name implied, to be more than a gallery. It sold artists' supplies ranging from art by numbers to what looked like high-class tools for highly professional artists. From its window displays and what she could see beyond them, the shop impressed her more than she might have expected from her brief encounter with Kelly. The gallery, a large airy room at the side of the sales area, looked equally varied, selling prints, cards, original drawings and water-colours, concentrating on local scenes.

As she walked in, she saw that the girl sitting at the desk was not Kelly. Georgia was hardly surprised, since Kelly hadn't struck her as a working woman – not in the art field anyway. She suppressed this bitchy thought immediately, amused at the ease with which it had come. There was no sign of any male presence, so Roy Cook must be in the rear rooms, if at all. This is where Zac might have come in useful, she acknowledged. He would be chatting up this girl within seconds with his own brand of irresistible charm.

She smiled amiably at the girl, and wandered into the gallery, where she did a quick tour in order to return speedily to the desk.

'I was looking for drawings by a young man called Sandro Daks,' she said to her brightly, waving vaguely in the direction of the gallery.

'I'm not sure if there are any left.' The girl rose immediately, registering definite interest, which was encouraging. 'We did have some.' She went into the gallery with Georgia trotting behind her, and stopped at a sepia-coloured drawing of the Canterbury Cathedral west entrance. Georgia decided that two hundred pounds was way too much to spend merely on acquiring goodwill, but fortunately the girl moved over to a large portfolio in one corner, a treasure-trove of odds and ends.

'There should be some unframed ones here.' The girl rummaged through, and produced small drawings, one of the Roman lighthouse in

Dover Castle and another of something Georgia thought she recognized.

'Isn't that the Dark Entry in the Canterbury Cathedral precincts?' she asked, and the girl nodded.

Georgia liked this one. Even in pencil Sandro had managed to suggest the dark versus the light beyond, and the atmosphere of past ages.

'He was very talented,' she said, wondering whether the Inland Revenue would accept this as a legitimate expense against tax. 'There was a murder in the Dark Entry, wasn't there? Years ago, of course. In the *Ingoldsby Legends*. How sad that Sandro was murdered too.'

For the first time the girl really looked at her. 'Terrible, wasn't it?' Trite words, but she did look genuinely upset.

'It was. In fact,' Georgia replied, 'I found his body. And it *was* terrible. That's why I wanted one of his pictures. It seemed right somehow.'

'I went for a drink with him a couple of times,' the girl volunteered.

Excellent, Georgia thought. 'I'm sorry. I can see it must have been hard for you. I was staying with my aunt near the pub where he used to work,' she continued smoothly. 'There was a girl there who said Sandro had come to Britain to find a man called Lance Venyon.' Exaggeration was necessary. 'She was wondering who this Venyon was, because it might have helped the police to find his murderer.'

'Sandro didn't mention him to me,' the girl

222

replied. 'Roy might know.'

At last. Georgia breathed a sigh of relief. 'Perhaps so. Is he around?'

'I'll check.' The girl walked over to the desk and spoke over the intercom. Whether it was the name Daks or Venyon that drew his attention, the reaction was positive. 'He'll come through,' she told Georgia, as though Her Majesty had condescended to drop by.

'Oh, thank you.' A bit of effusiveness never hurt.

Roy Cook quickly appeared through the rear door, and Georgia speedily assessed him. Late thirties, forties perhaps, over-smart, over-confident, slightly plumpish face that spoke of the good life. No starving in garrets with his artists for this one.

She advanced to meet him. 'Mr Cook? I met your wife at a wedding recently.'

'Whose was that, then?' The reply was guarded.

'It was at Badon House in Wymdown. My aunt's marriage to Terry Andrews.'

'Oh yeah. Kelly knows Terry.'

Relations, if not cordial, were at least established. 'I remembered Kelly talking about your gallery, and the police told me that Sandro Daks used to work for you. I found his body, you see. I know it's silly, but I thought I should buy one of his pictures, and this one of the Dark Entry is excellent.'

'Glad you like it.' He barely glanced at it.

223

'Great loss, Sandro. He could have become a pretty good artist.'

'A great one?'

'Who knows? He had something about him, that's for sure. It was great stuff for the tourists. I'll miss him.'

Time to move the conversation forward. 'I was telling your assistant that I heard he came over here to find a man called Lance Venyon. Did he mention him to you?'

To her disappointment, he looked blank. 'No. Who's he?' He seemed uninterested, so this was probably yet another dead end. The 'Who's he?' in the present tense came out so naturally, she was inclined to believe it was genuine.

'A friend of Sandro's grandfather.'

Perhaps it was her imagination but Cook did register something here, although all he said was: 'Unlikely. He said his family lived in Budapest, and before that in the Soviet Union. Not likely to have been much of a friendship.'

'Venyon died in the 1960s.'

'Then why so interested?'

The friendly note was fast vanishing, she noted, and the truth was called for. 'My father and I write up true-crime cases from the past, and Venyon's is one of them.'

'Is that so?' Cook shrugged. 'Daks was twenty-two. Not in the frame.'

He was definitely hostile now, and his body language suggested he was about to terminate this interview. Backtrack quickly, she thought.

'No,' she laughed. 'It can't have been important since Sandro never got in touch with the Venyon family. One of the problems in my line of work is that there are an awful lot of loose ends that might be completely irrelevant, but have to be followed up. Not like the provenance of pictures.' This had come out casually, but even so she received a sharp glance for her pains. Or was that her imagination too?

'Right. With us, it is or it isn't. Sorry I can't help over Daks.' The brisk tone told her the encounter was over as from now. 'Sandro was a nice kid. I was sorry to hear how he died.'

'Drugs, do you think?'

'No idea.' Still brisk. 'Too sensible, I'd say. Into women, was Sandro.' Loud false laugh. 'He had Fiona bang to rights, didn't he, love?'

A blush from the assistant, but whether it was irritation or modesty, Georgia couldn't judge. 'We only had a drink,' Fiona muttered.

'And I suppose Sandro didn't mention his grandfather to you either?' Georgia asked merrily.

A superior cool smile. 'No. Nor his grannie. Nor did we set a date for the wedding. Anything else?'

Definitely time to retreat. Georgia paid for her picture in silence, thanked Fiona profusely and turned for the door. As she did so, she was aware of someone who had just entered the gallery and was now talking to Roy as both men disappeared through the rear door. She had recognized the newcomer immediately, even with a partial view.

It was Mark Priest. What on earth could Jago's son be doing in a Dover gallery? He worked for an insurance company and lived in Tunbridge Wells. Dover was somewhat off his path, even if he did deal with art claims. Was he here on business? And if so, what business, and was it legitimate or otherwise? In that case, his appearance on a scene that had Zac involved in it was suspicious – even sinister.

She was still thinking about Mark Priest as she set off towards the car park. Then to her horror she saw that strolling towards her was the bad penny himself, Zac. She congratulated herself that at least she was sufficiently inured to his presence again for there to be no shivers down her spine.

'Georgia!' he cried warmly. 'What a surprise.' He deposited an uninvited peck on the cheek, turned round and walked along at her side.

'How did you get on with my chum Cook? Don't worry about me,' he said earnestly. 'I do understand why you went alone. We under-cover agents have to be careful. Are you all wired up and clad in a bulletproof vest provided by the Met?'

'Common sense is my guardian,' she replied as tartly as she could manage. 'You should try it sometime.' Should she mention Mark? No, not yet, she decided.

'Oh, Georgia.' He looked reproachful. 'For

226

you the glass is always half empty, not half full.'

That simply wasn't true. Georgia was about to jump on this, when she realized that's exactly what he wanted. 'Think of your work, Zac,' she reminded him amicably. 'We shouldn't be seen together for either of our sakes.'

'Nonsense. I merely bumped into my ex-wife.'

'Did you ever wonder why you got caught?' she asked, exasperated. Always so blindly optimistic.

He put on his guileless look. 'Peter was too good a cop for me.'

'If you carry on walking with me, you can tell him so yourself.' She should have guessed Zac would appear. Goodness knew how he found out when she was coming, but now she was here she could at least find out what he had been doing in Paris.

'Splendid. I'll come with you. Are you off to the castle?'

'Yes. Can you spare the time?' she asked sarcastically.

'For you two, of course.' He never could pick up sarcasm.

'You didn't answer my question. How did you get on with our Roy?' he asked, as back at the car park he slid into her passenger seat.

'So so. A blank on Lance Venyon, but then that was a long shot.' In fact she was still bearing in mind that although Cook had not registered the name of Lance Venyon he *had* seemed to react to the mention of Sandro's grandfather – though what that might imply she couldn't even begin to guess.

'Is Cook a suspect for Daks' murder?' Zac asked casually.

'No idea,' she replied firmly.

'I take it your lips are sealed.'

'Only because they've nothing to reveal.'

'But they do, they do...' he murmured.

She ignored him. 'He could be a suspect, I suppose. If Cook is up to no good, Daks might have been blackmailing him. Young to try that trick, though.'

'He was old enough to be a forger, if I'm right about the network being organized from Cook's gallery.'

'His father Leonardo is apparently a straight guy. He's been checked out,' she said. No harm in telling him that (she hoped).

'And yet,' Zac said earnestly, 'Sandro's grandfather was a friend of Lance Venyon.'

'Who was also on the side of the angels, so far as I know,' she countered.

'But how, Georgia, can you tell the good angels from the fallen variety? You made a mistake with me.'

Round One to Zac. She hadn't even a reply to give him, because he was right. 'How,' she asked firmly, 'did Cook get to know about Sandro, if you're right about the scam? He was over here for such a short time. It's understandable if he was just selling him legitimate pictures to sell to tourists, but as part of an ongoing fraud ring the time scale doesn't seem to fit.'

'It could be,' Zac said carelessly, 'that Daks used to paint the forgeries in Budapest, and they were brought over one by one. He probably paid brief visits to Britain in order to see the original hanging in situ, so that he could check the colours, then returned to paint the copies from reproductions. Roy travels a lot, I gather. He could have picked them up.'

'Mark Priest couldn't be mixed up in all this, could he?' she asked carefully, negotiating the traffic up Castle Hill.

'Not so far as I know. He works with me – sort of,' Zac added vaguely. 'Why?'

'He came to see Roy Cook this morning.'

'Did he?'

Georgia glanced sideways and saw that for once she had caught Zac off guard. 'Are you sure?'

'Positive. Does he work for the Art and Antiques Unit too?'

'Not sure.' Zac frowned. 'Could do. I've met him a few times in various places. He's well thought of. Everyone's reliable valuer, *too* reliable for me. Why don't you check him out with Policeman Plod. Mike, is it?'

'It is, and Mike's no Plod. You should know. And, incidentally,' she threw in, 'what were you doing in Paris?'

'Meeting Roberto,' came the prompt reply.

'I thought he worked in Budapest.' If she had hoped to catch him out, she was wrong.

'Georgia, dear, keep to Lance Venyon, there's a good girl.'

She fumed, but managed a sweet smile. 'I'll mention Mark Priest to Mike. He'll value your help, I'm sure.'

In theory it might be possible that Mark was in on the art frauds, perhaps one of the inside men with access to the houses; he would have the opportunity to take photographs legitimately for valuations, which Sandro couldn't in his role as tourist. It seemed unlikely to her, though. From the impression she had gained of Mark, he was a solid citizen. But then wasn't that what made a good con man? A *good* one, not like Zac.

She drove into the castle and along the winding route to the car park, handed over the entrance money at the visitor centre – both hers *and* Zac's, so nothing new there – then walked over to the disabled area, where Peter was waiting in his wheelchair. As they approached, his eyes went immediately to Zac and looked at her accusingly. 'You didn't go—'

'No. I went alone, and don't blame me for this,' Georgia said.

'I don't,' Peter replied grimly.

'No hard feelings,' Zac said kindly.

'Enjoy your time inside, did you?'

'It was profitable,' Zac replied seriously. 'I

learned quite a lot and now I can make an honest living. You heard I was working with the Serious Crimes Directorate?'

Georgia cringed. This was so like Zac. He actually thought they'd take this stuff about an honest living at face value. One glimpse at a con and he'd be involved up to his neck.

'I did,' Peter replied noncommittally.

'I gather from Georgia,' Zac continued blithely, 'that you're interested in King Arthur. I expect she told you about the Rossetti we saw in Paris. King Arthur and the Holy Grail, fake or genuine?'

'Trust you to upgrade it,' Georgia remarked. 'Not even Rossetti claimed it to be the Grail. It's a goblet.'

'Apart from that painting—' Peter began.

'Which Lance Venyon was connected with,' Zac continued for him. His nose was positively twitching, Georgia thought.

'I'm here merely to indulge a private passion of my own,' Peter finished airily, 'which Georgia does not at the moment share. And so far as you're concerned, Zac, no more.'

Georgia could say nothing, since Zac knew very well this visit must be linked to Venyon. Zac chatted happily about Pre-Raphaelites as they made their way down to the statue of Vice-Admiral Ramsay which stared out over the harbour to the Channel he had done so much to protect during the Second World War. Here it was easy to think in terms of King Arthur's fleet sailing back from France to save England from the Saxons or from Mordred's army, according to history or legend respectively. Looking seawards, not much could have changed in the view, although inland the rivers would have been much wider. On Barham Downs, though, the wind still howled as it would have done fifteen hundred years ago.

'It all seems most interesting,' Zac continued provokingly. 'You're hooked on King Arthur, Peter. Georgia is badgering Roy Cook about Lance Venyon, of whom he's probably never heard, Antonio Benizi had a Rossetti painting brought to him by the said Lance Venyon. Lance Venyon fell off a boat, by means unknown, and Sandro Daks is murdered. There must surely be a link?'

'Perhaps.' And that was all he was going to get in answer, Georgia decided.

'Call me a fantasist – as I'm sure you do, Georgia – but why therefore aren't you as fascinated as Peter in King Arthur?' Zac promptly replied.

She opened her mouth to explain, and found that she couldn't. Peter was doing his best not to laugh and Zac wasn't bothering to restrain himself. Another Zac trick. Divide the opposition. She shrugged, holding on to such dignity as she could muster, and turned the tables. 'And now Mark Priest takes a bow into Cook's gallery.'

'Odd, isn't it?' was all Zac said – which

instantly made Georgia suspicious. He usually liked beating an idea to death, not dismissing it.

Peter obviously thought so too. 'Very odd. Again, the link has to be the art world. You know Benizi, Zac, you know the Cooks, and you know Mark Priest. Now, let's consider this. According to Georgia, Antonio told her that he decided to keep that painting to see if anything developed over the discovery of the goblet, for that would mean the value of the painting would rise.'

'Did he?'

Zac had his blank expression on, but Georgia knew him well. That meant Zac knew something that they didn't.

'And,' Peter added, 'there were more paintings, weren't there? In Budapest.'

That was a leap and a half. Georgia hadn't expected that, but if Peter had hoped to catch Zac he was on a hiding to nowhere.

'Were there?' was all he replied.

'Roberto works in Budapest.'

That split-second pause that would be indiscernible to most people, but which Georgia recognized immediately, told her Zac was retreating into con-man mode.

'Right,' he said lazily. He could hardly deny it, so his only way out, Georgia realized, was for him to display no interest.

'Seen him recently, Zac?' Peter asked.

'Not in Budapest. Vienna maybe. Some time ago.'

Peter let it go, announcing that he was off to the wartime tunnels, but the point was made so far as Georgia was concerned. There were more paintings, they were in Budapest not Vienna – and Zac was somehow involved.

Perhaps Peter was hoping that by going to the tunnels next, Zac would get bored and leave them before they tackled King Arthur's stronghold, the church. If so, he was disappointed, and when after lunch and a long tour, Zac was still at their heels like a faithful puppy, Peter gave up, and made no demur when he followed them up to the Pharos and the Church of St Mary. He was actually a help in getting the wheelchair into the church and then stood by while Peter took centre stage.

'It must have been here, where the arch of the chancel of the early church had been, that the empty coffin was found during the restoration of the church in the 1860s.' Peter pointed to the spot. 'It was buried quite near the surface, which suggests this wasn't its original burial place. Wasn't Jago's theory that the chaplains might have taken its contents, bones, goblet and grave goods, if any, and left the heavy lead coffin behind?'

'It's possible,' Georgia agreed, conscious that Zac's ears were flapping.

'You old romantic,' Zac teased her.

Perhaps he was right. Standing here, she found that Jago's theory seemed tenable, as Peter pointed out where the foundations of the earlier church had been. As for romantic, on an impulse she had actually read the passage in *Le Morte D'Arthur* last night:

'And then was the noble knight sir Gawaine found in a great boate lying more then halfe dead. When king Arthur wist that sir Gawaine was laid so low, he went unto him; and there the king made sorrow out of measure, and took sir Gawaine in his armes, and thrice hee sowned ... And when paper and inke was brought, sir Gawaine was set up weakely by king Arthur, for hee had beene shriven a little before; and hee wrote thus unto sir Launcelot: "Floure of all noble knights ... And at the date of this letter was written but two houres and halfe before my death, written with mine owne hand, and so subscribed with part of my heart blood ... And I require thee, as thou art the most famous knight of the world, that thou wilt see my tombe." And then sir Gawaine wept, and also king Arthur wept; and then they sowned both. And when they awaked both, the king made sir Gawaine to receive his Saviour... And then the king let bury him in a chappell within the castle of Dover; and there yet unto this day all men may see the skull of sir Gawaine, and the same wound is seene that sir Launcelot gave him in battaile. Then was it told to king Arthur that sir Mordred had pight a new field upon Barendowne. And on the morrow the king road thither to him, and there was a great battaile betweene them, and much people were slaine on both parts. But at the last king Arthurs partie stood best.'

The first point that had struck her – irreverently – was that Sir Thomas's imagination had clearly run away with him if Gawain could foretell his own death so exactly in his letter. The second was that as Rossetti had followed the Malory story so precisely as to produce a watercolour of Lancelot and Guinevere at Arthur's tomb it wasn't a great stretch of the imagination to believe that he might also have produced a fine oil painting of the death of Sir Gawain.

She left Peter still musing in the church while she went to have a look at the Pharos at its side from the viewing platform, where she was interrupted by a shout from Zac.

'Come up here, Georgia.' He was standing on the grassy battlements looking out to sea, a spot where Peter's wheelchair would not be able to follow, she noted, perhaps unfairly.

She decided to accept the challenge, if that's what it was. If there was a battle coming with Zac, she must win it, and there was no point shirking the issue.

'Are you glad you came?' he asked, as she scrambled up the embankment to join him.

'In a way.'

'Which way would that be?'

Her exit line from this was easy. 'Your point about links between Lance, Arthur and Sandro Daks. I was almost ready to give up on the Venyon case before that.'

Zac was apparently intent on watching the ships going in and out of the harbour. 'And now?' he asked.

'It's easier to believe there's a story there, but I'm still not sure.'

'You never were.'

'Uncalled for,' she whipped back.

'Agreed. Do you miss me?'

'Irrelevant.'

'And thus the question is answered.' He grinned in victory.

It was too late to redeem the situation, so she ignored it, sensing he was about to make his move.

'I miss you,' he continued.

'I'm sure you haven't lost your technique with women.'

'Women in general aren't you. What's this man of yours like?'

'He's not *this man*. Luke's my partner. I live with him, and I love him. OK by you?'

'Much too defensive, sweetheart.'

'I'm not,' she exploded. The crunch had come, and she had lost the plot.

'No need to cry,' he said maddeningly.

Cry? To her horror she realized that she felt dangerously near it, but already he had taken her into his arms and was kissing her. Not on her cheek this time, and for one terrifying moment her body flared up, remembering, wondering what on earth might happen next. *Wanting* to know...

Then it was over. His lips were still on hers with the same intensity, but now she felt nothing in response. She had been crazy, but it was finished. Shakily she disengaged herself, sensing that she was free for ever, but hardly daring to believe it.

'I think not, Zac,' she said steadily, as he fell into perspective for her at last. He was a good-looking charmer, a weak con man, who deserved her compassion, but nothing more. It was past. It was over, thank heavens, and any tears he might arouse now would be those of relief, not passion or regret.

He must have read her tone of voice correctly – con men were good at that.

'Only a bit of fun. We had that, didn't we?' He sounded almost as if he were pleading with her.

Fun? She thought back to the agony of those years, but then she saw it in another way. Not the half-empty glass but the half-full one. She had clung to the bad times, and spewed out the good ones as invalid. But they weren't, and they *had* been fun.

'Yes.' She smiled at him with what she recognized with surprise as affection. 'Yes, we did.'

'That's what King Arthur is too, just Peter's fun.' It was hard to tell what Zac was thinking, but he looked amused as if he'd been somewhere else all the time. Although perhaps that too was Zac all over.

'Not where Lance Venyon is concerned,' she said as they strolled on.

'Maybe it was his fun too.'

'Well?' Peter asked when they returned to him, looking almost benevolently from one to the other. 'Found that missing link yet?'

'No, but it's there somewhere,' Georgia told him. 'Like Excalibur.' Perhaps someone would arise waving it before them. Or perhaps somebody just had. Perhaps, it occurred to her, Excalibur was in Budapest.

Eleven

'How was the day?' Luke was burrowing down in the cupboard for a saucepan lid, and Georgia couldn't see his face. Was it her imagination or guilty conscience that made her think Luke had been unusually silent since her return? He had been hard at work until gone seven and had then returned from the oast house with only a brief greeting before disappearing into the den – the name for their joint nest of books and computers. She told herself that the words guilty conscience hardly applied, and that therefore some preoccupation of his own or end-of-the-day weariness was all that was amiss.

'Very good.'

'Solved Daks's murder, have you?'

'I meant the Dover Castle visit. Peter was in his element.'

'But not you?' Luke stood up, his face flushed.

'Yes, in a way.' She pushed the memory of the battlements out of her mind.

'Something new on Lance Venyon?'

'Only firming up on Jago's theory.'

'So why go?'

There was something wrong.

'You sound very clipped.' Georgia took the bull by the horns. 'Peter wanted to put the theory into perspective by seeing the terrain for himself.'

'And did he?'

'Yes.' He had explained it to her, once they were alone. 'He said that if one imagined the boats lying offshore in the present harbour, the old fortress on the hill, with its chapel and Pharos beacon, would have been the obvious place to take the dying Gawain. And, he added, why should it be so incredible that forces should come by sea, whether from France or the west of England, to see off Saxon invaders? Or that their leader be remembered for this great deed on Badon Hill, otherwise known as Barham Down?'

Usually Luke would have entered into this discussion animatedly but tonight all he grunted was, *'Cui bono?'*

'To whom the benefit?' Georgia picked up, and then, as Luke didn't seem eager to expand, continued, 'You mean where does that get us? It gives a solid base for the discussion about the provenance of the paintings and the goblet.'

'Possibly,' was all he replied.

She held back the inevitable, 'Is anything wrong?' as Luke continued with obvious effort: 'Did you go all round the castle?'

'The lot,' she replied more cheerfully, and proceeded to tell him about the wartime tunnels.

'And Roy Cook? What happened there?' he asked, when she'd finished.

'I'm the proud owner of a Sandro Daks original.' She waited for him to ask more, but he didn't. 'Not much more. There was no reaction to Lance Venyon's name.' Still no comment. 'Did you have a good day?'

'Not bad.'

'I didn't see the beautiful Kelly,' she added, anxious to provoke a response.

No answer for a moment. Then: 'What about Zac? You didn't mention that he was jaunting along with you.'

So that was it. The worst. How on earth had Luke found out, and why on earth hadn't she told him earlier? So much for Luke the reasonable. From the expression on his face he had all cannons ready to fire. 'Because I didn't know he was coming,' she replied.

'Odd then that he rang here to ask what time you'd be there.'

Her heart sank. 'Zac was trying it on. He's a

con artist.'

'So talented that he can appear out of the blue after umpteen years and you show no surprise?'

'No, yes, I mean...' Georgia tried again, but her own temper began to rise. 'I met him again in France, he knew Roy Cook, he suggested we went to see him together, Mike vetoed it, I was glad. Zac still turned up. OK by you?'

'No. Because you omitted to mention it to me.' It sounded gentle enough, but she could see him stalking back from the barricades into a fortress marked 'Keep out'.

Work was the best antidote to relationship problems. For the first time Georgia blessed the fact that she had kept her former home in Haden Shaw as an office. It seemed a paradise today, and gave her a chance to readjust to normality before facing Peter's all too observant presence. On the way here she had convinced herself, Micawber-like, that all problems would solve themselves if she didn't panic, even Luke. He must realize, as did she, that the rock of their partnership was solid.

When she finally went into Peter's office next door, he took one look at her face.

'Margaret,' he said apologetically. 'That's how Zac knew.'

'She's no gossip about our movements.'

'No, only if a con man rings up, announces he's visiting Dover with Peter and Georgia and has forgotten which day they were going.'

Despite her annoyance, Georgia laughed. 'Your fault for keeping an open diary on your desk. Anyway, it's over. No problems.' Except with Luke, but she kept that thought to herself.

'Not entirely. There's Zac and—'

'Budapest,' she finished for him. 'Plus the fact that Cook only showed some interest in Lance Venyon when I mentioned Daks's grandfather.'

'Who died in Budapest. A city which boasts a branch of Benizi Brothers Antiques run by a chum of Zac's. I wouldn't mind betting he's a runner between Antonio and son.'

'Would a sensible man like Antonio choose Zac?'

'Who better to tread a fine line between the respectable and non-respectable. Ex-con man, we hope, now working for Scotland Yard.'

'Antonio wouldn't stop to work all that out, surely.'

'You have stars in your eyes, Georgia, where Benizi is concerned.'

'Nonsense,' she said indignantly, but Peter laughed. Unwillingly she began to concede that he might be right. 'What sort of go-between?' she asked cautiously. 'Email and phone take care of most business today.'

'One can't email paintings or objets d'art. I can't help feeling it's too much of a coincidence to have the Benizi Brothers and the Daks family in one city, both connected with the art world, both connected – however remotely –

with Lance Venyon and both with a question mark, so far as Sandro is concerned, over the legality of their dealings.'

'That's a kangaroo jump as a theory. So what next?' As if she couldn't guess.

'I've booked you on a package trip to Budapest for four days next week to see the Daks family and the Benizi emporium. It all seems very cosy, don't you think?'

'For whom?' she asked, alarm bells ringing.

'For the two of you, of course.'

For one crazy moment she thought he meant Zac. 'For Luke?' she checked. That was almost as bad at present.

'Naturally. Who else?' Peter smiled blandly.

'Where first?' Luke enquired.

As she stood on their hotel balcony in Budapest, this was a hard question to answer, since the city was new to both of them. Working visit or not, Georgia had been deep in guidebooks and tourist phrase books, partly as a ploy to avoid conversations with Luke. Consequently she had been less thrown than he had at the impenetrable Hungarian script when they arrived last evening. Furious at Peter's gambit, she had been inclined to come alone but that would have been playing into his hands. (And what if Luke ever found out?) She had half expected, even hoped, in view of their present stand-off that Luke would turn down the chance, pleading pressure of work and the suddenness of the invitation. Unfortunately, he didn't.

'You're not coming because you think I'll be meeting Zac, are you?' she had asked bluntly.

He had raised an eyebrow. 'If, Georgia, I thought you'd be so stupid I wouldn't come. As it is, I've always wanted to see Budapest. Any problem with that?'

Plenty that she could foresee, but she remained silent. Stand-off still in place. The space between them in the double bed was a no-man's-land and neither of them entered it.

Before her was the river Danube, winding its majestic way through the city dividing Buda from Pest. On their side, Buda, the dominating Castle Hill, the Várhegy, was the central point that drew the eye, with its churches, ancient houses and statues and the magnificent Buda Palace. On the far side of the river lay Pest, the more modern half of the city, with its museums, shops and the university. It was in Pest that she would find both the Benizi antique shop and the Daks residence.

She was tempted to answer Luke's question of 'Where first?' with the obvious tourist choice, the Buda Palace, especially since the heat made the effort of work harder. Nevertheless Lance Venyon had to take precedence. There was a possibility that somewhere out there could lie the answer to the riddles that he, fairly or unfairly, had come to represent. Hungary symbolized the meeting point of East and

West, and perhaps that might be a clue to the enigma of Lance. Nevertheless, as Peter admitted, they could be on a wild-goose chase, and the true story lie much closer to home.

That possibility didn't make this visit any less useful, even though both she and Peter were aware that it was bringing them perilously close to Mike's police investigation.

'I'll take the Daks family first,' she answered Luke.

'*You* will?' That eyebrow raised once more.

She silently cursed. She had put her foot in it again. '*We* will.'

'I can play by myself.' Luke let her off the hook. 'The Liszt museum is over in Pest.'

'Come with me today, and we'll play together later. We have two whole days here, after all.'

It was the right suggestion, and the atmosphere thawed as they took the bus across the river. 'Whatever you say, don't pronounce bus as we do in England,' she warned him. 'Here it means a four-letter word, not three.'

This produced a welcome laugh. The bus dropped them in Pest, and as she walked up the Rákóczi út and into the street where the Daks home was situated, she was even more glad that Luke was coming. For all their emotional estrangement he could be a great support in the meeting with Leonardo Daks, who was an unknown quantity. Mike had said that Leonardo was a retired academic. 'He's OK,' he had explained, 'but don't expect there to be anything behind the brick wall if that's what he seems to present.'

The fact that there was only one bell on the front door of this four-storey house suggested prosperity; most of the houses had three or four. The door was opened by a dark-haired girl, heavily pregnant, who announced herself cautiously as Magda. Leonardo had been equally reserved on the telephone when Peter called, and this girl, however she fitted into this household, was following suit.

They were led up several flights of stairs, since there seemed to be only a small anteroom on the ground floor, and on the first floor she glimpsed only a kitchen and dining room. They were shown into an austere but expensively furnished living room overlooking the street beneath, where Leonardo Daks – she presumed – rose to greet them. The girl stayed, so she couldn't be a maid. A sister? There were several pictures on the wall, but they looked like expensive prints rather than originals, which surprised her. She would have expected some sign of Sandro's work.

'Please come in.' Leonardo looked Jewish and in his mid-sixties, with greying hair; he also looked very weary, she thought, which natural enough. It was less than two months since Sandro's death.

'You bring me news of Sandro?' he asked immediately.

'We're not the police,' she explained, 'but we

know Chief Inspector Gilroy, whom you met. There are no arrests yet.' In fact Mike was making little progress. There was precious little forensic evidence and their one ace, a trainer footprint, had produced no leads so far. Nor had there been any success in finding the gun.

His face seemed to sag. 'He was your only son?' Luke asked sympathetically.

'Yes. Magda was his fiancée.'

'I'm very sorry about Sandro,' Georgia said. 'He was a very gifted artist. I bought one of his drawings at a gallery in Dover, where he worked for a man called Roy Cook. Did you meet him?'

No hint of recognition. 'I meet only the police and the people in the village.'

'I understand you also came over to Wymdown in 1990.' She thought at first he was not going to answer, but she was wrong.

'To Kent, yes. A short holiday. I taught art in Estonia and also here in Budapest. That was our first chance to travel freely to the West.'

'We are interested in a man who died accidentally in 1961. His job was tracking down antiques and his name was Lance Venyon. When your son first came to Kent, he asked where he could find Venyon, who was a friend of his grandfather. I wondered if you could tell us more about him.'

A frown, but she had caught his interest. 'My father is no longer living. I think, yes, he might have been a friend once. This man Venyon had property of my father's. My father say ask him for it if I go to England. I do not know what it was. No one know about Lance Venyon any more, say that he is dead, so I ask Sandro to make an enquiry too. He tell me he is doing so, but then no more. You bring news?'

'I'm afraid not. If Sandro discovered the property it would have been among his effects, and I think you have those. Could it have been a painting?'

From the flicker of reaction she realized she had scored a bullseye. But how and where? 'Was your father a painter?' she continued as innocently as she could. 'Sandro was excellent in copying as well as drawing, so his tutor said.'

A definite coolness now. 'Domenico Daks do not copy. Michelangelo, my brother, was artist; he create though, like Sandro, and has been dead for many years. Now Sandro gone too.'

Michelangelo? She was immediately back in Camelot with Professor Hoskin. Was this the source of his reference? No, this Michelangelo would have been much younger than Hoskin, although it could tie in with the reference to Raphael if Hoskin had been trying to convey something about a Pre-Raphaelite painting. Another thought. A young man called Michael ... Michelangelo? Was that too big a jump from Venetia's titbit of information? Could Lance Venyon have known him? Michelangelo Daks? He would have been living in Estonia, so it seemed unlikely.

'You all have such wonderful painters' names,' she said as casually as she could. 'Leonardo, Michelangelo, Domenico – is that after Ghirlandaio, perhaps?'

He shrugged dismissively. 'My father love art, that why we have such names. Sandro too–' he swallowed – 'for Botticelli.'

She felt her stomach knotting in excitement; she was teetering on the brink of a breakthrough. 'And there was Domenico Kranowski, the great art faker of the 1950s, whom Lance Venyon knew in Paris. Did your father work there too?'

'My father work in Estonia, and not as art faker,' he said sharply. 'My father no longer here to speak for himself. Nor, Madame Marsh, is my son.'

Point taken, and she thought they were going to be thrown out, but fortunately Luke came galloping to the rescue. 'Your son had a brilliant career in front of him. His death was a tragedy.'

Leonardo grasped the lifeline. 'He had good teachers here in Budapest.'

'Did Sandro ever talk to you about the work he did in England?'

The mask fell again. 'No. Did drawings, he said. For a lady.'

'Kelly Cook, perhaps?' Georgia asked. 'Or Cindy Priest? He seems to have sold his drawings to two galleries.'

He shrugged. 'I not know.' The interview was

clearly over, since he was rising to his feet, and after a few pleasantries to restore harmony, they were back in the street.

What, she wondered, had Leonardo hoped to learn from the interview? He had wanted any news of the investigation – and, she felt a rising excitement, of this property his father had sought so keenly. Domenico, Michelangelo, Domenico Kranowski, Domenico Daks – too much of a coincidence? If linked with Lance Venyon, no. Scenarios began to rush through her head.

'Luke, thank you,' Georgia said gratefully.

'Only protecting my investment.'

Back on firm ground. 'You haven't given us a contract yet, let alone invested.'

'It wasn't the book I was referring to.'

'Oh.' Georgia digested this. Did he really think she was walking in Zac's trail? 'In that case, protection isn't necessary. I'm armour-plated where Zac's concerned.'

'And inside the heavy metal?'

'Nothing, Luke. Like the Tin Man in *The Wizard of Oz*, there's an empty space where my heart once was.'

He looked at her questioningly.

'Mine's on permanent loan to you,' she finished.

His arm went round her.

'Sure?'

'Positive.'

'Then let's follow this Yellow Brick Road.'

He proceeded to jig along the Rákócszi út to the pleasure of a gypsy violinist in full Magyar costume who took this as a personal tribute to his playing and had to be duly rewarded.

The Yellow Brick Road continued down a side street, where Luke had wanted to see a garden with a Holocaust memorial at its centre in the form of a weeping willow. 'We're in the Jewish quarter here,' Luke explained. 'This is the Wallenberg Memorial Garden. He was the Swedish diplomat who rescued many Jews from being transported to Auschwitz from Budapest. They went through bad times in Budapest, first from the Germans, then the Russians.'

Sitting on a bench a girl glanced at them, and Georgia recognized Magda, who rose to greet them.

'You knew Sandro?' she asked wistfully.

'Yes,' Georgia replied firmly.

'I am fiancée. I have his baby.'

'That must be a comfort for you,' Georgia said sympathetically.

'I come to England to visit Sandro and go home with baby inside. Now I live in his home with family till the baby is born. Perhaps after that too.'

'Is that usual in Hungary?'

'To live with Daks family, great honour. Father Leonardo have sister, and she has daughter, but Sandro was only son. My baby another.' She patted her stomach proudly.

'Are the whole family artists?' Georgia asked as casually as she could.

'Only my Sandro left,' came the prompt reply. 'And then my son.'

Georgia hoped she was right about its being a boy. There might be a lot resting on this child, she reflected with growing excitement as they left Magda in search of lunch. Kranowski, Daks, Benizi, Venyon, Sandro...Surely the links were getting a lot stronger now? The Kranowski family disappears from Paris, turns up as Daks in Estonia, then re-establishes itself in Budapest, the city linking East and West. Which, according to her guidebook, was a city that in the 1980s was rife with art forgery and crime. And what could Domenico Daks' property be but the painting – or paintings?

'Circumstantial,' Luke said, when she put this thesis to him. He relented. 'But it's looking good. Equally you could be talking through your hat.'

'That's funny. Richard Hoskin used three words when I asked him about Lance: Raphael, Michelangelo and hat.'

Luke laughed. 'There you are then. Proof.'

'I am not,' Georgia informed him, 'going to return to Peter with a theory about Lance's old panama or homburg or trilby.'

'You should be grateful that the word Arthur hasn't passed anyone's lips today.'

She shuddered. 'Give it time.'

* * *

The Benizi premises were situated just off the Falk Miksa utca, a street filled with antique shops and near the Danube's Margit Bridge. Benizi Antiques looked unobtrusively expensive with three exquisite items in the window display, an icon, a painting and a Chinese vase. They spoke for themselves, suggesting it would be a waste of time to enter except with a large chequebook.

'You can leave this one to me, unless I'm positively drowning,' Georgia told Luke.

'Don't I have a part in your cunning plan, whatever it is?'

'Yes. Not to erupt when I mention Zac.'

Did she sense him stiffen? 'I'll stay out of this one, then,' he said. 'You'll do better alone.'

That was true and she was grateful. Luke gave her no time to argue, but strolled off towards the river. It was time to act, and in she went. The reception room followed the style of the window display. An elegant antique desk and chairs, plum-coloured velvet drapes and a sense that one was in the presence of great art (and wealth). A good-looking man in his late thirties appeared, thanks to closed-circuit TV she assumed, since nothing so vulgar as a bell had sounded. Immediately a chair was placed for her to be seated. To prevent her from fainting with shock at the prices to be mentioned? No problem. She sat.

'Signora?'

'You must be Signor Roberto Benizi.' And

254

when he nodded, she swept on: 'I'm Zac White's wife.' She beamed at him. 'Well, ex-wife really but we're on the best of terms. He's probably talked about me. He told me about the Arthurian paintings, you know, and since I was in Budapest on holiday I thought I'd ask if I could possibly see them.'

Nothing like jumping into a raging torrent. Roberto's smile barely changed. He looked puzzled but his eyes were studying her keenly. 'Arthurian paintings?' he queried.

She nodded. 'The Rossettis.'

'What were these paintings? Perhaps you could describe them? With Lizzie Siddal as model?'

The weak point and he'd hit it. She hadn't a clue what the other paintings depicted, or even how many there were. Time to play the ace. 'Not in the one I saw recently at your father's home in Paris. Such a magnificent painting of Sir Gawain, isn't it? I fell in love with the portrayal of King Arthur.' Mention the goblet? No, that would be a mistake.

'You wish to buy such a painting?' The eyes were boring into her, but at least he hadn't pursued the question of the subject matter of the others.

'Not me,' she said truthfully. 'But I have two friends who are keen enthusiasts of both King Arthur and the Pre-Raphaelites. If the paintings are on the market, I'm sure they would be interested.'

'I can make enquiries about such paintings, madame. Who are these friends?'

She smiled. 'Naturally I could not tell you that, if you do not actually possess the paintings. I was sure from what Zac said that you did. And of course since your father showed me the Gawain painting, the family firm would obviously have an interest in any others in the series.'

He frowned. 'It is our policy only to show or even discuss paintings with the principals themselves. At least I must have further information about these friends.'

The last card in her hand and the riskiest. 'Now you can't really expect me to divulge confidential information,' she laughed gaily, 'any more than I would reveal the secrets of the Daks family.'

A sudden stillness in the atmosphere. 'Domenico Daks?'

'Yes. If that, of course,' she said lightly, 'was his real name. Domenico, Sandro, Leonardo and Michelangelo.'

Roberto was *still* wavering. 'This Gawain painting,' he said casually. 'Is that the one with the priest in the background?'

You don't catch me out so easily. Georgia sensed victory. 'No,' she said. 'I don't remember a priest, just King Arthur holding a cup or something to Gawain's lips.' Please, please don't let him decide to telephone Antonio.

Another tense silence, then to her relief, he

relaxed. '*Scusi, signora.* Is necessary. You come with me, please.'

He beckoned to her to follow him. With her heart in her mouth, expecting to be coshed at any moment and grateful that Luke at least knew where she was, she did so, walking through the velvet drapes with a confidence she did not feel. Ahead was a corridor, but he beckoned her into a small side room. 'You wait here,' he told her. 'I fetch them.'

Was this a trap? She waited on tenterhooks, but there was no click. She hadn't been locked in at any rate. Either he *was* ringing his father, or the reason for her being in this small empty room was that he didn't want her to see his other stock.

With great relief she heard his footsteps returning and he hadn't been away long enough to have called Paris. He was carrying three paintings, which he stood against the wall, before removing the coverings.

Georgia caught her breath, hardly able at first to take in what she saw, and looking from one to another. The first was of a distraught woman holding a skull, with what was surely the Dover hill and Pharos in the background. 'The Lady of Farthingloe,' Roberto said, his watchful eyes upon her. For a moment this made no sense, and then she remembered Jago's recounting of the legend of Gawain's beloved who found his skull on the battlefield and gave it to the canons of the priory. The legend, he had said, that

Lance loved so much.

Interesting though that painting was, it was the other two that gripped her attention: Guinevere and Lancelot. One was of their final parting in the cloisters of the convent to which Guinevere retreated after Arthur's death. The other was of their tryst in Guinevere's bedchamber. Georgia had seen Rossetti's drawing of the discovery of Lancelot in the chamber by his enemies, but this bore no resemblance to it. For once guilt was playing no part in this relationship. With the casement through which Lancelot had obviously climbed behind him, he and Guinevere were just on the point of their first embrace. Georgia could almost sense movement in the figures as they approached each other, passion no longer suppressed, desire about to be fulfilled.

Roberto began to talk about the paintings in polished terms, obviously knowing every detail of Rossetti's career – and the provenance of the paintings through the Milot family. Now was not the time to declare that they were fakes, or even to think through the implications.

Instead, Georgia was riveted on the figure of Guinevere herself, the betrayer of Arthur, lover of Lancelot. She had seen that perfect face before.

It was Jennifer's.

Twelve

'So they're fakes!' Peter punched the desk in delight. 'I knew it.'

'It's very well to glory in our triumph,' Georgia replied practically, 'but where does this take us?'

She'd talked it over endlessly with Luke on the return flight from Budapest until he pleaded for mercy. They had devoted their free day to enjoy what Budapest had to offer, and that's how he wanted to remember it, he said. It was therefore Monday before Georgia had a chance to talk to Peter fully about the trip.

'Easy,' Peter replied. 'You have to be right. Domenico Kranowski equals Domenico Daks. It's making sense at last.'

'I'm glad you feel that way. What are we going to tell Jago? How's he going to feel?'

'Interested, but not devastated, I imagine, unless the use of Jennifer as a model connects her too closely with Lance. It's Gawain's bones that are his passion, and possibly the goblet that goes with them. He's not involved with the paintings.'

'Unless the Gawain story is blown to smithereens along with the paintings.'

'Why should it be?' Peter asked mildly. 'Jago developed his thesis before the paintings and goblet entered into it. *Then* the goblet rumours came along, and *after that* the paintings.'

Georgia felt a ridiculous sense of relief on Jago's behalf. 'You mean that Michelangelo or Domenico Kranowski painted them in response to the rumours about the cup? Why, though?'

'For cash, darling. That's what makes the world go round. Didn't you know that? The Jagos of this world may rise above it, but most folk can't afford to.'

'So one of the Kranowskis hears the rumours from whatever source, realizes a killing can be made from the Arthurian world and paints a series of pictures. Unfortunately Jago would recognize his wife and so might countless other people in their circle,' Georgia pointed out.

'If he saw them. Lance never got round to showing them to him, did he? We assumed that was because Jago's interest didn't lie in the paintings, only in Gawain's bones. Suppose Lance was just the Benizis' foil?'

Instinctively she found herself coming to their defence. 'Antonio told me that Domenico Kranowski didn't do the fakes.'

'He would, wouldn't he? And perhaps he didn't.'

She saw where this led. 'But Michelangelo did.'

Peter nodded sympathetically. 'And so the claim that the Benizi Brothers walk the fine line now has a distinct wobble.'

'Don't mince your words,' she said bitterly. 'It makes them fall headlong into the underworld and probably—'

'Dragging in Lance Venyon and Jennifer Priest with them. I'm bound to say, Georgia, that it does look that way.'

'But what motive for killing Lance?'

'When thieves fall out anything can happen.'

She slowly digested this. Antonio a murderer? She couldn't believe it. 'It doesn't fit, Peter. Michelangelo must come into this story some other way. If he *is* Venetia's "Michael", then he visited England in 1961, and Leonardo himself in 1990, probably both at Domenico's request to ask for family property back.'

'What property?' Peter asked sharply.

She had forgotten this was new to him. 'I assume the paintings. They could even have been in Hoskin's possession for a while at least, which would account for the reference to Raphael and Pre-Raphaelites. Leonardo didn't know what the property was.'

'Or said he didn't,' Peter retorted. 'You're not thinking straight, Georgia. Domenico died some years ago. If this property was so important he would have told someone in the family what it was before he died.'

She was momentarily silenced. Then: 'Probably,' she admitted. 'Although as we're dealing with fakes, Leonardo might simply not have wanted to tell *us*.'

'True.' Peter frowned. 'In that case, this property could equally well be the script about Gawain at Dover and his remains, or even a fake goblet.'

'No. The Kranowskis are art forgers, not metal-workers.'

'Are we sure? Anyway, as we agreed, just because the paintings are fake, it doesn't necessarily mean that Ruskin didn't discover the real existence of such a goblet.'

'Oh, come on,' Georgia shot back at him. 'Even if you're right, the bona-fide evidence is hardly likely to have been in the hands of a family of fakers.' She stopped in sheer weariness. 'This case is getting to me.'

'To both of us,' Peter agreed. 'We're stuck in the middle of a hall of trick mirrors wondering which way to turn.'

'Jago has to be the answer to that,' Georgia concluded. 'If anyone can judge whether Lance was victim or villain he can.'

'I assume that your investigation has moved on a stage.' Jago looked at them enquiringly, as she brought the drinks out into the pub garden. Too warm to sit inside on a day such as this, and much more pleasant for Peter.

'It has, in fact,' Peter assured him blithely.

'You know who pushed him overboard?' Jago looked surprised.

'No, but the range as to why someone should want to do so widens, and with that fingers of suspicion grow more confident.'

'Indeed.' Jago looked troubled. 'Poor Lance. He was the most popular man I ever met, but even the best of men can unwittingly get in the way of others' plans.'

'You did give us the impression that this popular man was somewhat hard on his women friends,' Georgia reminded him.

'Ah yes. That dear little Venetia. Since you reminded me about her, I've been thinking about her quite a lot, wondering if she had hidden claws and could have scratched back to the extent of pushing him overboard.'

'If she did, we'd never prove it,' Peter said lightly.

'So how long do you go on digging away at this theory of yours?' Jago asked.

'As long as you for King Arthur's goblet,' Georgia laughed, seeing Peter at a loss for an answer.

'Touché,' Jago said ruefully. 'Of course that might not be much longer. There's blog talk of a communal dig to take place shortly.'

'Where? When?' Peter asked.

'No details yet. I put it down to some movement on your part. Has there been one?'

'There has, though I can't see how it would tie up with digging for the goblet. We've proved to our satisfaction that the Arthurian paintings that Lance was in pursuit of, probably including the one with the goblet, were fakes.'

To Georgia's relief, Jago did not enquire

further and looked only mildly disappointed. 'I can't say you surprise me. There are always those that try to cash in on a current event. No doubt they were a crude attempt to persuade the unbelieving that there was such a goblet.'

'Not that crude,' Peter said. 'It came from the Kranowksi stable.'

'Now there,' Jago said, 'you do surprise me. Did Lance know that?'

'That's the question. He was so friendly with Antonio Benizi that it's hard to tell at this late stage.'

'Quite. Lance is not necessarily on the side of the devils,' Jago pointed out, 'even if he knew them for what they were. It was his job to track down such frauds, and to remain friendly with the fakers.'

'A thin line.'

'One which he trod with delicacy. Are you implying the provenance of the paintings led to his death?'

'It's possible.'

Jago nodded gravely. 'Not that that affects the goblet. That still exists, just as the bones of Sir Gawain do.'

Along with Prester John and Shangri-La, thought Georgia irreverently. She felt instantly ashamed as she saw Jago's blue eyes on her, as if he could tell what she was thinking. Zac's trick.

'Knowing Lance,' Jago said, 'if he had discovered the paintings were fake, he would have

264

redoubled his efforts to help me find Gawain's remains and any evidence connected with that. He might even have found it.'

'Then it's strange that nothing further has been heard of it. No one would want to stop their discovery, only to steal them.'

'We don't know that that hasn't happened,' Jago pointed out. 'Such is the secretive world of collectors that they make sure that rivals can't trace them. Today, with email addresses, that's much easier. With care, bloggers can make themselves untraceable.'

'Even the site's source?'

'Certainly,' Jago agreed. 'One could give false information using an external blog host and a valid email address.'

'Why such extreme secrecy?' Georgia asked.

'My dear Georgia, consider the hunt for Prester John. Man's quest for something beyond this mundane existence is a lonely one, a solitary pursuit: the search for religion, for the Grail – whatever. Each man has his own. Mine is Sir Gawain and there could be others on the same track. Amongst the bloggers there have been many theories as to the site, ranging from here to the Darenth Valley, though there seems a consensus for Barham Downs now. I shall not be joining any communal dig, of course.'

'So what is your next step? To dig on your own site?'

Jago laughed. 'Have you ever been poised on the brink of something you know will bring you complete happiness and yet be afraid to go forward?'

Oh yes, Georgia thought. That touched a nerve. She had. She was in such a situation now every time she was with Luke. Every time they made love, every time they argued over spaghetti, with every addition they made to the Medlars garden.

'The vision has become almost as precious to me as the object itself,' Jago continued. 'I fear to step forward, and yet I know I shall.'

'Travelling hopefully is better than arriving,' Peter said.

'Ah yes. How I agree with Stevenson. He was right, although I would put it differently myself. I believe perfection belongs to God. The medieval mason would build a flaw into his work, not wishing to step on the Almighty's prerogative. I feel somewhat the same, that the grail of perfect happiness should be left as just that.'

'Suppose,' Georgia said practically, 'that someone finds it first in exactly the place you now believe it is.'

Jago laughed delightedly. 'You are bringing me down to earth, Georgia. I cannot continue to live in cloud cuckoo land for ever. I might rush out with my shovel tomorrow evening to take one last brave step towards that grail. A step that might kill me, of course.'

Georgia looked at him curiously. 'How?' she asked quietly.

266

'You believe someone killed Lance,' Jago pointed out. 'It is not so inconceivable. So keep my possible plan under your hats.'

'Like Lance's hat?' Georgia asked idly, as he prepared to leave.

She was taken by surprise at Jago's reaction. He looked shaken, and, she thought, alarmed.

'So there could be something to Hoskin's idle words after all. What, I wonder, is so odd about Lance's hat?' Peter speculated as they drove home.

'What he kept under it?' Georgia asked.

Peter didn't dignify this with a reply. 'If I fed that into Google, I'd get—'

'Eighty million responses, no doubt.'

'Something,' Peter said optimistically, 'might crop up. You don't think it could be a blog, do you?'

'I don't. Lance wasn't privileged to know what they were.'

Peter sighed. 'Let's fall back on the tried and true. A reconstruction. We can start with his last day alive.'

'About which we know very little.'

'Last two days, then,' Peter amended. 'The day he left home and the day he left Hythe harbour, never to be seen again.'

'Not much better.'

'Correction. We know he gave a lift to an unknown woman.'

'Agreed. Could mean nothing.'

'He'd met Michelangelo recently.'

'Agreed. But we don't know whether it was about paintings or Ruskin letters.'

'We know he had a row with Venetia, who then went storming off to see Mary.'

'Agreed, with the proviso that we only have her word for it.'

'We think Lance was murdered.'

'Yes.'

A long pause. 'Can we take any of these givens further forward?' Peter asked.

'Only Venetia and Mary. We don't *know* one of them didn't go haring off after Lance.'

'It seems unlikely Venetia did. She said they were discreet.'

'Everyone can lose their rag every so often. She told us quite frankly that she did.'

'Could the visitor he was meeting that afternoon have been Jennifer? That would raise the temperatures to boiling point if Venetia found out.'

'It would give equal reason for Mary to boil over. Not to mention Jago. Suppose Venetia put Mary right on Lance's feelings for Jennifer?'

'Now that's a thought,' Peter said approvingly. 'Jennifer and Jago were in Paris, so no great problem about either of them coming to Dover. Mary never specified the meeting was in Hythe, did she?'

'Not so far as I recall. But Jennifer wouldn't want to kill Lance,' Georgia pointed out.

'Crime of passion? Jennifer comes over for an

unexpected dirty weekend with Lance, who cancels Venetia's trip. Jennifer sails back to France with Lance, finds out about the other two women and pushes him overboard.'

'Then jumps off the boat herself and swims to Boulogne. Not likely.'

'She takes the dinghy.'

'It was still on the boat,' Georgia said doubtfully. 'Strong swimmer?'

'And then emerges from the water with wet clothes, travel documents, money...? Drawbacks to a crime of passion.'

'Bother,' Georgia said crossly. Then: 'Suppose she planned it. Took a second dinghy on board.'

'You don't think Lance might have noticed it and thought it a trifle odd?' Peter said caustically.

'I give up.'

'Don't,' he advised kindly. 'There's an answer somewhere.'

Venetia's voice came over strongly on the telephone, more strongly than Georgia would have guessed from remembering her tiny frame. Peter had slept on the problem and by the time Georgia had appeared in his office the following morning had chosen to ring her, putting on the speaker phone so that Georgia could hear as well.

'How is it going?' Venetia asked.

'Step by step,' Peter answered blithely.

'How's Falstaff?' Always ask after the pets, he constantly advised Georgia.

'Guarding me like Cerberus.'

'From what?'

Venetia didn't answer that. Instead: 'What is it you'd like to know?'

'Whether you and Mary went together to Hythe to talk to Lance or you alone?'

A laugh, fortunately. 'I like the direct approach. Will you believe me if I tell you?'

'Not necessarily.'

'I think you might this time. I went alone. Mary informed me that she knew all about Jennifer and could do without my help, thank you very much. She also knew all about me, and wasn't at all surprised that Lance had dumped me. She'd already had a word with my husband. A sweet lady, Mary. Like one of those scratch cards. Take off the glitzy surface and underneath is the plain truth. Usually that you've lost. Mary's unvarnished truth was that she was going to hang on to Lance at all costs.'

'She didn't succeed.'

A pause. 'And you think my being in the picture had anything to do with that? No, Mr Marsh. I did go down to Hythe, and guess what, Lance wasn't there. He'd told me he was meeting someone at the club, but there was no sign of him. I went to his boat, still steaming with fury, convinced he was skulking there. Everyone knew me, so I just marched straight on board without anyone thinking twice about it.

He wasn't there either.'

'Are you implying he might never have left Hythe? That someone else might have taken the boat out?'

'No, I'm not. When I found out he was missing, I was on the phone like a flash. I even went down there. There was no doubt that Lance took the *Lady Mary* out himself early on the 14th. He was well known and was seen by several people. And, unfortunately for your thesis, all of them said he was alone.'

'No one could have been hiding below decks?'

'That's just about conceivable but hardly likely. Lance would have been most surprised at such odd behaviour and undoubtedly would have turfed them off if he'd thought there was trouble brewing. There was nothing he hated more than having a row at sea. He was a great dodger of rows anywhere.'

'So why did you think he was murdered, and how?' Peter demanded.

'The answer to the latter is no idea. As for why he could have been murdered, I suppose that because I could cheerfully have killed Lance myself at times I could envisage his arousing the sentiments in others too. Nor could I face the fact that he merely had an accident. Though that, Mr Marsh, seems to be the conclusion you must be coming to.'

'I still don't believe it,' Peter exploded. He had

come up to Medlars for dinner so that Luke could be in on the crisis meeting. Was this case going forward or sinking in a storm?

'Believe the accident or murder?' Luke asked.

'Either,' Peter growled.

'That doesn't make sense,' Georgia said.

'All right, I don't believe *it*. I do believe her.'

'I would have put it the other way around, Peter,' Luke said calmly. 'But I'm only a publisher.'

'You're not even that in this case,' Georgia pointed out sourly. 'There's still no contract.'

'Would you like one? I'll do one tomorrow.'

She looked at him in amazement. 'Are you being kind to us, Luke? There's no case yet.'

'There is,' Luke said. 'I've always been a sucker for buried treasure, and at least there must be a story to be told about that.'

Peter went home happily, but her evening was not yet over. Twenty minutes after his departure, he was on the phone to her. 'There's a message from Mike,' he said.

'Can't it wait?' Georgia asked plaintively. Bed was looking awfully attractive.

'I thought you'd like to know.'

'Know what?'

'Mark Priest's been arrested.'

Thirteen

Mark Priest? What had been going on? Georgia wondered. It was only two weeks since she had seen him in the Pad and Palette. The investigation had obviously moved on quickly. But which investigation?

'Arrested for what?' she asked when she reported in the next morning. 'For the art-thefts scam or Sandro's murder?' She'd assumed the former, but now this more sinister thought had occurred to her.

'Organizing the art scam, according to Mike,' Peter told her. 'At present, anyway. If Sandro got in Mark's way of course it might become a murder charge as well, provided there's forensic evidence against him. Sandro is firmly tied into it, since the copies replacing the stolen artworks are all by the same hand as Sandro's legit work. The Met has had its sights on Priest for a long time, because he has some connection to every house or museum suffering from the scam.'

'One could say the same of Zac.'

'Do you see him successfully masterminding a scam on this scale?'

'No,' she admitted. Even so she couldn't get her mind round its being Mark. An organizer yes, but a crooked one has to see round more corners than a straight one. It was true she'd only met Mark once, however, which wasn't a lot to go on.

'Mark Priest fits the frame,' Peter continued. 'Outwardly unassertive, he's in the middle of the game, and could have set up the thefts to switch the originals with copies, and dealt with the insurance problems later.'

'Are the Cooks involved too?' Somehow Georgia couldn't see Ratlike Roy or Kinky Kelly working avidly for Mark Priest, and yet if Sandro was working for them surely they couldn't be sparkling clean.

'Not proven. Priest has to talk first and at the moment he's putting on a fine show of complete innocence.'

'What about the Benizis?' she asked reluctantly. 'Do they come into it?'

'Question marks over the business, if not your chums in particular. There's nothing to link them with the Kentish art thefts, only the tenuous connection of the Daks family and Roberto Benizi in Budapest.'

'And Zac,' she pointed out.

'As you say, Zac. Who at the moment isn't in the frame, let alone the picture. That might be because nothing directly leads to the Benizis or to the Daks family, except Sandro. And if he chose to copy masterpieces and someone bought them – so what? There's nothing illegal in copying. It's a question of what you do with it and how you present it. I'm quite sure Sandro would have put a discreet mention of his own name on the back of each copy, which has no doubt been picked up by the Met. No intention to deceive, ladies and gentlemen, none at all.'

Georgia had mixed feelings. At the moment she would undoubtedly be persona non grata with Antonio and Madeleine, thanks to her Budapest caper. There would be a price on her head at least. She could visualize Antonio shaking his head sadly, even as he signed the execution order. That's enough, she told her imagination firmly.

'This will be another almighty blow to Jago,' she said.

'With luck King Arthur will help keep his mind off it. Look at this.' Peter passed her the morning's newspaper and she quickly scanned the item he pointed out. It carried the headline 'England's Hour of Need':

Speculation grows on the Internet that King Arthur is preparing to come to the aid of the nation. The late king still reclines in a coma after his mortal wound at the Battle of Cam-lann, but his supporters are claiming that his return is imminent. According to his spin doctors, his loyal party activist Sir Gawain has offered to reveal the whereabouts of his own bones and grave goods in the hope of discovering His Majesty's long-lost golden goblet, a magnet which, it is hoped, will draw the king from his resting place. Sir Gawain, best known for his epic battle with the gigantic Green Knight, expired off the Channel coast some years ago, and is now thought to be slumbering close to his former liege lord in Kent.

The article continued in this vein for another two paragraphs, concluding:

His Majesty's followers are preparing for Gawain's resurrection by meeting on Barham Downs near Canterbury on 6 July. Reports that a magician by the name of Merlin is expected to attend are as yet unconfirmed. A spokesman for the local archaeological society made it clear that the society had no plans to take part in the dig but would be keenly interested in the outcome.

Georgia laid the newspaper down. 'Do you think they *really* plan to dig?' she asked incredulously.

'Almost certainly.'

'Is this Jago's big moment? While the Arthurian world and his wife are digging on Barham Downs, he might be scuttling off to his own selected site.'

'Probably – with or without his son.'

* * *

Georgia could hardly wait to push the news-paper under Luke's nose, and took the rare step of suggesting he join them for lunch at the White Lion on the grounds that it might affect the contract he was drawing up. It was rare only because Luke preferred to remain glued to the oast house during his so-called lunch break.

'At least King Arthur's in command now,' he said cheerfully, once they were settled at the White Lion, Haden Shaw's local. 'Either he turns up with Gawain next week waving his sword and clutching his goblet under his arm, or he doesn't. You can't do a thing about it.'

'Thank heavens for that,' she said fervently. 'Shall we go along to watch the fun?'

'Jago's movements might be more interesting,' Peter said.

'Perhaps, although he might leave it for a few days, even weeks or months, before he makes his own move.'

'How will they organize this thing?' Luke had been reading the article carefully.

'According to the blogs, admission to the sacred spot is by ticket only,' Peter said. 'They can't be pleased at this wide publicity. Someone must have leaked it.'

'But what if the meeting's a practical joke? Remember the magician who heralded his arrival with a big poster campaign advertising "He is coming!", sold all the tickets, and when the eager audience arrived they simply found another poster announcing: "He has gone!"?'

Georgia duly laughed. 'Suppose something *is* dug up. Bits of Gawain's bones, as in the Piltdown fraud.'

'Modern tests would dispose of that.'

'Technology might have moved on since Piltdown days, but human beings are just as daft. It's a question of what people want to believe. If enough want to believe something is genuine, then the scam succeeds.'

'No,' Luke said. 'I don't agree. With this announced in the press, there are going to be doubters out in force.'

'Doubters have been overruled before,' Peter pointed out. 'Despite all the museums, including the Hermitage, who refused to buy Ruchomovski's Tiara of Saitaphernes, the Louvre went ahead and bought it.'

'Times have changed,' Luke argued, 'and that's where Arthur's goblet will fall down – that's if it ever pops up. There'd be so much ridicule that no one would dare stand up and proclaim it the real thing.'

'By real,' Peter came back at him, 'do you mean really King Arthur's or really genuine gold? I've no doubt about the latter, it's the former I'm more interested in.'

'How do you define *real*,' Georgia asked, deciding to stir it, 'where King Arthur's concerned? Do you mean King Arthur as portrayed by tradition, or a minor leader who repelled a horde of Saxons?'

Both Peter and Luke turned on her, but before

either of them could demolish her, Charlie Bone appeared at their table out of the blue. 'Guessed you'd be here,' he said, 'skiving as usual.'

'Look who's talking.' Georgia moved up on the bench and her cousin slid in beside her. She hadn't seen him since Gwen's wedding, and his arrival was opportune.

'I'm not.' Charlie looked injured. 'Peter asked me to come. I'm early, that's all, so eager am I to help you at all times.'

'Blogs,' Peter explained succinctly. 'I asked Charlie if he could trace them back to source.'

'I haven't got far,' Charlie said blithely. 'Terry and I played for hours this morning, but no more success than you did, Peter. They're all such secretive sods that no one wants to stick a head above the parapet in case he loses his fifteen minutes of fame.'

'So one of them could well be Jago himself.' Peter beat Georgia to the obvious conclusion.

'You mean Jago deliberately whips up this furore over a site well away from his own patch, so that he can keep all the glory for himself?' Luke said. 'Wow, what a gent.'

'I doubt if he would put it in those terms,' Peter said drily. 'He is an academic protecting his research, after all.'

'Picturing himself holding up the goblet as if he'd won the Grand Prix?'

'Good publicity,' Charlie observed.

Charlie had a knack of expressing the obvious

that had been too obvious to see for herself, Georgia thought. That could be exactly what Jago had in mind. 'So,' Charlie continued, 'are you all off to Barham Downs next Thursday, shovels and metal detectors in hand? Good pub at Barham.'

'No doubt King Arthur stepped down for a pint in the midst of the Battle of Badon,' Luke joked.

'There'll be another bunfight next week,' Charlie said happily. 'According to those blogs, half the lads think the goblet has nothing to do with Gawain but was dropped in the middle of the battle as someone stopped to take a swig of ale, possibly Arthur himself. The others think Gawain died at Badon, aka Barham Downs, and not at Dover, so why couldn't it be called Gawain's cup and not Arthur's?'

'Let's not spoil the story,' Georgia said patiently.

'What happened to that Lance Venyon you were investigating?' Charlie asked. 'Is he mixed up with this?'

Silence. How, Georgia thought, could they say yes, when they still didn't know *how* he tied in with it, if at all.

'No clues at all, Sherlock?' Charlie persisted.

'There might be,' Georgia said, 'but if so they're locked inside the memories of (a) a scorned woman, (b) an antiques dealer who won't speak in case it rakes up nefarious doings from his own past or (c) a professor in his nineties with Alzheimer's.'

'Ah. No way out?' Charlie asked.

'I'll eat my own hat if there is,' Peter said gloomily.

'Don't follow. Who else's would you eat?'

'The only words the professor could utter about Lance were Raphael, Michelangelo and hat. The Michelangelo could be a reference to the Kranowski family, known forgers of the 1950s. Raphael is perhaps a reference to Pre-Raphaelites and therefore to Rossettis, and the hat is a blank.'

Charlie looked interested. 'Did you try them all together?'

'Yes. Nothing interesting came out of it.'

He thought for a moment. 'Let's get back to your office and have a go.'

Luke decided to leave them in the interests of his own office, but Georgia was amused to see that he looked reluctant to do so. Could it be that he really was getting gripped by hidden treasure?

Once back in Peter's house, Charlie sat himself down at Georgia's computer – tactful of him not to usurp Peter's, she thought – and his fingers were soon busily clicking.

'Oh *yes*,' he said after a few minutes. 'Look at this, art and hat.' Peter wheeled himself over to peer over Charlie's shoulder as he scrolled through the list.

'Oh yes, what?' Georgia asked impatiently since her own view was impaired.

'*Bruno* Hat,' Peter crowed softly. 'Of course. Thanks, Charlie.'

'Who's he?' Georgia asked.

'No one. That's the point. It was one of the master scams of the 1920s when such jokes were highly rated in the fashionable world of celebs. Bruno Hat was a fictitious artist supposedly discovered in a small Sussex village and hailed by Evelyn Waugh and his chums as a genius. His work was sensational, and an exhibition was mounted of his frightfully avantgarde works. A catalogue was produced and Hat even made a brief appearance at the exhibition. The cognoscenti promptly bought paintings like hot cakes. Naturally they had to be pretty good anyway, and it's still not certain who actually painted them. Hoskin was remembering that.'

'But why?' Georgia asked, though ideas were beginning to spark off in her mind. Hat and Kranowski, Michelangelo Kranowski, Domenico Kranowski, Richard Hoskin...

Obviously Peter was galvanized too for he was on his own mission. 'Charlie,' he said, 'I have an important personal engagement with Google.' He turned the wheelchair round and in a trice was busy with the search button.

'The problem is that pretty nearly anything one feeds in comes up with something,' he grumbled. 'There's too much information in the world.'

'Or disinformation,' Georgia pointed out.

'The Internet's only a medium.'

'Hey presto,' Peter cried. He stared at the screen. Before Georgia could see what had caught his attention, he clutched his head, and cried out again: 'A fool, I met a fool in the forest and it was *me!*' he said.

'Never mind the Shakespeare quotes, what have you discovered?' Georgia peered over his shoulder.

'I knew those Benizis and Dakses were fooling us. There's the link between them.'

'Where?' she demanded. All she could see was a site about faked art.

'Domenico,' he howled.

'Explain.' She was hopping up and down in frustration.

'There *was* no Domenico Kranowski, and no Domenico Daks either. Part of the maze. He changed his name completely, naturally enough. He was heading a family of fakers, for heaven's sake.'

'So?'

'Antonio Benizi knows the Daks/Kranowski family well. He never lost touch with Kranowski. He knew the change of name, forename and surname. It's how the firm's operated all these years between East and West, and be blowed to the Iron Curtain. He was misleading you, Georgia.'

'Because of the paintings?' She was still in the maze.

'No,' he snapped impatiently. 'Look at this.'

She peered closely at the screen, with Charlie equally glued to Peter's other side.

'*Raphael* Kranowski,' Peter read out. 'Silver- and goldsmith. Faker of the Weimar Bowl and the Samos Rhyton, et cetera.'

'Antonio spoke of him as an art forger,' she stammered. 'Domenico, anyway.'

'There was no Domenico. We've both been fools, Georgia. You swallowing everything Benizi told you, and me' – at least he was including himself, she thought wryly – 'for not checking it on the Internet. How could I have been such an idiot? Am I getting old?' He looked at her in appeal.

Georgia couldn't answer. The sudden collapse of his usual confidence had shaken her and it was left to Charlie to come to the rescue. 'Even Sherlock had to call in Brother Mycroft on occasion.'

That rallied Peter. 'Very well, Mycroft. If it's so elementary, where do we go next?'

'Obvious,' Charlie said blithely, 'this chap forged the goblet.'

Peter's eyes gleamed. 'Which no doubt is the property Raphael was so eager to recover from Lance Venyon. So eager that Michelangelo pursued it in 1961 and Leonardo in 1990.'

'Charlie,' said Georgia fervently, 'if I wasn't in love with Luke, I'd marry you for this.'

'Why punish me?' he moaned. 'What have you got against me?'

'Nothing in the world,' she replied happily.

'You've given us the path forward.'

'It's Mum's eclairs, you know. They're good for the brain. Anyway, I'm getting interested in the Arthur story. I always fancied myself as the jolly fat one.'

'I think you'll find that's Robin Hood,' Georgia said gently, looking at Charlie's scrawny figure.

'So it is. Merlin, then.'

'You've achieved magic this time,' she said gratefully.

Georgia followed Peter into the garden after Charlie had taken himself off, rather regretfully, to return to his London flat. Hot days weren't good for thought, but then neither were claustrophobic offices, so the garden was a good compromise. She was all too well aware that the gate through to her own garden was rarely used now. Perhaps the time had come to sell the house. Or should it wait until next season? Just in case...

'Let's put this together,' Peter began. 'Fact. Benizi misled you over Raphael Kranowski.'

'He deliberately let me think Domenico was an art forger, because he didn't want us to follow up the goblet. Why?'

'A possible scam.'

'Whose? We suspect that Lance was mixed up with it, but did he organize it, or the Benizis?' Even now it cost her something to think of them as villains.

Peter took up the baton. 'The Benizis must be at the heart of it, since it's in their interests to develop the Arthurian market. If this goblet is first rumoured to exist, then proven, the provenance of that and the paintings is strengthened. If the chaplains' script and Ruskin letter also turned up, the price would be sky high.'

'The rumour is that the goblet was buried,' Georgia continued, the bit between her teeth now. 'It couldn't be just any old gold cup, it had to be linked with Arthur. So they draw Lance into it, but why should Lance help them? He had his reputation to consider.'

'Money. Friendship. And perhaps,' Peter added, 'he was killed because of this scam.'

'Unless Lance brought the scam to Benizi.' *Yes*, surely that was it? 'You're forgetting Richard Hoskin.' Was there a ray of light at last?

'In what way?'

'He was a historian and interested in archaeology. It's clear he knew about the scam.' Steady. She tried to keep a cap on her words. No thesis ahead of the facts. But, oh, how those facts fitted. 'He has a museum full of Arthurian-type artefacts.'

He caught her excitement. 'Old bones. Sir Gawain's bones, and,' he gloated, 'possibly his sword, belt buckle, shield, who knows what. Georgia, we're on our way. The goblet might even be there.'

'Where?'

'Glorious Sussex. The most wonderful county

in the world at present. No wonder the Benizis tried to charm you out of any suspicion of them, Georgia. Thank your lucky stars. If you hadn't been so gullible, he'd probably have shot you.'

'How very kind,' she said savagely, uneasily aware that he could well be right.

Georgia was looking forward to seeing Peter's reaction to Camelot, even though Barry Hoskin had been reluctant for them to come. His father was far from well, he told them, was already agitated over the King Arthur blogs, and he didn't want him upset any more. Then he had relented and called them back. His father, he admitted, was extremely anxious to see them after he had explained what it was about.

'I hope he doesn't think he's going to this gathering at Barham Downs,' Barry said gloomily, as he led them to the living room. 'When there was a hue and cry like this a few years ago, he was in better health and not only wanted to go, but to take half his museum with him. When I refused, he wanted to invite every-one for tea. Luckily it proved a damp squib, and no one was in the mood for a drive to Sussex. If,' he added hopefully, 'you could lay his worries to rest today, I'd be awfully grateful.'

'If we find out what they are, we will,' Georgia assured him. 'The problem is that we're looking for guidance from *him*.'

'Then we're all doomed.' Barry helped Peter manoeuvre his wheelchair round the furniture, placing him strategically close to his father.

Peter immediately hit off with Professor Hoskin, through nods and pictures of Anglo-Saxon objects which he had brought with him. The professor studied each one closely and handed it back without comment. Until, that is, Georgia saw Peter pass him a picture of an ornamented wooden goblet of the early Anglo-Saxon period.

The professor shouted out something that Georgia did not catch, but Barry supplied the word: 'Zoomorphic'. It meant nothing to her, but Peter was nodding enthusiastically. 'Animal ornamentation,' he said. Immediately Georgia was back before the painting of Gawain. That goblet had been decorated with some kind of animal shape.

The next was a picture of a buckle from the same period, also ornamented. 'Filigree,' the professor supplied with great satisfaction. When he struggled to his feet, beckoning to Peter, Georgia grew more optimistic still. Richard Hoskin seemed oblivious to the presence of Georgia and his son, who had nevertheless taken firm control of him, and he chattered meaninglessly to Peter. Peter manoeuvred his chair outside with Georgia's help, where he then wheeled himself rapidly to the professor's free side. No prizes for guessing they were off to Camelot.

'Here comes the conjuring trick,' Barry declared, once they were all in the barn. Camelot flooded into life, and having been forewarned, Peter was clearly in no doubt as to how to react. 'Oh, I say!' he exclaimed in delight. Nevertheless Georgia could see he was genuinely impressed. He had more of a gift than she did for transporting himself into the pleasures of others, however alien to his own.

'Sir Gareth,' Peter cried, of a blond-haired knight sitting at the round table, and Richard Hoskin nodded in delight.

'Sir Perceval,' Peter tried, then corrected himself. 'Geraint of course,' and he received a nod. He passed muster with Sir Bors, Lancelot was a no-brainer, then came Lamorak, of whom Georgia had never heard, Tristram, and another stranger to Georgia, Sir Segramour.

By this time Peter was obviously in high favour and Hoskin might have sat there all day, but Barry turned the lights out on Camelot and on in the museum itself, where Georgia took over. The problem was that she wasn't sure what she was looking for.

'King Arthur's goblet?' she tried on Hoskin hopefully, but there was no response. Even Peter's ace, 'Raphael Kranowksi', brought nothing. She was beginning to lose hope, until Peter mentioned Bruno Hat. Now it was a different story.

She listened amazed as the professor burst out laughing, his hands slapping his frail legs. 'Lance, Lance...' and a flow of words followed though nothing that she could understand.

'Benizi,' she tried, but it was only Lance that he stuck with.

'Lance – die,' he managed and a thrill of optimism ran through her.

'He drowned in an accident,' Peter tried.

Unbelievably, there was a vigorous shake of the head in reply. It might not mean anything, Georgia warned herself, but it was a sign that he was on track at some level. He could point if not answer, and he was doing so at what looked like pieces of a broken sword.

'Lance? Painting? Rossetti? Pre-Raphaelites?' she tried again, but this time he just shook his head, putting a hand out lovingly to the artefacts.

Barry was indicating that his father was tired and that it was time for them to go. As they left, he pushed a diary into their hands. 'Let me have it back when you've finished with it. It's not much, but it does have Lance Venyon's name in it several times.'

Georgia could see that it was for 1958, and as soon as they were away from the house she stopped the car so that they could look at it. There were indeed several mentions of Lance Venyon, first as Mr Venyon, then Lance Venyon, then LV or Lance, six meetings in all over the summer of 1958.

'I think that the professor was trying to tell us that Lance had something to do with these artefacts. That they were part of a scam. Lance's Hat. Suppose,' Peter said slowly, 'they were waiting here for Lance to pick them up on the Benizis' behalf, and then when he died they just stayed here. Those items wouldn't have a lot of value in themselves.'

'The dates don't work. Any cache of bones and artefacts would have to age in the ground. They wouldn't still be in this collection.'

'Bother. You're right. Suppose what we saw were the rejected ones? Suppose Lance took what he wanted and left the rest?'

'Possible, but too many supposes. Are you implying the professor forged all that stuff?' Georgia asked.

'No. These could be the real thing. The professor would have access to all sorts of collections hidden in museum basements, which might never be missed. Think of the value to the Benizis' scam. Pop some of these authentic bones and artefacts in and it would make the goblet appear genuine in a collection. Gold is difficult to date.'

'Theoretically the goblet still might be genuine.'

'Less and less likely, darling. I think it's time for a word with your Antonio.'

'On the phone?'

'Of course. No one gets shot that way.'

Georgia forbore to point out that the Benizis could easily find out where she lived if they were intent on getting rid of her, but acquiesced.

'Shall I do it?' Peter asked sympathetically.

'No, I will.' It was her job. She'd been too gullible with them, but no more.

She rang from Peter's office as soon as they were home, and Antonio answered – somewhat guardedly. No surprise there. If he was waiting for her to mention the Budapest paintings, he'd be pleasantly surprised. It was the past she'd keep to, not the present – if only for her own safety.

'We know about your arrangement with Lance, Antonio,' she began after the opening skirmishes.

'Georgia, what arrangement is this?' he asked plaintively.

'Lance provided you with enough genuine old artefacts for you to stock Gawain's grave so that the Kranowski goblet should appear genuine and the paintings' value soar through the roof. Did you tell Raphael he and Michelangelo could have a share of the booty, or did you pay them cash?'

Silence.

'You told me Raphael, alias Domenico, was an art faker,' she reminded him.

He spoke then. 'No, Mrs Georgia, you assumed he was, because we had just been to the Louvre. We talked about paintings. I do not believe in giving unnecessary information. Raphael liked to be thought of as art faker, so he can keep real work secret. Big joke. He called himself Domenico when he painted. But he was not as good as his son Michelangelo.'

'A big joke like the one you and Lance were involved in for the King Arthur market. Is that why you killed Lance?'

'Kill him?' he exploded. 'No, no, no. You have it wrong. It was not my funny joke. You think I would do something as foolish as that? We did not know about Lance's game, Madeleine and I. We guess something naughty going on, but not what. We only find out later. We very cross.'

'When did you discover? Before or after he died?'

There was a muffled voice, then the receiver was snatched from Antonio, after a scuffle, which Madeleine obviously won. Her calm voice said: 'A week or so before he died, Georgia, when Michelangelo telephoned us. We were living in Rome, and at that stage Lance had only talked to us about the painting of Sir Gawain and its provenance, convincing us that it was genuine.'

Some hopes, Georgia thought.

'We knew nothing about any goblet until Michelangelo told us, nor did we know about the other paintings, which he sent to us a few days after Lance's death. He was furious because he had gone to tell Lance that the Kranowksis were about to be exposed as fakers, and his father was intent on getting the goblet back. After all, his exposure would ruin Lance's plans, he might have thought. Lance refused to let him have it, however, and Michelangelo suspected he had sold it.

'I could not work out what was going on,' Madeleine continued, 'so I decided to go to see Lance. I was due to visit London anyway, so I saw Lance on my way back to Dover. He was not pleased, and told me I was too late. He had been working on this scam for a long time; everything had been in the ground for over two years to allow time for the earth to settle around it, and the joke was about to spring. He wasn't going to ruin it now by digging up the goblet, the prize of the collection. No one would think the goblet was a fake because the other artefacts weren't. Besides, he had taken his inspiration for the scam from the painting of Sir Gawain, and he was positive the provenance of that was secure. Like a fool, I believed him, since I hadn't seen the other paintings at that point. I would have had no doubt about their being fake. Lance told me to take my ferry home, and he would drop me off at Dover. I needed to talk it over with Antonio, so I agreed, but the next thing I received was Jennifer's letter. The Kranowskis' exposure as fakers took place hard on the heels of our receipt of the paintings and we heard no more. The scam seemed safely buried, which was good.'

'Even though it would have made you rich?'

An exclamation of annoyance. 'You don't understand, Georgia,' Madeleine said. 'The whole point of the scam was that it was a joke – of sorts. Lance was going to pay Kranowski out of his own pocket, and had already paid Hoskin. Lance confessed to me that day that his aim had never been money, but revenge.'

Of course, Georgia thought, kicking herself for not realizing it sooner. Not money, but the game!

'Lance was hell bent on making Jago Priest the laughing stock of the Arthurian world,' Madeleine continued, 'by building up the hoax to the point where Jago was so obsessed that he could never admit anything was a fake. The world's press would be present, Jago would luxuriate in his glory to the full; he would officially authenticate the find – and then, he, Lance Venyon, would tip the press and experts off that it was all a fake. It was Lance's revenge for Jago marrying Jennifer.'

'And Jennifer knew about it?' *Never forget Jennifer.*

There was a long silence, then at last Madeleine answered her. 'I don't know. That's the torment.'

Fourteen

'How can we tell him?' Georgia asked. Jago already had Mark's arrest to battle with, even though the charge was still for the art thefts, not murder. So far, Mike had said, they were still lacking forensic – or indeed any – evidence to connect him with the murder of Sandro Daks.

'How can we not?' Peter asked reasonably.

For good reasons, Georgia thought. However robust Jago might seem, he was in his mid to late eighties, and the shock of his life's dream being shattered, just at the point where they suspected he might be about to dig once again for Gawain's bones, might well be too much for him. Added to that, he still considered Lance to have been his best friend. Two central props to his life would be knocked away.

'In hindsight, it was a good plan,' Peter observed.

'Was it?' It seemed to Georgia fraught with risk.

'Our Lance must have had patience. He worked on the scheme for several years. Jago married Jennifer in 1956; Lance at some point conceived the idea, set the rumours going

296

himself without benefit of the Internet, then pretended to pick up on them, fitting them in to what Jago already believed, then organizing and ageing the collection in the ground.'

'The question is: *did* he put it there?'

Peter ruminated. 'My money would be on the assumption that he had already buried it when he died. Otherwise what happened to the goblet? It wasn't presumably found amongst his belongings after his death, and the Benizis would have known if it had come on the market.'

'They wouldn't have told us, though,' Georgia said. 'And if you're right, and the collection was buried, you must see where that takes us.'

'Of course I do. It's still there where Lance buried it; he was about to spring the joke.'

Georgia grappled with this. There was a flaw somewhere. 'Buried it *where*?'

Peter whirled his chair round irritably. 'Georgia, I don't *know*. There are a thousand don't knows. What, for instance, about the chaplains' script and the Ruskin letter? Do they exist? Are they buried with the hoard? Can't be. So where are they?'

'Perhaps Lance had a further flourish planned with the paintings, script and letter to turn up. But he died.'

'I notice we've stopped using the words killed or murdered.'

'We have to,' she said gloomily.

'If Jago found out about the hoax,' Peter said

wistfully, 'that would have given him a first-class motive.'

'We've been down that cul-de-sac,' she replied. 'He had the time, but no opportunity. Even if he had learned or guessed about the hoax and dashed over from France to be the mysterious visitor Lance arranged to meet that day – who must surely have been Madeleine – how could he have overcome his loathing of water sufficiently to choose that method *and* plan his escape by water?'

'Risky, I agree. Lance might have been a trifle wary at Jago's sudden enthusiasm for sailing? No, if we're talking murder, it's back to the Benizis, Venetia or Mary, or persons unknown.'

'Or Hoskin,' Georgia added.

'I hadn't thought of that. You're right, but where does that get us?' Peter looked at her. 'Shall we wipe our hands of the murder angle? Luke still thinks the story of the scam alone might make a book, depending on what happens over the dig.'

'Back to square one. That means Jago finding out about the hoax.'

'He will anyway.'

'Not through us.'

'We've committed the unthinkable. We've become personally involved in this case, particularly you, Georgia.'

She could say nothing in her defence, because it was true. Even now she was taking the Benizis' story at face value. 'Yes, let's press on with dear old King Arthur,' she agreed. 'One odd thing is that when Lance died, Jago *didn't* find the hoard in the place indicated and that's where Lance must surely have buried his collection. So why didn't Jago find it?'

'Sometimes you excel yourself, Georgia.' Peter didn't seem to be joking.

'Thank you,' she replied modestly. 'Either Jago must have changed his mind, or he missed it. Or he lied about where it was to us. Or,' it occurred to her, 'he *did* find it and is gloating over his hoard in secret.'

'In which case he's still in for a big shock when he discovers it's all a scam – and, if you're right, why should he be making a song and dance about it now?'

She made a stab in the dark. 'Because he's going to *re-find* it, to get his hour of glory?'

'Why take over forty years to do so?' Peter cut neatly through her argument.

'The time is ripe now. He's bored with just looking at it once in a while, and the recurring rumours have given him the perfect opportunity for public glory, especially with the bloggers meeting on Barham Downs. Jago doesn't know, remember, that the goblet is Raphael Kranowski's, not King Arthur's.'

Peter finally delivered his verdict. 'You could be right, but I don't think you are. It seems to me we could be missing a trick here.'

'A trick about what?' Her voice came out as a squeak. Not another U-turn, surely?

'It could be Jago is the guiding blogger behind the Barham Downs gathering. He's busy keeping the opposition employed elsewhere while he digs away. I'll ring Jago. We should be there, just in case.'

'He's in his late eighties. He won't be doing it by himself, and he'd arrange for press to be there. Anyway, I repeat, we know it's all a fake.'

'As you said, he doesn't know it's fake.'

Georgia closed her eyes in despair. 'I can't bear it. It gets worse all the time. I can picture him at Wymdown digging away in his field in the confident hope that his life's dream is about to be fulfilled. He'll have enduring fame as the greatest Arthurian of them all. And after that it will all be exposed as a hoax.'

'That's life,' Peter agreed.

'You're very callous.'

'I do believe you're beginning to have Arthurian stars in your eyes, Georgia. Secretly you want King Arthur to come galloping down from the hills to scoop up his goblet just as much as I do.'

'The world could do with him,' Georgia replied with dignity.

Only another day to wait. Several times Georgia had wanted to warn Jago, and she suspected Peter still did too.

'No,' he had decreed. 'We can't take the responsibility. But he's agreed we can join him, and says he'll let me know the location tomorrow afternoon.'

'Should we warn Cindy or Sam?'

'They have their heads screwed on sufficiently to know the risks.'

'Neither of them knows there's really something to be found.'

'How,' Peter asked, 'do we know there is? All we know is that there probably was something somewhere forty-odd years ago.'

She moaned slightly. 'Your meaning?'

'Look at it this way. As you pointed out, the hoard wasn't in the expected place. Our Lance had a valuable gold cup in his possession. Less valuable than if it belonged to King Arthur but nevertheless undoubtedly solid gold, since Kranowski would have used old gold from the Byzantine period.'

'How would King Arthur get a goblet made of gold from the East?'

'Easily. Trading arrangements in those days were less hampered by HM customs and import taxes. As I was saying, what does Lance do with this goblet? Suppose it was a double scam. Suppose he pays some paltry sum for the goblet from Kranowski, sets the whole scam up, with bones and what have you, but flogs the goblet for himself?'

'We've been there. It would have come on the market.'

'Not necessarily. He could have given it some entirely new provenance, nothing to do with

Arthur at all. When Michelangelo comes over in 1961 and asks for it back, Lance can't hand it over, fobs off Michelangelo with some story and Lance breathes again, briefly.'

'Michelangelo kills him?'

'Theoretically, though how remains a mystery. Final reconstruction: he gets in contact with the Benizis in Rome, says he thinks Lance has pinched the goblet, then the Kranowskis flee. The building of the Berlin Wall in August 1961 seals the borders between East and West Europe, bringing virtual silence until 1990, when Leonardo zooms over to have another go. With me so far?'

'Agog.'

'He's told Lance is dead, can't track Jago down, because he's living in France, Sandro comes, still thinking there's a chance of finding the goblet for his family. Sandro gets hold of Jago, this time to confirm Lance is dead and fish around for news of it. As a result, he too believes Lance stole it.'

'Then why was Sandro killed?'

'It has to be over the art thefts. Blackmail.'

'Then what was he doing in the churchyard?'

Peter stared at her. 'Damn. I'm out, checkmated.'

'Someone to see you.' Luke came into the kitchen with an expressionless face just as Georgia was scanning the newspaper to see if

302

there was an update on the Barham Downs meeting.

'Who is it?'

'Zac.'

She choked on her coffee.

'I offered him pistols or swords at dawn,' Luke said affably, 'but he declined. He's kicking his heels in the living room.'

'Thank you,' she said weakly. 'Do you...' she began uncertainly.

'No way. I'm off to the oast house. Your problem, darling.'

'Thanks a bunch,' she thought mutinously. She found Zac standing in front of a painting she and Luke had bought in Italy two years ago.

'Nice,' he said, as he turned round to greet her.

'What do you want, Zac? she asked crossly. 'Eight-thirty in the morning is a fairly unsocial time.'

'I could do with a coffee,' he answered her plaintively, and she had to laugh.

'The kitchen's the place for that. I can finish my breakfast and you can tell me what you're after.'

'Luke seems a nice bloke,' Zac said approvingly, following her lamb-like to the kitchen.

'He is. Are you married again?' She'd never thought of asking him.

'Sort of. Didn't bother with the ring this time. Too much trouble.'

He didn't seem disposed to say more and she

wouldn't ask. That would mean involvement, whereas this needed to be over and done with. Otherwise the next thing she knew would be that he would be telling everyone that she and Luke and he and Mrs Sort-Of were all bosom friends and no doubt getting credit on the strength of it.

'Tell me what you're here for,' she suggested after he had been presented with his coffee.

'I'm in a mess.'

'When weren't you? What is it this time?'

'The Art and Antiques job.'

'Mark Priest?' she asked sharply. 'You've been caught out too?'

'Sort of.'

'Explain, if that's possible.' Zac's explanations were usually as cobwebby as his scams.

'The thing is, Mark's been charged, and I could be next.'

'You mean you're involved in it? You idiot.' She should have guessed this.

'No. I'm innocent, I really am, Georgia. I might have one or two things on the side but not this one.'

'Like running fakes to Budapest.'

He shot a glance at her. 'Maybe. Close, anyway. It looks like I could be roped in for bringing Sandro's copies back here.'

'And did you?'

'No,' he said virtuously. 'I wouldn't be such a fool. The trouble is that Mark knew I was running for the Benizis. Not,' he added hastily, 'that there was any truth in that, but it doesn't look good. Mark could have set me up, you see, and it wouldn't be hard for the police to make a case that I'd been playing both sides. Which I haven't.'

'No disrespect to you, Zac, but why should anyone, let alone Mark or the Met, set you up?'

He shrugged. 'Don't know. The thing is that I know I'm innocent, but I've worked more closely with Mark than I let on to you. When the Art and Antiques Unit asked me to co-operate, I thought Mark was the best bet to help me out. He didn't seem the type for a master villain. So he gave me an idea of what was worth checking into to see if it was fake or not. I had a fling with his sister a few years ago, and she put me in touch with him. I did some valuations and so on, and it always seemed to be those houses in which the copies turned up.'

'What can I do about it?' she asked cautiously. A fling? Zac with the cool calm lady? It didn't fit.

'Put in a good word for me, if it comes to the crunch.'

She tried not to laugh. 'I'm not the police, Zac.'

'But you know I wouldn't be such a fool again, Georgia,' he pleaded.

'I *don't* know. That's the problem.'

He sighed. 'Then just do some looking out for me, then. You and Peter *prove* I'm innocent. The thing is, Georgia, Mark's not cool enough to organize an art ring like this. Someone else is behind it. I reckon it's a woman, I know a lot about how women's minds work.'

'Really?' she asked drily. 'Are you saying this is Kelly's doing?'

'Kelly? She wouldn't know a Watteau from a Warhol,' he said rudely.

'That doesn't stop her organizing the scam.'

'Agreed. But think about it, Georgia. If Mark's guilty that's that; if he's innocent, look to those closest to him.'

For one crazy moment she thought he meant Jago, but of course he didn't.

'Do you mean Cindy?' she asked incredulously. 'Why on earth would she set up her own brother?' Cindy was surely too small a player in the art world to be able to organize something on this scale. Or was that the point? Appearances were deceptive, and it would certainly explain the fling with Zac. She needed contacts, and Zac was good at that.

'I don't know, but it adds up, don't you think?' Zac replied. 'I thought you might mention it to Mike.'

'Mike doesn't like bright suggestions from outsiders.'

'I knew I could count on you,' he said happily.

'But not today,' she said firmly. 'Today is the Barham Downs gathering. The Priest family will be otherwise occupied.'

'Not at Barham Downs. Jago's got his own thing going. Might be fun. We know it's going to be a fake, don't we?'

'Do we?'

'Come off it, Georgia. You've been to Budapest. You've talked to Antonio. We know what we're talking about.'

Caution needed here. 'About the paintings, yes.'

'Goblets, Georgia, goblets.'

So he did know. 'There's nothing fake about a golden goblet unless it's sold under false pretences.'

'That's true.' Zac looked worried. 'You're not thinking of pinching it, are you?'

'It wasn't at the top of my list of priorities,' she whipped back tartly.

'Good. I'm pretty sure Jago is digging tonight. Are you going? The Barham Downs dig starts at six-thirty.'

'Yes.'

Zac looked even more worried. 'Remember you and Peter are the only ones who both know it's fake *and* have no reason to conceal it. Just be careful.'

It was a warm day and after lunch Peter had made it clear he had other fish to fry on the Internet, and Georgia decided to spend the afternoon in Medlars' garden. The Barham Downs meeting wasn't until six-thirty and in case Jago had also arranged his dig for tonight, Peter had offered to check whether this would be later or earlier. Either way, she had an hour or two to herself.

The cottage garden had been overgrown and neglected when Luke took the house over, but during the summer they had worked on getting the original shape back, planting and scattering seeds partly at random. Already the work was bearing, if not fruit, then at least signs of perking up, with old rose trees regaining hope, and producing flowers. The age of King Arthur seemed a long way from this and so did 1950s Paris. Earth and gardens were real, not cloaked in the garb of time or mystique. Beyond the garden, the fields stretched out almost to Haden Shaw and though there was a footpath to the lane past their house it was seldom used. There was a gate from their garden into the fields – their escape valve, Luke called it. There would be a plentiful supply of blackberries shortly, and few rival pickers.

She glanced up from the file she was reading, shading her eyes against the sun, which was too strong even for her sunglasses. Today there was a walker – a woman – who had obviously seen her and diverged from the footpath to approach her gate. As she grew nearer she saw to her amazement that it was Sam. No mistaking that bright spiked hair, and boots.

'What on earth are you doing here?' she asked, surprised that anyone Sam's age would walk anywhere. Then with alarm: 'Jago's all right, isn't he?'

'Fine, as far as I know. Looking forward to

tonight. That's why I'm here.'

Georgia blinked. 'Why?'

'Because' – the girl was still smiling – 'it's not going to be ruined, least of all by you and that legless old fart.'

It took Georgia a moment before she realized she meant Peter, and she froze. What was all this about? Not good. Zac's words came back to her. Take care. 'How could we ruin it?' she asked as calmly as she could. The girl must be unbalanced. She would ignore the reference to Peter – for the moment.

'You going?'

'Probably. How would that ruin it?'

'The press are coming. You're not going to get your hour of glory by telling them it's all fake.'

So that was it. No time now to think round this. She had to get out, and quickly.

'I don't want your grandfather hurt either. That's why I'm going, and so is my father. If it is fake, it will come out anyway.'

'Only if you shoot your big mouth off. For once in his life Grandpops is going to get his big moment and you're not going to stop it with your lies.'

'We don't propose to tell him anything, Sam.' Calm, keep it calm.

'You don't understand a thing, do you? Only one word and everyone will believe it's a fake. And it's real. It's the real thing. I know it is. Grandpops knows it too. He's not a fool. He's been working all his life on this, but one word of fake, and that would be that. Sandro was going to tell him it was a fake too. Some arty-farty story he'd made up.'

'You shot him.' The words jerked out. Georgia was ice-cold. Now she did understand, all too well. The only person in the world besides Jago who would go on believing in this goblet no matter what proof was produced was Sam. And she would murder for it.

'Of course I did. He was going to dig the goblet up and make a stupid claim that it was his. The fool pretended it was fake. I saw him off, that's all. I had to.'

Georgia's mind whirled into action. She was in danger – she was not even within earshot of the oast house, where Luke was working. For the first time she noticed Sam's shoulder bag. A bag she had one hand inside. Should she keep her talking? If she ran, she'd be dead before she reached safety.

'Why do you care so much, Sam?' Keep the voice quiet, genuinely interested.

The girl smiled. 'I'm the only one, that's why. The others laugh at him. Mark, Mum, the lot. Why? The fools can't see King Arthur's a symbol. He's God. He means something. Grand-pops has been waiting for this all his life and he's going to get *his* day of glory.'

'It's gone too far, Sam. The goblet won't pass the tests. Even if it did, there's nothing to prove whose goblet it was.'

'*You've* gone too far, Marshy girl. It's real, not a fake. And so's this.' Sam was waving the gun around now. The gun that had killed Sandro. She looked insane, laughing hysterically, first pointing the gun at Georgia, then waving it over her head.

'Your grandfather wouldn't want this, Sam,' Georgia managed to say steadily. 'He'd be cross with you. King Arthur was a symbol of life, not death.'

Sam began to cry, then hiccupped in hysteria, and the gun was kept straight at her.

Keep talking, Georgia thought with dry lips. Talk of King Arthur, that's your only chance. Sam had moved between her and the house now, and there was no one to run to, no one to hear.

'You fucking fool, of course he'd want it. The goblet and bones are all he cares about. Not you and the old fart. It's his own personal Grail, and he's going to have it.'

Through a daze Georgia saw the pistol rising, Sam coming closer, and she froze. She'd never had time to tell Luke how much she loved him, never have his children, never see Peter again. Everything was still, waiting —

Then there was shouting all round, the gun rising in front of her, the flash and the explosion followed by pain and the ground she was sprawling on. Voices – Luke's? No, *Zac*'s. Men's voices, shouting, pounding feet. Painfully she sat up. She was dizzy, and as her eyes

311

cleared she saw Sam spreadeagled on the ground with Zac at her side. What on earth was he doing here?

'I've got the gun,' Zac was saying in a pleased voice, as Luke pounded towards them. Dear God, was he going to shoot her – or Luke?

No. She could see Mike Gilroy too.

'What did you do?' she asked Zac faintly, as Sam showed no signs of coming round. Guns weren't Zac's style. He was scared of them, she remembered.

'I hit her with a melon.'

Melon? What kind of sense was that? Zac seemed as shaken as she was. 'I was first round the side of the house, and saw her. Your green-grocery delivery was sitting outside the door so I grabbed it and chucked it at her.'

'A *melon*?'

He looked rather pleased with himself. 'I was always rather good at cricket.'

'That's it, Georgia. It's time for the showdown.' Peter thumped his hand on the desk.

'I'm all for it,' she agreed heartily. The morning after was the time for showdowns. The evening had been spent with Luke alone, safe at Medlars. Sam, having recovered from concussion, was under very voluble arrest and if forensic science supplied sufficient evidence that the gun matched, as Mike was sure it would, she would be charged with Sandro's murder and the attempted murder of Georgia Marsh.

Zac, having recovered his aplomb, was preening himself for being a vital witness, Peter had told her. His story was already all over the newspapers. 'Man foils Murder with Melon'. The look Mike had given him had suggested he only had a temporary reprieve for good behaviour, however. After all, he had pointed out, it had been Zac who had gaily let Sam know Georgia was planning to be present when Jago made his bid for stardom.

'Thanks, Zac,' she said wryly.

'He did save your life,' Peter said. 'And he was worried enough to call Mike.'

'Yes.' Someday she'd have to think about that. Now she could only think of how soon she could be out of this maze and back with Luke. Jago's dig had been postponed, thank goodness, since he had not unnaturally been horrified when Cindy broke the news to him at the police's request.

'Nothing has altered so far as Lance Venyon is concerned,' she pointed out.

'It has,' Peter said soberly. 'Do we really believe that Sam didn't know it was a scam?'

'How could she know?'

'Through Mark, or more probably if you're right through Cindy; she organized the art thefts and knew the Daks family all too well, and probably the Benizis.'

'The art thefts could still be Kelly's venture,' Georgia said doubtfully.

Peter eyed her thoughtfully. 'The melon has

got to you, Georgia. It was Cindy, of course. She was under our noses all the time. Cindy setting up her brother. Sibling rivalry there, I think. I gather dear Zac told you he had an affair with her four years ago and remained in touch; he chatted to her – as Zac will – about his contacts with the Benizi set-up and the brilliant young copyist they employed' – he saw her face – 'no doubt for strictly legal reasons. Anyway, it gave Cindy the idea for the art thefts.'

'More than that.' Georgia saw how it all fitted now. 'It also gave her the idea of setting Mark up as a fall guy in case one was needed. A game I suppose she would call it. Like Lance Venyon. Jago said he played life for the game.'

'The game,' Peter repeated thoughtfully. 'The only explanation for Jago being so slow on this fake is that he's so obsessed with finding the bones that he has persuaded himself that Lance was indeed his best chum, and that his original theory was correct. He had just misjudged the exact site. But it's there, he claims, not far from the point Cindy showed you. That's where he intends to dig.'

'Believing it genuine or a scam now?'

'We're assuming Jago is either a collector prepared to blinker himself to the truth, or a man with the nerve to knowingly laugh off a scam, or lastly a straight dealer: that implies Jago is right, that a fake never existed, that Hoskin's museum is just that and that the Benizis are lying through dislike of him.'

314

Georgia gulped. 'Is that all possible?'

'Oh yes,' Peter replied. 'It is. And even if it's fake, we can presume that the hoard is buried convincingly deep in specially prepared earth to look as though it's been there since the sixteenth century.'

'Jago would have a hard job convincing the Kentish Archaeological Society that it was King Arthur's.'

'It would fit Jago's thesis and that's all he requires, no matter what arguments go on amongst the cognoscenti afterwards. Look how long it took to disprove the Piltdown Man, and even now there are question marks over who was behind the hoax if any.'

Georgia nodded. 'I still think we should be there at the dig.'

'I agree, together with the police of course. Did you see the newspaper today?'

'Only the front-page story, about the melon.' She managed to laugh. It *was* rather funny.

Peter passed the newspaper to her, folded back to page three: '"Barham Downs waits in vain for King Arthur." You can read for yourself the account of what happened last night – a wash-out. Nothing found, except a couple of pieces of old iron which could be from British or Saxon swords. It's this paragraph might interest you though.' He leaned forward and tapped the page.

'"In an Arthurian hoax in the late 1950s,"' she read, '"four paintings with seemingly im-

315

peccable provenance as the work of Dante Gabriel Rossetti gave credence to the story of Sir Gawain's burial in Dover Castle, but were later discovered to be fakes. The current rumours of Arthur's golden goblet being buried with Gawain's bones are thought to stem from a revival of the same hoax." Where did *this* come from?' She was staggered. 'Zac?'

Peter laughed. 'No way. There's only one answer to that. Your chum Antonio. Nice move, yes?'

'He does indeed walk the fine line,' Georgia said admiringly. 'Quick thinking on his part. This distances him nicely from any goblet scam, while curiosity value will shoot the value up nicely, temporarily at least. I might even put a bid in for one of them myself.'

'Come in.'

Jago seemed to have aged tremendously. His shoulders were bent, and his whole demeanour was of weariness and defeat. 'Help yourselves to a drink, please.' He waved towards the kitchen as he led them to his study. Georgia took the hint, and after ensuring Peter was safely into the room, went to make tea for them all. Jago had asked them to come over immediately, when Peter took the bull by the horns and telephoned him. It took some time locating everything, and when she returned to the study bearing the results, Peter and Jago were in full flow about arrangements for the postponed dig, which Jago was explaining would be in a week's time. She had mixed feelings: revulsion at the whole idea and a desire to get this case finished, and – she admitted – genuine curiosity.

Jago broke off immediately. 'I have to apologize to you, Georgia, for what happened. Sam is heavily partisan where King Arthur is concerned. She'd never have used the gun, of course. She runs wild...' He didn't sound as if he even believed this himself.

'I gather that Mark is clear of charges of art theft,' Peter said less than tactfully. So he wasn't letting Jago off the hook yet.

'He is,' Jago replied. 'Cindy is not. Poor Mark. He never can see what's happening before his eyes. It's his own fault for becoming involved.'

Georgia shivered. He didn't, she wanted to say. Surely Jago must see that? He was as much a dupe as Zac had been, and that was saying something. Goodness knows what he now believed about his precious theory and the hoard. She bit back any reply, however. It would do no good, and Jago had enough to contend with. Even so, his reply had been chilling.

'I've had every journalist in the world ringing me up,' Jago continued querulously. 'In vain I tell them my theory has nothing to do with fakes. I suppose you told them about the Kranowskis.'

'No.' Peter answered this, to Georgia's relief.

317

She was still grappling with the speed with which Jago had moved from his grand-daughter's attempted murder and daughter's involvement in an art-theft ring back to his beloved theory about Arthur.

'Then it was Madeleine and Antonio Benizi. They never did like—' Jago stopped, and passed a hand over his forehead. 'Do you know, I really feel I'm getting old. Stupid, isn't it? This great scam, do you believe it?'

'I'm afraid so.'

He shook his head. 'The goblet exists. It all does, and it's real, not fake. These are simply rumours of a scam put about to devalue the collection when it is found.' His eyes lit up. 'Yes, I see it,' he cried. 'Antonio Benizi, of course. Just like him. Put around the rumour that it's all fake, and he can buy it for virtually nothing, and then prove that it is real after all. Money, you see...' He looked uncertainly at them, as his voice trailed off.

Georgia said nothing. She couldn't. She'd taken enough shock herself in the last day, she couldn't add to Jago's.

Peter, it seemed, could. 'It wasn't Antonio,' he told Jago in a neutral voice. 'It was Lance who organized the scheme and commissioned the goblet.'

'I don't believe it,' Jago said harshly.

'I understand, but it is so. You can check with the Kranowski family, in due course. That was what Sandro wanted back, when he telephoned you.'

'Who?' Jago looked bewildered, then shook his head. 'I can't take all this in. I really can't. I can't believe that Lance would ever have tried to trick me so. It wasn't a trick, it was a decoy, that's it. He hoped by drawing the competitors off on a false trail, he would leave me a clear field to find the real burial place for Gawain's bones.' The light of hope shone in his eyes.

Please let Peter let him think that, Georgia prayed.

'No. Lance would have revealed the scam, once you had dug up the hoard,' Peter said briskly.

For a moment Jago looked at a complete loss, then replied, 'I don't know any more. I just don't understand.'

'Perhaps there's a much simpler explanation,' Peter said, gentle again. 'And with the story now public, it might be possible for you to face it.'

'I've faced enough in the last few days. One more horror won't kill me.' Jago rallied slightly.

'You're behind at least several of the Arthurian blogs, aren't you?'

Jago bridled. 'Why not?' he said indignantly. 'One doesn't get much fun out of life at eighty-six. One has to make one's own.'

'Fun,' repeated Peter meditatively.

Where was Peter going with this, Georgia wondered, feeling too sick to grapple with his route. It was no great surprise that Jago was hosting a site, but several of them? What did that imply? Jago, from being the victim, seemed now at bay. Control had passed to Peter, and he was in a place where she couldn't follow him. Yet, at least.

'Fun is an interesting word,' Peter continued. 'And you're an interesting man, Jago. There are two sides to you, the academic and the gamester.'

'One has to relax at my age.'

'But you can't relax too much, can you? Not even now with all that's happening to your family.'

Jago looked at him in surprise. 'You didn't come here to talk about King Arthur, did you? You're harking back to Lance Venyon. Have you discovered how he was murdered?'

'He wasn't,' Peter replied.

'Then there is hardly any need for you to disturb me or to attend the disinterment of Gawain's bones.'

'On the contrary,' Peter said, almost sadly. 'There is a murder we have to investigate.'

'Whose?' Jago shot at him.

'The murder of Jago Priest. You are Lance Venyon, aren't you?'

Fifteen

How strange to be back in this village pub, Georgia thought, where only two months ago she had sat with Luke and Peter, while Jago – Lance, as she must think of him now – spouted happily about Arthur with Cindy and Sam. A lifetime away, it seemed. This didn't seem the same man; with that one accusation he had turned into a stranger.

'It was puzzling me,' Peter said. 'Here was the Jago we all liked, but all we heard about was the man whom nobody seemed to like at all. Including, presumably, his wife Jennifer.'

'Do we have to bring her into it?' Lance said. 'I can deny all this, of course. I doubt if you could prove it.' He had no conviction in his voice.

'Of course you could deny it,' Peter replied. 'But DNA would, if push comes to shove, prove you wrong. Mark is Jago's son, Elaine your daughter, as is Cindy. Do Cindy and Sam know, incidentally?'

Lance said nothing for a moment, then: 'Blast DNA,' he said amiably. 'And the answer is no, they don't. None of them does. I can't see proof

321

of any crime, thus no arrest and thus no DNA sample. Your tame policemen can't take samples against my will.'

'So where is Jago Priest?'

'Not my problem. It is yours,' he replied merrily. He seemed to have revived very quickly. The game, Georgia thought. The game was indeed afoot, and the game now was to outwit Peter. She was still recovering from the shock. She'd have it out with Peter later for not telling her, though she reluctantly conceded that the less she knew the better, perhaps.

'I doubt if the answer will be too difficult to discover,' Peter replied.

'I do,' Lance replied blithely. 'The mere fact that I took the opportunity of stepping into Jago's shoes when the rotter walked out and deserted Jennifer does not make me a murderer. I merely resigned from the Sorbonne in his name, and took a new job in Toulouse.'

Walked out? Georgia thought. Good one.

'Identity theft?' Peter asked.

'There was no financial gain, I assure you. Forfeiting my own savings and pension was more hardship than gain, since Jago's are less good. Moreover, Jennifer had more money than Jago.' He was obviously enjoying this immensely, and Georgia was almost hypnotized into forgetting there was a murder to consider.

'It's always the game with you, isn't it?' Peter said.

'Indeed it is. Still. I always loved the game. I

have greatly enjoyed feeding you titbits of bait, then watching you hare after them – rather too efficiently, I fear, in the case of the Rossetti painting, and of course my disappearance.'

'How did you manage that?' Georgia asked.

'I had a clever wife, or rather partner, if it makes any difference. We celebrated our fortieth anniversary in 2001.'

'Did she help you plan her husband's murder?' Peter asked dispassionately. No letting him off any hooks, she noted.

Lance's expression grew harder. 'What murder?' he asked again. 'Jago went on a few days' holiday to – where was it, Outer Mongolia, perhaps? – and never returned.'

'Without knowing he was dead, why did you go ahead with the theft of his identity?'

If Peter had hoped to throw him by this, he was out of luck. 'Ah,' Lance replied immediately, 'because he'd been missing for the whole of that summer, it was clear to me he must be dead. He would never have stayed away from Jennifer so long otherwise. When it was clear he was not returning for whatever reason, Jennifer suggested I should move in with her. Mark needed a father, he was very young.'

'Why take his name, then?'

Lance looked shocked. 'Society in those days would not have tolerated our living together otherwise, and there were of course poor Mary's feelings to consider. We didn't want to wait the necessary seven years or so for Jago's death to be formally declared. We decided we could make a new life in Toulouse, and perhaps eventually England, to benefit from my King Arthur coup in due course. I was reluctant about the latter; it seemed to me one dice thrown too often. Apparently I was right, but Sam was insistent that I should have another shot at the dig, so I thought why not? Coincidentally – what a surprise – the rumours began again. A chip off the old block, is Sam.'

'So it seems,' Peter said. 'Even in murder.'

'Diminished responsibility,' Lance said quickly. 'I couldn't bear ... Enough of that.' He caught himself briskly. 'To resume my tale: I took the new position in Toulouse, at a somewhat lower academic standard. I knew enough about art to teach its history admirably and was a far better teacher than Jago himself. I have quite a reputation you know, even now. In those days there weren't quite so many conferences so it was possible to keep to my own turf; Jago and I were much the same build, and with the help of a beard and change of parting, that sort of thing – and of course with Jennifer at my side – it proved quite easy to avoid recognition. Friends and family were a problem, of course. Fortunately, only one of Jago's parents was alive, and she was senile.'

Fortunately? Georgia felt sick.

'My parents, of course,' Lance continued, 'believed I was dead, and it was easy to lose contact, as it was with friends. As we were in

324

Toulouse, distance made their hearts grow considerably less fonder, and for those stalwarts who were more clingy, it was possible to invent excuses for not seeing them, or for Jennifer seeing them alone. As the years passed, it grew even easier, until we were able to return to England – not too close to Wymdown or Dorset, of course, until Mary died.'

'You were listed as being at the funeral,' Georgia said puzzled. 'Your wife would have been there, surely.'

'Quite. I did take a few risks. I had taken the boat out on 14 September, with an extra dinghy on board, to near the French coast, where Jennifer was waiting for me. It was a wrench to part with my beloved Hillyard, but needs must. As for the funeral, well, that was a problem. I had missed the memorial service through tactical illness, though Jennifer attended. When it came to the funeral it was a different matter. Mary had been obsessed with the thought that she had to see a body before she would believe I was dead. Otherwise she hoped I might come marching home, or so she told Jennifer. Today this would be understood, but then the police merely thought her a nuisance, clamouring to view every body that could possibly fit the bill. When one did pop up, Jennifer went with her for company. I suspected that Mary knew about Jennifer's role in my life, but in an odd way that made her more dependent on Jennifer after my so-called death. Mary was set on the body being mine, and Jennifer gently helped her to believe it. As for the funeral, it was ultimately simple. Jennifer gave my name to the undertakers and to the journalists there, each time indicating some other man as if that were me.'

'But Mary would have noticed you weren't there.'

'I had to leave promptly, Jennifer explained to Mary. Poor dear Mary was in such a state that she believed I rushed right away because I couldn't take the emotion of Lance's death. I wrote her the most charming letter afterwards, of course. In Jago's handwriting naturally, since that was something I most certainly had to acquire. As for my voice – well, I never rang Mary. Only Jennifer did, and Mary was too diffident to make international calls. They're commonplace now, but it was quite a fandango in those days.'

'If Jago went to Outer Mongolia, he'd have taken his passport with him,' Georgia pointed out.

'So he would. Fortunately, my line of work, shall we say, allowed me to overcome this difficulty. Ten years ago, with Mary no longer alive, we thought it safe to move back to Kent, and reacquaint myself with my daughter. My appearance had by then changed with age, and no one would remember the old Lance's voice – save perhaps darling Venetia, but fortunately she too had moved away. She was a highly inquisitive sort of person.'

'So the mysterious visitor the afternoon you went to Hythe wasn't Jago?' Peter asked.

'Good heavens, no. There was no visitor. I lied. Needed time to myself.'

'Madeleine visited you that day.'

'So she did.' Lance laughed. 'How could I forget? Most unwelcome. She wanted to probe into the scam on Jago. She felt protective of Jennifer and was convinced it was all my idea. A stupid woman.'

'How had she heard of it?'

'No idea.'

'It couldn't be that Michelangelo Kranowski came over to warn you that Raphael Kranowski was about to be exposed as a fake? That you fobbed him off with the same story that the great scam was about to be sprung but you weren't going to tell him where the goblet was buried; that he thought you had pinched it, and went back to ring Madeleine in Rome?'

Lance still didn't look fazed. 'I suppose it was possible. Dear me, such a long time ago.'

'It must be. According to what you said just now, Jago had been missing for some weeks, even months, and you thought he was dead so it seems unlikely the scam would still be sprung in his absence.'

A split second while Lance realized he'd been trapped. He wagged an indulgent finger. 'Words, Peter, words.'

'Which can be fatal.'

'If verbal, not worth the paper they're written

on, as Sam Goldwyn once famously said.'

'Was the scam all your idea? Or Jennifer's too?'

'Forget Jennifer,' he snapped.

'And the murder?' Peter asked.

The gamester was beginning to tire. He shrugged. 'Very well. That prat Michelangelo bleated to Jago about the goblet being Raphael's work, and revealed the whole damn scam to Jago. Jago came hot foot over to Dover; I met him after I'd dropped Madeleine off. God, what an afternoon. What a day, come to that. We had an interesting discussion. I put him on a ferry back to France and he went off quite happily – well, not happily, he didn't even like ferries very much.'

'He didn't come aboard your boat?'

Lance snorted. 'Jago? You have to be joking. One of the less pleasant sides to this particular game has been my inability to sail any more. Fortunately having Jennifer made up for that.'

'So did Jennifer murder Jago to get him out of the way so that she could be with you? You knew he was dead, so if you didn't kill him then she did.'

He went very white. 'That's a dastardly thing to say.'

'A Lady Macbeth?'

His face was strained. 'No.'

'She came with Jago that day, didn't she?'

He hesitated. 'Yes.'

'And you both murdered him.'

'No.' He was shaking with genuine emotion now. 'Jennifer's dead, so I might as well tell you. Lady Macbeth my foot. You just don't bloody understand. She was crazy to have married Jago, and she knew it. We had had a spat, and she did it in a temper.'

'But Mark was Jago's child?'

'He didn't get a chance at another. He was...'

'Shot?' Peter said inexorably, when he paused.

Lance glared at him. 'No. Jennifer came with Jago that day. For all his jabbering on about the Round Table, there was nothing gallant about our Jago. First he was raging because he'd found out about my joke – no sense of humour – then worse, called Jennifer a whore and anything else he could think of.'

'He'd seen the other paintings?' Georgia asked.

Perhaps it was the suddenness of her intervention that threw Lance off course. He looked startled, taken off guard. 'What other paintings?'

'Two of them had Jennifer as a model for Guinevere; I presume they were Michelangelo's work.'

'Means nothing to me,' Lance said dismissively. 'It was the scam. The scam was everything. Nothing would satisfy Jago but to come to Badon House that day. He was raving, but for heaven's sake there's no crime in a practical joke. So I drove him there with Jennifer. I'd buried the stuff near the church. It had been in the ground maturing like vintage wine. Once there, he went berserk all over again, and attacked me. For an unathletic man he had strength. SAS training, of course. I defended myself, he slipped, fell against a gravestone, and the fall killed him. Jennifer saw what happened. I was beside myself and couldn't think straight. She said she wasn't going to lose us both, and if we just scarpered together there would be enough evidence around to put one if not two of us in jail. We waited until the small hours, got Jago's body into the car and drove hell for leather for Folkestone where I dropped Jennifer off to get a ferry; I went on to Hythe, got the body on board, waited till early morning so that I'd be seen to depart alone, then climbed into the dingy, set the boat adrift and that was that.'

'Not quite,' Peter said. 'A dinghy was left on the boat. How did you get an extra one in such a hurry?'

A split second, before he replied easily: 'Two dinghies on board. I told you. I'm a careful sort of chap. Overanxious, Jennifer always said.' He smiled. Of course he would, Georgia thought dully. Lance would always win his game.

'And now,' he chuckled, 'you must, I'm afraid, permit me my last game. The unveiling of Arthur's goblet by Jago Priest. Poor Jago must have his hour of glory.'

* * *

The same spot in the same field as Georgia had looked at with Cindy. Of course it was here. That too had been a game. Talk of geophysical surveys and metal detectors was a smoke-screen. So was Lance's claim of having dug every inch of this field. There hadn't been any digging here since the late 1950s.

Lance seemed to have recovered his strength, if his jauntiness was anything to go by. He'd even produced a yachting cap to wear, as if deliberately to taunt them.

'Now we're all here, let's begin. I must say I'm looking forward to seeing it again. Poor Sam. If only she could have been here. Cindy was against the whole thing – I see why now.'

'With the police forces of umpteen countries on her trail,' Peter said, moving his wheelchair to one side as the digging began, 'I can see why.'

'Thanks to your meddling,' Lance said grimly. 'We're hardly the Borgias, you know. All I wanted was to be one of the great hoaxers of history, like the Bruno Hat scam. No harm done, only a lot of red faces. That was my idea and look how it ended up.'

He glanced round at the assembled company. Mark – at least – Peter, Georgia, Luke, Mike Gilroy, two sturdy uniformed policemen and half a dozen diggers. 'Anyone would think,' Lance said drily, 'that you were expecting to find a body in here. Well, you'll be lucky. There is one.'

Mike moved forward.

'Sir Gawain's,' Lance laughed. 'What did you think I meant? Jago Priest's?'

He could still laugh, Georgia thought with amazement. Yet there had been two deaths, and half his family arrested. Did he *care*? Yes, she thought, for two people. Sam – and Jennifer. Peter was still sure there was more of the story to come out, however. 'I don't believe this fall against a gravestone, do you?' he had said on the drive there. 'I suspect his old army training came rather readily to him.'

'He had no need to kill Jago,' she had pointed out.

'Unless he realized that with Jago dead, not only could he wriggle out of blame over the scam, but take Jennifer too.'

'That's possible,' she had agreed, but was aware that neither she nor Peter really believed they had the full facts.

Here on a late July afternoon in still swelter-ing heat, she could imagine the chaplains with their precious cargo, and it was hard to believe the story had all been built up in her mind thanks to Lance's playacting, a charade he had clearly relished. And yet, she had to remember, Jago really *had* believed this theory because that's why the scam had been possible.

'Why did you leave it buried here after you sold Badon House?' she asked, watching as the diggers progressed. Conversation had petered out, as the hole gradually grew deeper and tension grew. Even Lance had been silent. They were down six or seven feet now.

'Why not?' Lance replied. He carefully kept his voice low in Mike's presence, Georgia noticed. 'I was the only one who knew it was here, and I kept the field. I couldn't afford to draw attention to myself as Jago Priest in connection with something that had connections with Paris in the 1950s. Suppose someone noticed I wasn't the sort of person as the Jago they knew? Besides, there was the goblet. Kranowski wanted it back. I meant to pay him, but never got round to it, thanks to Jago.'

'Seven feet,' Mark called up. He was leading the diggers. 'Any time now.'

'You know,' Lance remarked, 'I almost feel that it's real. Camelot is coming our way. Perhaps I *am* Jago after all.'

Georgia could detect a tremble in his voice. Peter's eyes were fixed on every spadeful of earth and Luke was getting equally enthralled. She realized that she too was tense. What was she waiting for? King Arthur? Was the ghost of Jennifer here too? Or Jago's?

'There!' Lance cried, shuffling forward to the very edge and pointing down. The diggers stopped and Mark scuffled in the soil as some scraps looking like decayed wood appeared. Luke had appointed himself photographer, as had Mark, who was already busy snapping away – for the family archives? she wondered.

'Be careful,' Lance said plaintively. 'I took

such pains with it.'

He had. Over the next hour the shape left by the wood scraps formed a rough oblong about four feet long and two wide. Within that, the earth was being eased away from what had been the box's contents – no, Georgia caught herself, there *was* no box. This was a modern scam, not a sixteenth-century drama.

Luke was in the hole himself now, vowing that his archaeological competence was well known. Not to Georgia, but she said nothing. Impatiently, she clambered down the ladder to join them, feeling like Hamlet leaping into the grave of Ophelia. Lance was not pleased, but so far as she was concerned, he had no right to object.

'Look,' Luke said. He was squatting down clearing away earth. 'Bones.'

Lance heard and was almost dancing with anger. 'Come out,' he ordered the entire crew. 'One person only.'

The diggers took him at his word, but Luke and Georgia ignored him. Peter was urging them on, telling them to take no notice, and had his own camera in hand. Mike was now physically restraining Lance from following them.

'Take care,' Lance shouted in anguish. 'The skull is separate.'

'Here,' breathed Luke, as a bone protruded through a round mass of earth.

'Give it to me, you fool. It's Gawain's skull,' screeched Lance – and for a moment Georgia almost believed it was.

Luke stood up and handed it up to one of the uniformed PCs. 'It had to be separate,' Lance said more quietly. 'The chaplains left in such a hurry, they wouldn't have had time to arrange the bones and skull together. All hugger-mugger. By his side, you should find the buckle, and bits of sword.'

'And the goblet?' asked Luke practically.

'To your right,' Lance called.

Georgia felt around for some minutes, but neither she nor Luke could find anything. 'I can't see it,' she called.

'Dammit, woman,' Lance yelled. 'Let me go down, if you please, Mr Gilroy.'

Mike glanced at Peter, who nodded. 'Not you, Georgia, nor you, Mr Priest,' he said to Mark. 'Luke can stay.'

Georgia knew they were right; if Lance grabbed her down there she would be a potential hostage. Nonsense of course; but, she remembered, he had had SAS training. It wasn't a pleasant thought. Reluctantly she clambered after Mark up the ladder and she and Mike steadied Lance for the climb down, with Luke ready beneath. Lance managed the descent remarkably nimbly in his eagerness.

'Now!' he said. His face disappeared from their view as he bent down slowly and tugged at a dark bundle. Luke, to Lance's obvious annoyance, helped him pick it up and bits of old cloth fell away. 'The only thing I couldn't get to be authentic,' he said lovingly. 'Sixteenth-century velvet, which is why there are mere scraps here. Look!'

The goblet had loomed so large in her imagination that the size took Georgia by surprise, as Lance clung on to the mound of earth. Then he began to pull lumps of earth away, until what remained was still a mud ball, but only now of four or five inches. It was still covered in mud, but now the clear shape of a goblet could be seen.

Lance held it aloft with one hand, and Georgia watched, fascinated. 'The golden goblet of King Arthur,' he cried. Lovingly he began to wipe it with a handkerchief. 'Water,' he commanded, and one of the diggers obliged with a watering can from the cemetery. Gradually she saw the gold begin to reveal itself, gleaming in the late afternoon sun. Still dark, still muddy, but soon it would shine out in all its glory.

Lance made the climb back, refusing to let anyone take his precious goblet from him, and when finally, with a great deal of help, he reached the top, Georgia saw tears in his eyes. He looked round in triumph at the assembled group as though he were victor, not loser.

'Here!' he said softly as the last bit of earth fell away, and he held it up again, clasped in both hands.

King Arthur's goblet. It was impossible here to think of it as Raphael's goblet, or Lance's, or even Sir Gawain's. For a few moments, even to

Georgia, it was Arthur's alone, gleaming out in the sunshine. She recognized that ornamentation from the painting: it had been an animal, and it could indeed have been a bear surmounting something she didn't immediately recognize. A primitive crown? A Christian symbol? It hardly mattered. She knew what Antonio would have said if he were here: *it has soul.*

Georgia felt a few tears in her own eyes. Stupid. However good, it was fake. Yes, but Antonio had said that for a true artist there were no fakes, there were only creations. A fake was unique in itself. As was this gleaming masterpiece.

At last Peter held out his hand towards Lance, who handed the goblet to him, with Mike's eye carefully watching every movement.

'You know,' Lance remarked at last, 'I feel I own this goblet.'

'Forget it,' Peter said gently. 'You don't. The Kranowski family does.' Even Peter, his daughter observed, didn't have the heart to point out that Lance's grand-daughter had murdered Sandro for its possession.

'Morally I do. I brought it into existence.'

'Tell that to Leonardo Kranowski.'

'I suppose you are going to insist on taking it back to him. Suppose I challenge it? The land is legally mine, therefore so is the goblet.'

For a moment, Georgia froze, but Peter made short shrift of Lance's challenge.

'Jago Priest owns this land,' he said flatly,

'and after him his son Mark.'

'Then there's no problem,' Lance said genially, 'is there, Mark?'

Mark had been silent all this while, and Georgia held her breath. For a moment she thought he would side with Lance. 'No problem at all,' he replied steadily. 'I'm sending it back to the Kranowksis.'

Georgia breathed a sigh of relief. Jago Priest had taken his revenge.

'He's still alive, isn't he?' Venetia asked. Georgia had elected to drive down to see her to break the news, rather than merely telephoning her.

'We can't prove it without his DNA, of course, although since Sam's has been taken it shouldn't be too hard if it comes to that. We don't know yet. The police are pondering it.'

'I knew it, you know. That's why I was sure he was murdered. Lance wasn't the type to disappear over the side of a boat. Too careful and manipulative for all his hail fellow well met line. That's sincere too, of course.'

'Do you want to meet him again?'

'No thanks.' Venetia pulled a face. 'Jennifer won and that's that. Besides, that would mean having to ask you where Jago is. Ah,' she continued, 'I can tell the answer from your expression. Lance did him in, didn't he?'

'No body and all Lance says is that it was an accident.'

'Not one through his falling over the side of

his boat. Jago would never have set foot on it, not if he was alive. No, I don't fancy seeing him again. I'd rather delude myself over the Lance I remember during the good times. The next thing would be his conning me into moving in to take care of him. Forget it. I've a dog to look after. I don't need a jackal.'

Georgia laughed. 'Did you know about the scam?'

'I guessed, and from that it wasn't far to considering Lance's disappearance as fishy. I stopped halfway on that, which is why I said nothing to you. I didn't want to know what happened, and still don't. But come with me for a moment.'

Georgia followed her into a study with a sleek-looking computer and desk. Venetia opened a cupboard and took out an old carrier bag. 'I got it down from the loft for you. Such a lovely thing. I couldn't bear to throw it away.' She shook the bag upside down and out fell a mass of scraps of parchment with ancient calligraphy and ornamentation.

'These are beautiful,' Georgia exclaimed, once she had got her breath back. 'Could they possibly be Lance's chaplains' script, the provenance for the cup?'

'I imagine that's what Lance wanted them for. And there's a letter too.'

'From John Ruskin?'

'Yes. I was keeping it for him. It's all fake, of course.'

'Do you know who faked it?' Georgia asked.

'I did.' Venetia cast a mischievous glance at Georgia. 'I always had an artistic gift.'

'It's at this stage I'm glad it's not up to me as to what happens to Lance. There's no proof of murder, or of accident now. What will Mike do?' Georgia asked Peter on her return.

'Without a body, not a lot forty years on. Even the DNA evidence wouldn't prove he killed Jago.'

Georgia shivered. 'Do we have to go down there?'

'It's where it began.'

'The Gawain site?'

'No, Sandro's death.'

They were staying with Gwen and Terry at Peter's request; he felt it only fair to fill them in on events, and had taken them to show them Gawain's grave and such objects as Lance hadn't taken with him.

The churchyard, where she and Peter had come alone, was a far creepier place, and, despite Peter's presence, back came all her previous revulsion.

'So it was here,' Peter said reflectively, 'you found Sandro.'

'Why was he murdered in this place, though? Chance?'

'No. Sam kidded him she was going to pose with the goblet in the nude on a gravestone. Then the row broke out as he realized that was a joke. Her claim is that the gun was Sandro's and she grabbed it from him in self-defence.'

'Oh yeah? And then she stalked me and needed it for the same reason,' Georgia said. She shivered again at the memory. 'This corner is still creepy. Let's get away. Lance could have buried Jago's body anywhere.'

'A moment, Georgia. Let's get to the bottom of this story now.'

'Aren't we there?'

'You know we're not.'

'But his story about putting the body over the side of the boat could be true.'

'Too much trouble getting it there, and too risky.'

'You mean – he is buried near Gawain?' She tried to convince herself that must be the answer.

Peter shook his head. 'I mean *here*. Where easier than a grave not long dug, with a coffin in it? Look, Josephine Jones, 1960.'

She swallowed, trying to distil logic from emotion. 'It's possible.'

'Probable. I've already talked to Mike.'

'Then why bring me here again?' she cried.

'We need to concentrate on Jago and Lance before Jago is forgotten and Lance prances off into a happy sunset.'

'You're sure it's accidental death?'

'Are you?'

How could she say yes when all her gut instinct told her that the story wasn't yet over?

'He murdered him.'

Peter nodded. 'Planned murder.'

'Never forget Jennifer,' she said slowly.

'You're right.'

'When Madeleine threatened to reveal the scam?'

'Before that. What was going to happen *after* the scam? Have you asked yourself that? Jago would be humiliated, but what help would that be to Jennifer and Lance's relationship? None. Murder would undoubtedly have taken place in due course. After the scam, Jago would apparently commit suicide in his humiliation, and after a decent interval she and Lance would marry. That would leave Mary dangling, which would be a problem, but one they could live with. Unfortunately this plan went drastically wrong.'

'Because of Michelangelo.' She was following it now.

'Yes. Jago discovers the scam and Jennifer's plans rapidly change. She accompanies Jago, and somehow Jago meets his death, no doubt at Lance's hands but at Jennifer's planning. Her power must have been remarkable.'

'But there's no proof it was premeditated.'

'Oh, but there is. For us, at any rate. A jury might be hard to convince after all this time.'

'What's the proof?'

'Two paintings, Georgia,' Peter said simply. 'Sir Gawain's painting in 1959 to fit in with the scam was no problem, nor was a painting of the

Lady of Farthingloe. What is interesting is the other two sent to the Benizis by Michelangelo after the supposed death of Lance Venyon. If the scam was successful, sooner or later Jago would have seen those paintings.'

'And seen Jennifer as the adulterous Guinevere.'

'Yes. He would have known Jennifer was involved with the scam, realized her relationship with Lance – and sued for divorce. Divorce wasn't highly rated in those days, and would not have suited Jennifer or Lance one little bit. No, how could Jennifer have risked being the model unless she knew Jago would no longer be alive to see the paintings?'

Georgia remembered the last time she had sat on this terrace, drinking wine and eating. Only then the gathering had included Zac. Now it was Luke – thank goodness.

'I'm sorry we had to be so suspicious of you,' she said.

Antonio beamed. 'It is our fault. We did not want to be part of tricking Jago, so we ask Lance very few questions and he tell us nothing. We only know when Michelangelo tell us.'

'It was delicate,' Madeleine said.

'*Si*,' Antonio agreed. 'Delicate. Paintings, you see. Lance bring first one to us. If we ask too many questions we might guess it a fake. Then we see the other three when Michelangelo bring them to us after Lance's death. We took them because of Jennifer and hide them. One day perhaps we can sell them—' He looked angelically innocent. 'So now you know we tread careful line. Not deal in fakes.'

'Of course not,' Georgia agreed solemnly.

'Good, good. So have more wine.'

Luke accepted with alacrity, but she held back. No more mazes of confusion for her.

'You are a good man for Mrs Georgia,' Antonio said. 'Better than Zac.'

'Thank heavens for that,' Luke murmured.

'So now you have the goblet...' Antonio said thoughtfully.

'To hand back to its rightful owner,' Georgia said sweetly. She wasn't going to stand for any belated claim that it was his.

'Madeleine and I wonder where *real* goblet is,' Antonio finished.

Georgia almost choked. 'What real goblet? There *is* no real goblet.'

'Oh yes. That is very funny, now we know that Lance killed Jago.'

'Nothing funny about that,' Luke pointed out.

'No, but Lance killed the man who actually knew where the real goblet was. Jago did not trust Lance, so he said nothing to him. He realized it was not in that field. Lance was wrong, he told us.'

'Where, then?' Georgia cried.

'Oh, Mrs Georgia, he did not tell us. What a pity.' Antonio chuckled. '*Ciao*, goblet. We could all have been very rich, yes?'

344

Epilogue

'Blow this wheelchair.' Peter had been determined to come, heat or no heat, to Budapest with her. Once the formalities of the Treasure Act and coroner were over, made much easier since the goblet's ownership was now beyond doubt, Mark had agreed that Peter and Georgia could return it in person to the Kranowski family. They had wasted no time, and no sooner had they checked into their hotel in Pest than Peter was eager to call a taxi to the Rákóczi út.

'I won't be able to get up the stairs you told me about, but perhaps Leonardo will come down,' he said hopefully. 'I just want to see the damned thing handed over.'

'It's no palace,' she warned him. 'You might be disappointed in the goblet's new home.'

Fortunately Leonardo himself came to the door to greet them. He was smiling with pleasure. 'You have it, our goblet?' he asked eagerly.

'Ours?' Georgia wondered. Was he speaking on behalf of all Kranowskis, past as well as present?

'Yes.' Once inside, Peter opened the bag they had brought it in.

She was surprised when Leonardo stopped him from going further. 'Wait, please.'

He led them straight to the wall at the far end of the entrance hall, painted with the dull murals that Georgia had seen before. He motioned to them to wait, went to the end of the wall and pressed what looked like a light switch. Some light switch. This one rolled the apparently solid wall back like a sliding door, neatly enclosing itself behind the stair well and revealing a corridor in front of them. It was immediately clear to Georgia that *this* was the main part of the house (and, no doubt, business). 'Please to come with me.'

Georgia needed no second bidding and escorted Peter as Leonardo led them into a little room with a table and several chairs, reminding her of the Benizi store she had visited. But this was no empty room. The walls were covered with exquisite tiny miniature paintings and cabinets displayed small golden ornaments and objects that wouldn't have disgraced Fabergé, and icons. Bemused, Georgia sat in one of the ornate chairs, by Peter, to wait until Leonardo reappeared. When he did, however, he was not alone. He was pushing another wheelchair.

Its occupant was a bearded old gentleman with carpet slippers and a red velvet jacket with cap to match. He looked older than Jago, older even than Richard Hoskin, in his mid-nineties at least. It took only a moment for Georgia to realize who this was, however, and for Peter too.

'You must be Raphael Kranowski,' he crowed in delight.

The old man inclined his head. 'Of course,' he almost whispered in good English. 'We goldsmiths live long. We are a family firm. We must see the family continue.'

'We were sad about Sandro,' Georgia said.

He acknowledged her sympathy graciously. 'We have a fine baby coming, Sandro's baby. I will teach him much before I die. I will give him my goblet. It is for him.'

'I have it here,' Peter said, handing him the velvet bag.

'Ah.' His frail hands fumbled with the draw-string, and Georgia wondered whether to help. She decided not to. This was Raphael's goblet. She could see tears in his eyes as he unwrapped it, and saw the goblet as it must have left his hands. No shiny glitter, but the true soul of the gold.

He held it up for Leonardo to admire. 'I told Leonardo that Lance had stolen the goblet, but he said Lance was dead. If so, the goblet would come on the market, so I knew something was wrong. But now I have it.' He stroked its curves lovingly.

'It's magnificent,' Georgia said sincerely.

She was fixed with a steely glance.

'Yes, it is magnificent,' Raphael agreed. 'But one day they find my Holy Grail. Much, *much* better.'